❊ BANNER OVER ME

BANNER OVER ME

A tale of the
Norman Conquest by

MARGERY
GREENLEAF

illustrated by Charles Mikolaycak

FOLLETT PUBLISHING COMPANY
Chicago ✵ New York

The lines from The Song of Roland, *translated
from the French by Charles Scott Moncrieff,
are quoted with permission of Chapman and
Hall, Publishers, London.*

*Text copyright © 1968 by Margery Greenleaf.
Illustrations copyright © 1968 by Follett
Publishing Company.
All rights reserved. No portion of this book
may be reproduced in any form without written
permission from the publisher. Manufactured
in the United States of America. Published
simultaneously in Canada by The Ryerson Press,
Toronto.*

Library of Congress Catalog Card Number: 68–25634

First Printing

Jacket Design by Allen Carr

FOLLETT PUBLISHING COMPANY
1010 West Washington Boulevard
Chicago, Illinois 60607

T/L 0673

For encouragement and patience
to my children

Priscilla, Carol, Betty, Charles,
Stephen and Sally

OUSE RIVER

YORK STAMFORD BRIDGE

DERWENT R.

HUMBER RIVER

NORTH SEA

THE WASH

ENGLAND

Thames River LONDON

MOUTH OF THE THAMES

BLEAN WOOD

ANDREDES LEAG
(The Weald)

CANTERBURY

DOVER

STRAIT of DOVER

WINCHESTER

LEWES

HASTINGS

ENGLISH CHANNEL

ST VALERY

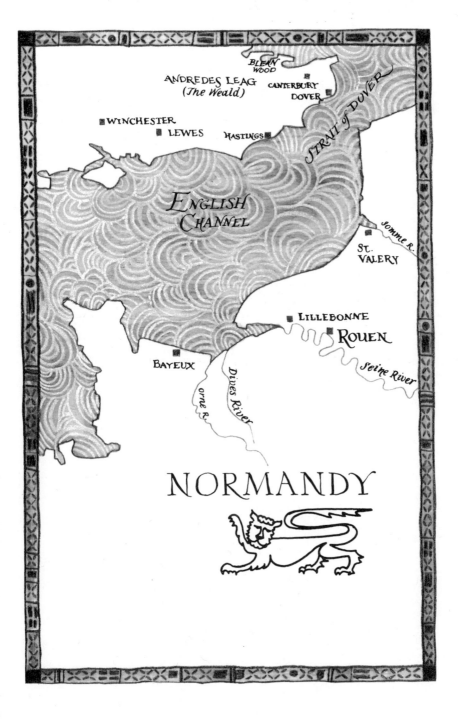

BLEAN WOOD

ANDREDES LEAG
(The Weald)

CANTERBURY
DOVER

STRAIT of DOVER

WINCHESTER
LEWES
HASTINGS

ENGLISH
CHANNEL

SOMME R.

ST.
VALERY

LILLEBONNE
ROUEN

BAYEUX

Dives River

Orne R.

Seine River

NORMANDY

UROLD, son of Engelric, was on his way home, trotting along through Blean wood in the fading light of a Yuletide afternoon. The path ran along a brook between the silvered ranks of the ancient beeches.

How still was the forest now—the trees, the small woodsy creatures, all things deep in winter rest. And where lay Boughton herd? All day he had not found a single deer track.

At the fording that men called Brothercrosse, where the ruts of Canterbury Way ran on toward London town, Turold stared for a space or two at the dark copse that lay beyond. He saw no rogues in ambush, so stooped to drink, splashing the water into his mouth with his hand and wetting face and hair. The water shone like the polished metal of a knight's shield and he saw his face—blue eyes and high cheek bones.

Turold laughed aloud.

What a strange face, he thought. I look like some kind of fighting man—a doughty man-at-arms! Indeed, I am like to Cerdic—as like as two peas in a pod. And rightly so. Were we not born of our lady mother in the same hour? And she passing to another world beyond our ever knowing her? He crossed himself.

If I belie my looks, Cerdic matches his, for he truly is

9

a warrior—a house carl with the Earl Harold. A soldier these three winters, since we came to the mark of ten and six. Aye, Cerdic is a soldier!

And what am I? A minstrel? In Saxon land there be no honors for minstrels. I am a thane's son, yet I serve as a plowboy, a very churl!

His resolve was hardened. This night he would run away and head for Normandy across the Narrow Seas.

He picked up a stone and threw it far into the wood.

Leaping the stepping stones, he ran to the grassy knoll where stood that greatest of all beeches, Beech of the Rood. The setting sun touched the bare branches soaring above the other old trees and turned to gold the scar of the cross slashed into its massive bole. He knelt a moment before the cross, then turned at a sound. Someone was clawing through the yellow leaves at the foot of the tree —a skinny ragged youth.

Turold stepped quickly to him, jerked him to his feet. "It's no use, no use digging here all the time for that gold chain! Years and years it's been. It's no use, Pig-Boy!"

Pig-Boy seemed to shrink into himself.

"What could you do with it, anyway? It's mine! When Duke William passed here that day with his Norman knights, you saw him throw me that gold chain. But we never found where it fell."

"Engelric will ne'er let you have it! Hating the duke and all Normans like he do." Pig-Boy had no words to tell how he felt about that chain, shining as it fell and never seen again. Sometimes he didn't feel like a pig-boy at all and tried to imagine himself a churl, lying at night with the house churls and the dogs, feet to the ashes of the fire pit in hall. But God had made him a pig-boy, and a pig-boy he must be.

Turold took a firmer hold of him. "We're standing on bones, lad, sacred bones. They'll be hantin' round yer sty come dark."

Pig-Boy's teeth chattered. "Lemme off this place!"

"Bones," Turold insisted. "My grandsir was buried here and two other thanes who fell here defending the great Canute, beset by Blean men. Canute had a cross cut into the trunk of the tree, and a finger-bone of our good Saxon saint, Althege, buried with his lieges to hallow the place. My poor lad! Never dig here again."

Pig-Boy uttered a despairing cry and wriggled free. He felt cold clean into his bones. But as he leaned weakly against a sapling it seemed as if strength and warmth flowed into him. A childhood memory rose of an old man who had told him tales of glory when the dark people—his people—had been lords in Albion. Now he felt that close by in the darkling wood were small, swarthy men like himself. But they walked as masters, not thralls, and Pig-Boy gathered the shadows about him like a cloak and knew that in some far-off time his people, rather than Turold's, had walked here master of moor and forest.

Suddenly he shouted at Turold, "Ye'll never get away! Ye'll rot here a churl all yer days. Churl! Singer of songs! And think you that Rolph, that prideful Norman, will e'er let you wed his girl? He sits in his castle on yonder hill and laughs at the likes of you! All Saxons are but as dogs to him!"

"Be quiet now!" Turold's voice was sad. The woods were hushed around them, almost like an animal breathing softly in the gathering dusk.

Now Pig-Boy remembered many things. He looked at Beech of the Rood—was something rising there through the mists of evening to clutch at him? He turned and ran blindly toward his nook in the sties.

Turold wrinkled his nose. There'd be a half sheep roasting above the fire trench in hall. He headed up the lane and around to a place in the manor wall where an oak tree flung a branch over. He was reaching up to it when something came down on him from the wall. Down he went, breath knocked out. He rolled over, got to his knees, shook his head. Beside him a man in a dark hooded cloak was getting up, picking up something, running off into the shadows.

"St. Mildred!" muttered Turold, "a stranger-man! What was that thing he had? It gave me a bump!"

Engelric sometimes talked about having this tree cut down. It offered easy entry to thieves as well as to truant sons. Yet nothing was ever done. Saxons! Talk but never act. Yet he was of the same breed, letting his father make churl of him, whereas Cerdic served with the earl's carls.

Ah—he mused upon the remedy. Yet to run away from home was a terrible, a chancy thing. To be a master-less man with no protection in a world of wolves and men that were worse than wolves. Masterless man . . . master-less man . . .

It was the song of the night wind, the one that women listened to with a certain expression on their faces—if some-one they loved wandered in far places with no lord to help them, save only the Lord of Heaven.

Kyndritha the bake mistress listened like that for her

12

sons who had not returned from the sea. And sometimes Adela the grandam seemed to hearken to the night wind. But for whom did she listen? The churl women sometimes whispered of another son. But surely he would know if she had another son besides Engelric.

He sat a moment on the wall looking down at Adela's bower where it leaned against the side of the great hall. More strangeness! The wind-door was open, swinging in the wind, and the room was empty. His grandam should be in there with her maids, stitching on the Dragon banner.

Dropping from the wall he ran to the hall, leaned against the heavy door and went in. At the fire pit a sheep was scorching, untended on its spit. Adela the grandam stood in the center of a huddle of maids and churls, laughing at them. How tiny she was, like a silver-haired doll!

"Come now!" she told them, half scolding, half comforting. "It is nothing. There was no one."

Kyndritha, the grizzled old bake mistress, cried, "I tell you—I saw him! A man—a pixy, or worse! His face was hooded, he looked not to right or left but came in and went straight to the bower door. And there he be unless he's flown up the smoke vent."

Adela spoke lightly. " 'Drithy, you are always seeing things. We can't stand around talking; the banner's to be finished. Three days' work and it will be ready for the earl."

Kyndritha shrieked, "Turold, don't 'ee let her go in. I tell 'ee, it were a ghosty man!"

But Turold only laughed at her. He saluted the tall maiden with the long braids, Cerdic's sweetheart Brunhilda, then in three strides he flung the door open. They all crowded to peer in. The room was quite empty, the corner fire smoldering, wisps of smoke creeping out the wind-door.

Said Adela quietly, "Why, the fire's almost out. Build it up, will you, Turold?"

Turold got some wood and knelt to blow up the coals. Kyndritha was, he knew, telling only the truth. There was a stranger-man roaming about. What was that thing he had dropped at the wall, then hastily put under his cloak?

With Brunhilda's help, Adela spread out the long Dragon Banner. "Look, Turold, is it not bonny?"

He looked at it. Bright embroidery, the work of many months, the head and tail crusted with jewels. How sinister the curve of the tail, yet how noble the head with its flashing eyes!

"Nay, it is grand! And never had a Saxon king such a banner to float over him!"

"A king! It is for the Earl Harold!"

"Aye, so it is. But he will be king, grandam."

2 THE BODE

THE great hall was murky with wandering smoke from fire pit and wall torches when Kyndritha handed Black Jarn the dinner horn.

He rubbed his black beard. "Now 'Drithy, can't a man set after a long day? Had to run all over for some lost sheep. Those feckless herders!"

"They're just boys!"

"Just boys," he growled. "And the big boy, where was he?" But the brown eyes, deep set in his long-jawed face, were not cross. "Blean wood again, I warrant."

He opened the door and the blast of the horn echoed across close and moor. The manor folk came trooping into hall and settled noisily onto benches along the big trestle table. Someone said, "Tough old sheep again!" and the laugh went round.

They waited until Engelric seated Adela in the high-backed chair beside his own at the upper table, and until the maids had served the meat and bread, then attacked the victuals with knives and napkins. Boys passed foaming mugs, and the talk got louder. Some of the younger churls raised an old war song and beat the board with their fists.

Turold came in from feeding his stallion and slipped into a place at the foot of the big table.

Engelric suddenly shouted, "Be quiet!" Then to Black

Jarn, "Jarn! Has Turold helped you this day?"

In the silence Adela's fingers tightened on her napkin. Somewhere a wolf howled.

Black Jarn scraped the trencher with his fingers. "Turold?" he growled. "I made out. And the ricks are all capped . . . yes, all capped. I wasn't very busy."

Engelric crashed his heavy cup against the board. "But Turold's been busy, eh? Busy in Blean wood! Turold, come here!"

Standing before his father, Turold spoke boldly. "Am I never to have time for myself? You keep me here, though Cerdic serves with the carls. For fortn't I've scarcely drawn breath of my own!"

"Breath of your own! Time of your own! By all the saints—who has time of his own?"

He turned to Adela. "My lady mother, I must score you for this. You taught him the Norman tongue, you helped him to make that long song—some drivel about an ancient king and men who died in a pass. It's ruined him for the farming, like that other one who should be here, for the son's duty he owes . . ."

Adela stiffened. Her face was a mask.

Turold cried out, "Don't blame the grandam! She only gave me what I starved for."

"Starved! Did you say starved? That's what you all will be doing some winter after I'm gone. Who then will look after our folk? I never thought to see my own blood so niddering." He reached for more meat. "I hear you've been seen keeping tryst with that Norman wench and hunting with her brother. I forbid you to have aught to do with any Normans! And after this you are to bide in

16

the demesne. I will set your tasks hereafter. Black Jarn is too easy on you."

Turold lifted his head and looked his father squarely in the eye. "I will see Roger and Lucy when it pleases me."

Engelric glared at him.

"And I will no longer be used as a churl. Do not press me too hard. I wish not to fail in son's duty!"

Engelric shouted, "Duty!" He rose and gave Turold a mighty buffet on the side of his head. He was felled by the force of it and lay with his feet in the ashes. A brown mastiff came and licked his hand.

When his head cleared, Turold sat by the wall blinking at the shadows playing across the dark walls. Eating a choice morsel Kyndritha brought him, he sang softly to himself and knew what he must do, and how to get his white stallion through the manor gate, for he could not go to Rouen on foot like a churl.

Aye, now is the time . . .

"*. . . now is the time for it, now is the time!*
This time and no other!
The wind sings and the wolf sings
And the downs will be white under the moon."

The wind was making a great song for him now. How it shouted, how it sang, over moor and manor and sea, over the Blean wood which moved like a harp under its hand. Always there were songs, in trees, the wind, the brooks, and in the great deeds of men. And he had made a song of the greatest of them all, of Charlemagne fighting the pagans in Spain, and of his paladin, Rollant, dying in

17

the pass of Roncevalles to save his lord. But only William, duke of Normandy, could know the glory of that song.

A churl came into hall babbling of a stranger at the gate, and at his heels came the old gateward, Ulfnoth, crying out, "Let me turn him away! No honest man knocks at such an hour."

Adela looked amazed. "Ulfnoth! We never turn travelers away."

The door was flung wide, and a tall man bearing the banderole of a royal messenger stood looking at them. Adela hastened to welcome him, food and drink were brought, and they asked his news.

"I am Breame, king's bode," he said, "and I bear news for the Earl Harold at Canterbury. It's—"

Engelric interrupted him, "The earl is at Dover, we heard."

"Then I must ride to Dover. The earl will surely set forth as soon as he can get his carls in motion."

"Then," said Adela, "we must work all night on the new banner, for he wants to take it with him. The great meeting, the Witan, comes soon."

"A new banner?" The bode swung round. "What banner will it be? Is it for war or for peace?"

"Why, there is no war, we have peace," answered Adela. "It is the Dragon of Wessex, all wrought with jewels and silken colors. We will show you."

Turold hurried into the bower and brought the banner, which he spread out, standing on a bench.

"I see!" The bode's voice was grim. "I see what this is—the old emblem of Uther Pendragon, who saw a dragon in the sky and had two banners made, one for war and one for peace, and they hung always in the cathedral at Winchester. But I like it not that here is only one. For this one is going to be for war, my masters!"

Adela, holding the tail of the dragon, put her hand to her heart, and the maids made the sign of the cross.

Engelric banged his fist on the board. "War! You must be mad. We have had peace many years, since the Danes ruled England—for eight and twenty summers—peace, I tell you!"

The bode shook his head. "Peace do you call it? It is slumber—like the sleep of a hog who recks not the time of slaughter. The king is holy. But he has poured out treasure for relics and to build the new minster, while all the defenses fell into decay. On our east coast we are likely to see again the Danes or the Norsemen."

There was silence a space, then he added, "And to the south, a leopard ready to spring." He looked earnestly around on them. "I think ye be true English hearts all."

Engelric answered, "Aye, and haters of these Normans that the king gives good English land to."

The bode leaned forward. "Look you! Call in your churls from the outer crofts and teach them to fight. Whet your blades and make spears of your pruning hooks!"

The silence made Turold's skin prickle.

Breame went on, "The old king is dying and there is no prince of the blood. William of Normandy means to have the English crown even if he has to fight for it."

Engelric clenched his hands. "But Harold! It is known of all men that Harold will be king. He has ruled the kingdom under Edward for many years. And last summer we all swore to the old bishop that we would hold to

19

Harold when Edward dies."

The bode persisted. "What I tell you is true. Last summer while you were swearing to make Harold king, Harold himself was in Normandy swearing away the crown of England to William. Didn't you folk know that Harold was shipwrecked on the French coast?"

Engelric answered, "No one seems to know what really happened, only that William took Harold from Count Guy, who held him for ransom."

"I know—I was there! William feasted us; we helped him in one of his little wars. Nonetheless, we were prisoners. At the end, when he sent Harold home with many fair words, he made him swear to help him get the English crown. William claimed that King Edward had promised it to him."

Engelric cried out, "By Holy Cross, it cannot be!"

The bode shrugged. "What else could Harold do? Rot for the rest of his life in a Norman dungeon? Harold took the oath. But let me tell you the terrible part. After it was done they lifted the altar cloth and under it we saw the bones of many saints—relics from all over Normandy."

Engelric shouted, "It was a trick—it cannot hold him!"

The bode assured them, "William will use this oath to get the English crown."

"It can never be. And Harold has strong brothers to help him."

Breame nodded. "All but one. Where is Tostig?"

Turold felt the chill the name brought. Tostig! They were all silent now as if thinking of that false brother to Harold, who had made so much trouble in his northern earldom and had been banished at last.

Said Breame, "We saw Tostig last summer in Normandy; he'd been visiting with his wife's people in Flanders. He came to Rouen—to mock Harold. There's a rumor he is going to raid our coasts."

Black Jarn cursed. "He's a bad one."

Breame rose. "Aye, that he is. I give you thanks for refreshment. Have you a horse for me?" He picked up his banderole.

"My son will get you a horse," Engelric told him.

"Your son!" The bode looked Turold up and down. "By God's grace! Does he ride, does he wield the two-handed sword? There may be work soon for young blades."

Turold handed the bode his cloak. "Come and pick your mount from the horse barn, master. You mistake," he said. "I only play the churl."

When Turold came back to the hall his father was slumped over a long sword, fumbling with a whetstone. Turold looked about him. His father's men had eaten and drunk themselves into a stupor and lay where they had fallen, useless as sheep. He took his old cloak off a peg. If it snowed he would need it over his new one.

He went to the bower where the women bent over the banner. He would need the old harp Adela kept there. So he spoke of it, and Adela lifted her dark eyes and gave him a long clear look. It told him what he wanted to know. "Yes, take it," she said.

He turned to the wall, but the harp was not there. Suddenly he knew what it was that the stranger-man by the wall had dropped.

"Where can it have gone?" she asked wonderingly. No one but Turold ever touched it. That is, not since another young singer long ago . . . She roused herself. She must not weaken now.

Turold did not notice the slight quiver of her lips. It was late, late. And he must be far away by daybreak. She pointed to the corner of the bed, to a little leather bag. As he tucked it into his jerkin, he felt the hard edges of coins. He did not go to her, but looked at her a long moment. It was more than a caress, for she was the only mother he remembered. He went quickly from the bower.

In hall his father was shouting to no one in particular, "Harold is my lord! Norman curses can't make us take—"

Turold went out into the night. The moon was already above the manor wall. He went to the bakehouse and made up a packet of bread, cheese, and cold mutton. He went to the horse barn, found his horse furniture, and led out White Boy, slipping on bridle, cinching saddle, tying on the bundle of food.

From the darkness where the byre churls lay huddled in hay he heard Black Jarn grumbling, " . . . and now he rides at night. For sure, the night mare will chase him."

Someone moved like a shadow along the wall. Was it Pig-Boy the snooper?

At the gatehouse he climbed over, went a few feet from the wind-door where the old man slept and blatted like a lost lamb. Soon Ulfnoth came and opened the gate and tottered out along the wall. Instantly Turold had White Boy through and was riding across the moonlit fields toward the bulk of the Broken Tower.

NDER the gray wall of the castle Turold looked up at the opening leading to Lucy's bower and whistled till he saw a flutter of white. It was too high for them to speak, and he wished to touch her hand and look into her dark eyes. But all that would be his reward when he had won a fame that would make her father listen to his suit. He sang a Norman lullaby she had taught him, saluted her, and turned away.

Down the slope trotted White Boy on the track that led into Blean wood and so to Canterbury and the sea. When day came, his father would be hunting for him. But at this hour, it was sure that Engelric was asleep on the rushes on the hall floor. There was yet time to get away beyond all catching in the far mazes of the weald. He was not afraid; he did not believe the tales that dragons of Old Time still lurked there in deep and awesome marshes. He had ranged In Blean since he could walk, and Blean wood was feared of many.

To cover an emptiness he began to sing of Rollant:

"High were the peaks, and shadowy and grand,
The valleys deep, the rivers swiftly ran . . ."

Abreast of Beech of the Rood he pulled up and looked down at a man who was lying there beside a little fire. There were often such fellows, wayfarers or pack men who slept under the protection of the beech with a fire to warm them and keep off wolves. While Turold got down and knelt a moment under the beech, White Boy nuzzled at the sleeping figure, so that when Turold mounted again the man unwound himself from his cloak and sat up. Turold took up the reins.

"Your pardon, master," he said and then was gone, splashing through the ford, riding gaily along singing again of Roncevalles.

But he had hardly gone beyond sight of the beech when he heard shouts behind him—cries for help in the French tongue. *"A l'aide . . . garçon! A moi! Secours! Secours!"*

He reined White Boy around. He could not go back! Yet Blean men were right savage. To them Christian folk were only creatures who supplied clothes, as deer gave them meat and crofters' sheep yielded warm skins. If they left the stranger alive, he would be naked. It was winter night and snow coming.

He shouted and dug his heels into White Boy. He could hear the howling of the wild men as he raced back.

The stranger was standing against the massive bole of the beech, slashing and darting with his sword at the men who leaped about him, ragged—and hairy as animals. Turold rode into them, swinging his sword, and they suddenly shambled off into the night. Laughing, howling like a wolf, he harried them to the fordway, where they melted into the blackness of the copse.

There was silence as Turold sheathed his blade and turned to see if the stranger was harmed.

24

The fellow was wiping his face with the hem of his cloak. "My thanks, young master," he said. "Are you of France? You understood my call."

"No, but I know the tongue." There was something strange about this man. Though sleeping unattended in the wood, it was sure by his voice and bearing that he was some noble one, used to the command of men.

"Be you man or spirit?" asked Turold, and his neck prickled as he thought of that other one who had stood in the same way against the tree forty years since, and defended himself against Blean men.

"Why do you ask?"

Turold said, "That is a holy tree." And he told him about Canute.

"Who saved him?"

"They say the rogues were fierce that day, and some had swords. My grandfather and four others were with him; he was wounded. They were saved when some of Canute's lagging men came down that hill. Two king's men were killed."

"Was it so?" said the Norman. Turold had a feeling that the man was laughing. But what was there to laugh at?

"An omen," said the Norman. "A tree where kings stand to defense."

As Turold turned White Boy, thinking of his need now for speed, for his father's stallion was the fastest in all Scray, the stranger called to him, "Wait! I lost my companion in this accursed forest yestereve. I lost our horses too. I dare not move from here till I get help. Do you know this wood?"

"Master," said Turold, "I wish I could help you fur-

25

ther, but I have urgent business now—out yonder. Go up that lane and the manor folk will help you."

The stranger scowled. "Saxon rustics! They'll be churlish—and my need is desperate. My friend is a great minstrel of Normandy; he has been ill, distraught. We brought him here to see if Saxon air would help him, for he was Saxon—he came from Scray somewhere long ago, poor Taillefer!"

Taillefer! How could he tell this man what that name meant to him? He cried, "All my life I have longed to see him. And this night I am running away from son's duty to go to Rouen, that he might hear my great song ere I offer it to the duke."

"You too are minstrel," said the man. "Then you cannot refuse."

In that moment Turold knew it was too late, too late to escape, too late even to help this man. For now he heard what he should have heeded some moments before—horses coming on the gallop, men shouting and torches flaring, down from Farthingwold home place.

Turold spoke quietly. "It is too late. Here are my father and his men, and I can go nowhere now. I must be churl forever." So he turned to face them and made no protest when Engelric rode close and took him roughly by the arm.

"Do you want to leave your bones to bleach in An- dredes Leag?" He sagged in the saddle. And yet Turold, looking from him to the stranger, felt a thrill of pride. Both were big men, yet the Saxon did not suffer by comparison. Engelric went on, "Maybe when you get this nonsense knocked out of you, then you can be proper

26

thane's son and remember where duty lies."

Turold thought, Aye—press me into the mold, like butter from the churn. No more nonsense now, only the farming, pigs in the mud, men like pigs swilling food and drink to lie gorged on the rushes. Endless work and never a song at day's end . . . *But I am not butter.* . . .

But he said never a word, only looked into the dark wood, and it eased his pain to think of the stranger. Engelric held no love for Normans, and this man was a Norman. Yet they must help him; they must find Taillefer the minstrel. But before he could speak of it, the stranger himself was beside them.

"Good Saxon," he said, "your son would have been a league away and out of your reach had he not stayed to succor me, beset by outlaws. He is a brave lad. I pray you, give me his help further. My companion, sick and confused, is lost in this cursed wood. It was down there . . . I fear he will die."

Engelric turned in the saddle. "Master, this lad is a wayward son who shirks duty. Let me give you one of my men who knows the wood. Black Jarn, come here!"

The Norman shook his head. "I pledge my honor for his return to you. He is light of heart and strong of limb, and he is the one I must have."

To Turold's astonishment Engelric bowed his head in assent. With a quickening of pulse he felt that here was some strange new pattern. He had not escaped to Normandy, he was in chains again. And yet . . . things would not be the same. He had succored a king, and life was beginning at last for him. No, no! How foolish! This man was no king. But who was he?

Engelric was saying, "But the lad must keep watch while my mother prays at the Beech as always on the year-day of Canute's besetment here. My father's bones lie there beside his shoulder-companions, many years it is now."

The thane and his men rode back up the lane. Night was fading, dawn was near. Turold and the stranger hid the horse, found a bush for their own concealment, and sat down and ate from Turold's bundle of food.

The stranger sighed, wiped his mouth. "A thousand of thanks! I had hunger." He pointed to the copse. "That dark thicket! That is where those wild men hid."

Turold agreed. "A useful place from which to way-lay travelers. They'd have pulled me off my horse had I not galloped through the brook."

"It happens often?"

"Oh—aye. Twice since All-Saints Day."

"Splendor of God! Why don't your people cut it down?"

Turold laughed softly. "Now I see you are but newly come into Saxon land. By St. Mildred! Were you born in Scray you would ken that it be an honor to be robbed from the very ambush that betrayed Canute and others. A most noble and notable thicket!"

The stranger laughed, then hushed, for Adela was moving through the aisles of the beeches, the hood of her cloak laid back from her silver hair, shining from the candles of the seven-branched candlestick.

The stranger whispered, "Beautiful!"

She mounted to the knoll and knelt for some time. In the blaze of the tapers the scar of the cross shone like

28

living gold. A woodcutter came from the west, driving a two-wheeled cart toward Canterbury. He made a reverent sign and drove on. While they watched the moon sank, leaving a misty grayness. At last Adela rose, and holding the candlestick before her, walked slowly up the lane and was gone around a bend.

The Norman stood up, absently brushing himself. "Where did she get such a thing? Never have I seen a finer."

Turold stiffened. "Sir Norman, my grandam is of noble Norman birth. She came to England with the Lady Emma when Emma did come to wed Canute. But the candlestick of the seven branches is a treasure that has been in the family of my Saxon forebears for generations."

The Norman's dark eyes gleamed.

Leading White Boy down the brook path, he asked about Harold, how men held him in affection, and Turold, unthinking, answered that he was beloved above every man in the kingdom, adding hastily, "After King Edward, of course."

The Norman fidgeted with the tassels of his hood. At last he asked, "Why must you run away to Normandy? Why must you be a minstrel?"

How could Turold explain? He was both Saxon and Norman, save that he could never stick a churl as if he were only a pig, as Rolph of the Tower did. In feeling for men he was Saxon.

And now he was searching for the greatest minstrel of all, for Taillefer. He felt a great wonder. St. Mildred is watching over me. My life is beginning at last!

N a path leading into the far dingles, they found a glove belonging to the man they sought. They went on, leading the white stallion. The Norman asked Turold about Duke William. "Do you not fear him? Men say he is treacherous and fierce."

"That I cannot believe. I saw him once, long ago."

The Norman stared. "Why, you were only a little lad when William came to visit King Edward."

"Still I remember. I saw William—he rode the biggest horse that ever came up Canterbury Way. He is like a warrior king of old—oh, he is royal!"

The stranger's eyes gleamed. "Are you sure you would know him again? You were young, dazzled by the trappings."

Turold answered, "Not the trappings, but the man! I have long served him in my dreams."

He tried to tell this man about that procession passing along the old Way. The heavy-footed stallions, the long line of riders, two by two, dust rising. And banners. Cloth of gold, everything of rich and shining stuffs had those knights of William's, with gold and jewels too.

And he told him how the duke, stopping by Beech of the Rood, had loosed his hawk, how it made its stoop upon his own pet dove. "I ran with a stick and beat off the falcon. It went back to the duke's wrist—he was roaring with laughter as he hooded it. And just as he was riding on . . ."

The Norman picked up the tale. "—and just as he was riding on, he turned back and tossed a gold chain to the brave little Saxon."

"Master! You were there! You must be of the Norman court—you saw me that day."

The man smiled. "So you have William's chain."

Turold hesitated, "We have not the chain. It was lost in the leaves, and—" He took the Norman's arm. "Quick, someone is coming!"

They led the horse behind a wide beech and held his muzzle. There was the sound of horses; then a file of riders appeared on the slope above.

Turold said, "That is Rolph of the Tower, but we'll do better without his help. Hunting with all those men— blundering about! And a good chance for those who hate him to make ambush." And he told him how, some weeks since, a churl had attacked Rolph with a knife, adding, "He is well hated of our people, and with good cause."

"Cause!" cried the Norman. "What cause could a churl have to touch his lord? It is not so in Normandy."

Now it was Turold's turn to stare. "But life is splendid there. Here all is work and much thought for our cattle. There you have pageantry and grace."

"But we maintain discipline. How do you think that lords can dwell in pageantry and grace, as you put it, unless the lower orders toil for them? God has set lords over the rabble for their own good. And a lord's vileness is better in the eyes of the Lord than a serf's righteousness."

31

Turold said, "We have but few thralls. Adela says they are from the old conquered ones, their children's children."

The Norman laughed. "I suppose you give them the best place at the board and clothe them richly?"

"Well, no," admitted Turold, thinking of Pig-Boy, and how, once a year, he threw him his old breeches.

"It's the way of the world. Some are created to serve and some to rule. If you are not lord, you are slave."

"Oh, no! Those born to rule must care for all their folk, not just themselves. There can be beauty without tyranny and work with splendor too."

"Not on this earth." Then he pressed Turold with questions concerning Harold and the kingdom, and of King Edward's promise to pass the crown to the Norman duke.

Turold protested: "The king cannot pass on the crown, he can only indicate preference. The people of England, through their great meeting, the Witan, choose a new king."

The Norman laughed. "Many Normans now hold English land; they will shout for William."

"No, no! You don't understand. We have already chosen. With the times so disordered . . ."

The stranger gripped his arm. "What did you say?"

Turold cried wildly, "The old bishop has already gathered our wise men, and they have sworn to him and to each other that when Edward dies they will choose Harold!"

Suddenly the Norman seemed to be beside himself. He covered his head with his hood, he plucked at the strings, tying and untying them. At last he asked, face turned away, "Will Harold then be forsworn of his oath? He dare not! 'Tis but the attempt of the foolish old bishop to stay the sure event."

He laughed. "By the splendor of God! We cannot be checked so!" And he strode on so quickly that Turold had to run to catch up.

Suddenly he knew what folly he had done. This great secret babbled to a Norman! Yet he hurried along, wishing above everything to hear his voice again, to look into those glowing eyes.

White Boy stopped and pricked up his ears. There was a sound like horses running, or deer.

"The deer! They'll be coming through here!"

The running became a thunder, and deer fled past in great leaps, the antlered ones as frightened as the does and fawns. In a space they were gone, the mashed-down ferns were moving, the broken twigs settling onto the forest floor.

It was very still.

Said Turold, "Let's go see what frightened them."

They retraced the herd's tracks to the place where the running began but saw nothing. Then as they skirted a marsh, they heard a sound not belonging to the wood— a moan, a man's moan.

On a mossy bank lay a man in a dark cloak. They ran, knelt beside him. His eyes were closed, and there was an arrow in his shoulder, and blood around it. They cut open jerkin and shirt. The arrow was deep. The Norman shook his head. "Poor Taillefer! Did Rolph's men do this?"

Turold stood up. "Perhaps. They are very careless! I'll get the horse, and we'll take him to my grandam; she's

33

a famous nurse." He ran up the bank.

The Norman looked down and saw a small harp with a gilded leopard's head on the frame.

When Turold led up the horse, the wounded minstrel was saying, "Sire, you should not have come to this place. Old joys and new sorrows walk here . . . the hall I saw . . . I cannot remember . . ." He closed his eyes.

Turold looked down at the little harp. "If this man is Taillefer, he is also the thief who walked boldly into my grandam's bower and took this off the wall."

"That is strange," the Norman said. "At his best he is a singer who can enthrall you all night long. But he was hurt—he saved the duke in a battle when both were young men. That is why we call him Taillefer, Cleave-Iron. But he is bemused more often than not. We have to lead him by hand to get him to table. He was Saxon once, as you are."

They lifted the wounded man with some difficulty, for though he was thin his frame was great, and the arrow was in the wound. While they led the horse through the wood, Turold sang—Saxon lays and Norman lullabies. And then he sang of Roncevalles.

> *"Rollant hath set the great horn to his mouth,*
> *He grasps it well, and with great virtue sounds.*
> *High are those peaks, afar it rings and loud,*
> *Thirty great leagues they hear its echoes mount.*
>
> *"Great Charles canters with fury made,*
> *And all the Franks dismay and wonder have . . .*
> *That they are not with Rollant the Captain,*
> *Whereas he fights the Sarrazins of Spain.*

34

"God! Sixty men are all now in his train,
Never a king had better Capitains . . .
That emperor bids ten thousand horns to blow;
Brave Franks—now on to Roncevalles they go!"

When at last they came out on the Way, the Norman said, "Young man, you must go to William. He will welcome such a singer!"

Near Beech of the Rood, Taillefer swooned, so that they must ease him from the saddle. Gently they laid him on the bank under the tree and bathed his face with brook water.

"Our hall is only a step further. I'll run ahead and have our people bring a litter."

So he ran off up the lane. Yet when the manor wall loomed before him, he turned back. It seemed that the wood echoed with strange noises. It was as though a company of men passed the Way, and he thought he heard his name shouted.

He ran back with all speed and came again to Brothercrosse fordway and Beech of the Rood, dusky and hushed under the lengthening shadows. The whole winter day had passed as if in a dream while he walked In Blean with the stranger.

And now Turold stood staring. He stroked White Boy, who rested, hipshot and head drooping. There was no one, nothing else in sight in all the wood. The Norman was gone, Taillefer was gone, only the ferns pressed down showed where they had laid him. There was a current in the air, an odor and sense of things unseen that made Turold draw his cloak closer.

Had he been pixy-led this day?

35

Yet there was blood on the flank of the horse, and underfoot the track was churned as by the passing of many horses. Had these horsemen been friends or foes? Did they have the Norman prisoner? Or were they perhaps Rolph's people returning from the hunt? Perhaps Rolph was the "friend" of whom the Norman had spoken—he was the nearest Norman in Scray.

Now that Turold thought upon it, he had leaked information like a sieve but the Norman had told him nothing.

Now his dream was shattered. Yet he had seen Taillefer, had helped him. And he had talked with that uncommon man, that princely stranger. Since dawn of Thor's day he had known all this and now he was alone on Freya's eve, with the winds mournful and he honor bound to return to churlhood.

There was a thin sound, and whirling about, he saw Pig-Boy slipping behind the Beech. He was reminded that Pig-Boy had certainly roused up Engelric to come after him. He moved fast and easily caught the boy on the other side of the tree, held him by his rags, dragged him to the brook and heaved him into the cold water.

Pig-Boy clutched at a branch, fell with a splash, rolled over and got up. His wet rags lay flat against his bones. He bounded off, hunching one shoulder, his eyes like dark coals.

Turold felt sharp pangs of remorse. "Come to hall, and I'll find some dry clothes for you."

"No . . . no . . ." panted Pig-Boy, "none o' yer old rags!"

He picked up a stone.

36

"Look at yer horse," he yelled. "He'll lead you through cold and wet, through briar and marsh till you be as I am!"

Turold cried, "Wait!"

But Pig-Boy threw the stone. It took White Boy in the neck, and he tossed up his head and cantered wildly off into the darkening wood.

"You little devil, you rogue!" Turold pulled up his belt and ran off after the horse.

T was morning of Freya's day when Turold brought White Boy to the gate of Farthing-wold and Ulfnoth the ancient warder raised his hands in wonder to see young master and his horse covered with mud.

To the thrall who ran to take White Boy Turold gave word for a rub and a hot mash, and to another he said, "Come to the washhouse and fill a tub for me." Clean and dressed, he stood by the bakehouse door and wondered whether the bad feeling inside of him was real sorrow or only the pangs of an empty stomach.

He began to croon a sad little song, then laughed.

Oh, those wondrous smells coming from the bakehouse. Man is but a stomach on legs! He uttered his special howl—the old boyhood signal between him and Cerdic, known to all the manor folk. Kyndritha, laughing, appeared at the door with a wooden bowl of steaming meat and broth.

Turold bowed. "This poor beggar thanks thee, fair lady. And what are yon good smells from your oven?"

"Turold! What happened to 'ee in the wood?"

He held a chunk of meat on the point of his belt knife and tossed it, caught it in his mouth.

"'Ee don't fool old 'Drithy! Summat bad, I ken!"

"Lady! The oven!" he cried.

She smacked his rump, but shortly brought him a crusty loaf on a wooden paddle. He pretended to kiss the top of her gray head. He finished the meat, ate half the bread and asked, "Where's Adela?"

"Sewing!" Kyndritha snorted. "She was! But the banner's done now, with Brunhilda's help. We put the grandam to bed this morning—I tucked her in myself. But with the earl coming, there'll be hundreds to feed—and the ox not even ready for the fire!"

She gave him a push. "You be about to fall down! Go now to the loft and sleep. You can be a real help later—if you can stand up!"

When the sun was at the nooning he woke, hearing his name called. He jumped from the loft, brushing off his clothes.

Kyndritha stood inside the high door scowling at him. "I scarce got the words to tell 'ee."

"What is it?"

"A messenger came from the Tower."

"Bless you, 'Drithy! Where is he? From Roger?"

She shook her head.

"Lucy, then!"

"Nay, lad—it were one of Rolph's huntsmen. He brought a packet—said it was for 'ee."

"Good! Where is it?"

She gave him a long sad look. "The master took it and threw it in the fire pit—right under the roasting ox."

He stared at her. "I don't believe it!"

"'Ee knows how master is. Anything from that Norman . . ." She fumbled in her wide skirts. "Here, I saved summat of it for 'ee."

She held out a piece of parchment, scorched on one side. He seized it, turned it over.

"The writing's all here. Oh—bless you, bless you!"

He bent over it, but she pulled on his arm and he turned impatiently, "Please! Oh—this is wonderful . . ."

"There's something more. Don't 'ee want to see it? The best of all. For a king!"

"Stop teasing!"

"Nay—I took it from the pig-boy, scrabbling at the side of the pit he was. But I saw the flash as it fell out of the scarf it was bound in."

" 'Drithy! For God's sweet mercy—have pity!"

She took from her bosom a long heavy gold chain attached to a medallion cunningly carved with leopards. The ducal leopards of Normandy! He seized it, held the medallion against his cheek.

She laughed. "Best hide it from the pig-boy!"

"Nay—it's for Adela! The writing says—"

He didn't wait to tell her, but rushed off to hall and into the open door of the bower. Adela sat in her chair with Brunhilda kneeling to fasten the ribands of her slippers.

"Oh, look, look!" and he thrust chain and parchment into Adela's hands. She held up the chain, but returned the writing.

"You read it," she said.

"It's a message from that Norman I was with in the wood. I helped him to find Taillefer—he was wounded. I guess that Rolph's people took them to the Tower."

Adela smiled and shook her head. "Tell me later. But read the writing."

He smoothed it out, all crinkled from the fire as it was. "It says, 'This chain is the mate of the one that was lost. Give it in the keeping of the grandam. In days of sorrow she shall nail it on the manor gate, for the safety of all. As for you, honor and devoir to your father now. Nevertheless to Roncevalles you shall go.' "

"Let me see it." Long she studied it, then said, "I understand the good intent. Yet I pray we shall never need it. And now, Turold, it is time Mistress Brunhilda be escorted to her home. It shall be your happy duty."

"But Cerdic will soon be here. He will want to see her!"

Brunhilda explained, "It's a promise to Father. But you will be enough to go. The men are all needed here. And we'll be safe enough in broad day."

Turold went to the horse barn and saddled Brunhilda's palfrey and a big black for himself.

In half an hour they were out on the track and down into Blean, splashing through Brothercrosse. As they rode Turold was hoping that around each bend they would see Cerdic riding toward them. Soon the roads would be choked with carls, and there would be little to fear with so many earl's men about. So Turold rode with a high heart, careless that he had left his sword by the washhouse and was now unarmed except for a belt knife.

They came suddenly upon the Normans around a bend, three knights sitting their heavy horses, blocking the way. It was all over in a moment, Turold unhorsed and Brunhilda carried off on a Norman saddle. Galloping back toward Brothercrosse they were—and Turold on the ground.

Dazed, he lay for a moment, then struggled to his feet. The black gelding was not far off. He caught him and got stiffly into the saddle. A horse was coming from the east, and he prayed it might be a carl—or at least someone well horsed and well armed. When the rider came into view, he could not believe his eyes.

"St. Mildred!" It was Cerdic in linked mail, helmet on pommel, yellow hair hanging on the shoulders of his crimson cloak. In his hand was a lance, long and heavy with a pointed flag rippling from the tip. In his belt a sword, and a battle ax tied to the saddle.

"St. Mildred!" Turold yelled their special signal and spurred the black. They met, and Turold poured out to him what had happened. ". . . that French knight—Rolph's captain!"

"God help her!" Cerdic's horse leaped as spurs raked his flanks. Turold followed.

They must reach her before the Normans took her into the Tower, where they could easily hide her and not even Lucy know she was there.

At the ford they found Pig-Boy driving his pigs home. Cerdic yelled, "Pig-Boy, wait! Brunhilda's carried off to the Tower. Are there any of our men on work over that way?"

Pig-Boy cried, "Aye—at the edge of Blean, making hurdles, I think. They got billhooks with 'em. The Normans rode past but now. They didn't seem a-hurry. The maid has swooned."

Turold told him, "There's a passel o' men in the close. Run get them."

Cerdic set his mouth. "Hurry, boy—hurry!"

42

Pig-Boy, skinny legs flashing, disappeared up the lane. The brothers took a short cut through the wood where manor folk were working on wattle stuff. They rode up, told the tale, and rode on again up the shoulder of the hill with the sokemen coming fast at their heels, for Saxons, whatever their faults, were good men at footwork.

They were running like wolves, the savage bearded men, swarming like a black cloud onto the Tower path and they were just in time, for the three Normans were riding up the slope to the gate. Cerdic gestured with his lance and passed it to Turold. The men behind them raised a great shout.

Without words, Cerdic and Turold worked like the two halves of a perfect whole. They cut the Norman captain away from his men, harried him along till they could see that Black Jarn and the others were keeping the rest of the knights busy. The captain was in poor shape to give combat with Brunhilda across his saddle. Turold circled, kicked the black horse so that suddenly he was fair upon the Norman and struck him on the shoulder. He fell heavily and Brunhilda, hanging from the saddle, was in danger till Cerdic caught her up and riding off to a little distance, laid her under a tree.

Then he was back in the fray, for the other knights were attacking Turold and the Saxons able to deal little harm to armed men.

Almost at once there was a new sound, again the howling of enraged men. Over the rise they were coming, some a-foot, some a-horseback: Pig-Boy had done his work well; here were forty men from the manor to help them. Maybe they could overwhelm the Normans by sheer num-

43

bers. Down came Engelric, his men armed with clubs, stones, pikes, a few swords. They swept like a storm upon the Normans, and the brothers drew back for a moment, breathing their horses and themselves. They looked toward Brunhilda and smiled to see that one of their own men was lifting her to a pony, was trotting away eastward with her. But when they turned back to the fight, they did not smile. It was like to be a bitter day before it was done.

Norman men-at-arms were galloping down upon them from the Tower, and blood would be shed. His friends and Lucy's, killing each other! It must be stopped! He shouted above the tumult and saw Roger trying to do the same thing. Roger! He and Roger, they must not come to an encounter!

But at that moment there came a mighty thundering voice which commanded all men to hold their arms. It was a knight riding alone down from the Tower, hands up, unarmed.

This man shouted to Roger, "Stop your men!"

As all held their arms, panting, he cried, "Command your men to quit this senseless brawl. I saw from the wall the cause of this broil, and I commend the friends of the maid who came to rescue her. But the wench is safe; let there be no more combat."

The knight, in black hauberk with nose piece of the helmet down, rode to Engelric. "Saxon," he said, "let me beg pardon for this deed of shame. Rolph shall make amends to the maid's people. And now let me speak of another matter for which I ask your indulgence. You are the father of that young singer whom they call Turold. I will pay you well to let him go to Rouen, for William

44

ever honors minstrels. You can get many to farm, but few to sing. Let him go to Rouen in the service of the duke."

There was a murmur from Engelric's men—rather it was a growl such as a surly dog makes to an enemy. Turold heard the Norman's words with some surprise; he expected his father to answer as he did.

Engelric said shortly, "The boy will be a Saxon thane, not a singer in Normandy." He turned his back and rode off, his men running after him. Some of them limped, one man had a bloody arm, but they suffered no mortal hurts. The Normans had not come off so well. One of their men lay dead.

Turold and Cerdic rode home stirrup to stirrup and no words between them. They had not gone far when they heard behind them a rider coming in haste, so they turned and held ready their arms. It was Roger, shouting their names, coming right hand up.

He drew up and looked searchingly at them both. He shifted in the saddle. His dark eyes were sad. He said, "Turold, were you my blood brother I could not love you more. And you, Cerdic. But this concerns Turold, for there is a coil back there. One of my father's men was killed."

"I am sorry," Turold assured him. "It is bad business for neighbors to shed blood."

Roger's face darkened. "It is bad business when armed men carry off unwilling maidens!" He shook his head. "But you know how my father is! He does not see things as we do. He should blame only the captain, but . . ."

"Speak, man, speak!" cried Turold. "We can bear it."

Roger answered slowly, "They blame you for the

45

death, and they call it murder. The one who rode with him says it was you."

Turold shrugged. "I unhorsed that captain at the very first—and scarce got into the business again. But it was a chance they took, not murder."

"Aye!" Roger looked relieved. "But watch your way now, Turold. For my father will come to ask justice on you and by ill chance the reeve of the shire is at the castle."

"Ill chance it is!" exclaimed Cerdic. Engelric had kept long feud with this reeve over some missing sheep.

Roger suddenly blurted, "Now don't get roiled, Turold—but you are so careless about going with proper arms, though you never forget your harp. Here . . . my sword! Take it for my sake—never leave it off. Not that you would be my man—and I hold no land of my own yet, anyway. But because we are friends!" He thrust his fine French sword into Turold's hands.

Turold laughed. "I will take it. God be wi' ye!"

Roger pulled around and galloped off.

Cerdic remarked, "Let's give them their due. A Norman can be right gentle."

"Aye—and I marvelled to see Rolph and his men humble before that knight who stopped the fray. 'Tis sure he is the man I walked with In Blean yesterday." And he told Cerdic of what had passed between them in the wood and how he had betrayed the secret of Harold's choosing. "But you cannot know how clever this man is. I am a simple Saxon plowboy," he added bitterly, "and he sifted me quite to the bottom."

They went on in silence till they saw the manor place below them. Cerdic looked at Turold riding so moodily,

46

head sunk on breast, and softly he began to sing Turold's
song:

> *"High were the peaks, and shadowy and grand,*
> *The valleys deep, the rivers swiftly ran.*
> *The count Rollant, with sorrow and great pangs*
> *And with great pain, sounded his oliphant."*

Something rose in Turold that could not be put down
in spite of all sorrow. He touched his lagging horse to
a gallop through the empty fields, knowing his face was
still set to Normandy, and his deep voice rang out:

> *"That emperor bids ten thousand trumpets blow,*
> *And now with speed to Roncevalles we go!"*

HEY came at last to the gate of Farthing-wold and shouted for Ulfnoth who came trembling, babbling at the sight of Cerdic, his hands fumbling at the bars, "Did ye put the rascal Normans in their place?"

"Aye," Turold assured him gravely. "You can always trust us for that, old man." As they trotted into the close he said to Cerdic, "I'll wager that 'Drithy be tearing her hair out. First Grandam and the maids are up all night working on the banner and then food must be got ready for Harold and his carls. Now this afternoon everyone rushes off to the downs."

They walked their mounts between chapel and fire pits where an ox, sheep, and pigs were roasting, with a great pother of women and boys rushing about, Kyndritha presiding, waving her long fork.

When the crowd caught sight of Cerdic, they swarmed to greet him, the thralls kissing his feet.

Kyndritha hopped about, screaming that all the victuals were scorching. The young ones were shouting, "Masters, masters, come to the fire, we be making great feast, come and see!" The children, clinging with eager hands to their stirrups, tried to turn them that way. So, pressed by the crowd, they rode slowly up to the pits. Cerdic winked at Turold as he gently lifted Kyndritha's cap off her head

48

with his spear. She whirled about, shook her fork under the horse's nose, but what she said was lost in a roar of laughter from the crowd as the two riders made their horses execute a demivolte, Cerdic holding the cap on his lance tip, crying out, "'Tis my lady's favor; who will joust with me for it?"

When the bake mistress was quite speechless, Cerdic lowered the lance and dropped the cap neatly on her head. She looked up at him, gasping and laughing.

Suddenly all the merriment was hushed. Engelric was on the step of the hall setting the new banner on its tall standard. It moved in a gentle breeze, jewels flashing. Many made the sign of the cross as they looked at it. Quietly in the silence Engelric came through his people, his face hardening as he approached his sons.

"Get down, Turold!" Engelric's voice was harsh. "For your carelessness some of our folk are hurt—and lucky not to be murdered. We found your sword by the bake-shed. Had you gone properly armed . . . But now we will have the reckoning."

His sons dismounted. Two churls came to Turold, and they stripped off his cloak, tunic, and shirt. Someone handed the bull whip to Engelric, and his people huddled together, murmuring.

But as the master raised the whip, Cerdic stepped between his father and Turold. "Listen to me, Father," he pleaded. "Do not shame him so!"

"No, no!" Engelric planted his feet wide and raised the whip again.

"It's all right," Turold assured Cerdic in a low voice. "You keep out. I had this coming."

49

But Cerdic dropped his cloak, stripped off mail and shirt, and tossed them down. "You must whip me too," he said. "We'll take it together."

As Engelric, his face dark, raised the whip again there was a sharp cry behind him. All turned about, and by the light of the fires they saw Rolph riding through the gate at the head of a troop of mailed men and Ulfnoth vainly plucking at his stirrup till thrust aside. The manor people opened a way, and Rolph and his men came past the fire pits to Engelric.

Rolph pointed with his sword. "Come, reeve, there is your man!"

The high reeve of the shire rode forward; he was an old man, and he looked tired. "Your son, Engelric," he said flatly, "to answer to justice."

Engelric's hand closed hard on the long whip as he looked the riders up and down. "What are you doing in my close, pushing past my warder? And why have you brought this man, the reeve?"

Rolph said, "One of our men was killed on the moor—his fellows declare your son ran him through with his sword."

"My son bore no sword in the fray!" Engelric looked at Rolph sitting his horse before him, armed cap-a-pie in linked mail. The Saxon thane stood only in his breeches, boots, and farm-stained jerkin, and was unarmed, save for the whip.

"By what right do you enter here?" he demanded. "Here I alone have the right to give justice in my own demesne. I still render travel victuals to my lord with his men and in return he grants to me the high justice as well as the low." And Engelric turned his back on them.

"Take the Saxon boy," commanded Rolph.

Now Turold was looking at Rolph's men, and he felt a sudden excitement, for among them he saw the knight in black who had put a stop to the fighting on the moor. It was his friend of the wood, who only an hour gone had asked Engelric to let him go to Normandy. Turold's heart hammered, suffocating him, so that he had to breathe deeply. He tried to pray. By St. Mildred, this was all a trick, a splendid trick, to get him away. Let Engelric whip him—he deserved that. But this man would take him to Rouen, to the land of his dreams—he was going, going at last!

The two men-at-arms whom Rolph had bidden to seize Turold were not too quick at their work. They nudged their mounts over and looked uneasily from Turold to Cerdic and from Cerdic to Turold. The two Saxon brothers stood with naked torsos, long yellow hair streaming over their shoulders, of like height and identical in features. As like as two crows on a dead oak.

Suddenly Engelric raised the long whip and struck the horses of these two Normans such a cut that they reared and one backed into a fire. There were screams and shouts, and Rolph raised his lance against Engelric as he cried, "There shall be justice done—we will take him!"

Turold snatched up a hayfork, Cerdic a piece of wood.

But at this juncture the knight in black mail jumped his horse to Rolph's side as if to interfere, pushing down the lance. Before any harm could be done, the manor folk raised a great shout, "Harold, Harold!" So arms were lowered, and men turned about to face the gate.

51

And now one came riding on a gray stallion with
many men behind him. In the winter dusk the whole
manor-place was lighted by the glare of scores of torches
carried by those who followed him. He sat tall in the
saddle with his graying hair falling from his helmet, the
blazing belt of an earl girding the green cloak and holding
the rich scabbard which swung at his hip.

Behind him, row on row beyond the gate, up the lane
as far as the eye could see by the blaze of the torches,
still coming on out of the dark edge of the wood, rode the
house carls, all in shining mail with cloth-of-gold gonfalons
rippling from their lance tips.

The earl's horse stepped high and slow, shaking his
head. So rode the Earl Harold into the close and came
stirrup to stirrup with Rolph the Norman, and his men
came on behind and filled the close and filled the fields and
spread out over the downs beyond the wall, a thousand
strong. The sound of their coming, of the horses, was like
the sea on the shore.

In the close there fell a long silence.

The Earl Harold took his ease in his saddle and looked
at them all. He saw the bare backs of the two brothers, and
Engelric with whip in hand. He saw Rolph and his men.
He looked long at the reeve of the shire, and that one
wiped his lips with his glove and lowered his eyes. Then
Rolph spoke in a low voice of his charge against the
Saxon's son.

Harold said, "If it be the king's justice that you want,
let us look into the matter."

The reeve did not answer, but Rolph cried boldly,
"The boy is forfeit to me!"

The earl's lips twisted a little. "So you ask the high justice?"

"That I do!"

All this time Turold was watching the Norman in black mail, and he marked that as the earl came forward the knight edged his horse back into the shadow of the chapel.

The earl was smiling, laughing. "Let us have the high justice by all means. But where is the one you accuse?"

All looked at the two lads standing in the firelight.

Then Cerdic cried loudly, "I am the one, take me, take me!"

But Turold, grasping his arm, cried too, "My lords, he lies, he is trying to save me. Heed him not, I am the one!"

"Why, here is a lovely thing," said Harold, smiling. "Each of them cries out for the right to be hanged. But the accuser must prove which of them is the man."

Rolph said slowly, "The one I seek is a manor-churl, a very plowboy. His brother is your carl, I have heard. Come, you yourself know which is the lad I want."

Harold twisted sideways in his saddle, and his eyes were merry as he looked at the brothers. "You might try and see which one of them smells of the stable." The manor folk shouted, slapping one another in glee. Harold did not mean to give up his own to the scurvy Normans!

Harold went on, "Truly, at this moment, I do not know myself which is carl and which is farmer. And yet, Norman, let me tell you that both these lads are my men, and I am only making sport of you. Do you think I rule half of England to be faced by such as you? There are

53

at this moment a thousand men within call of my voice, yet were I alone you would not dare to take so much as a sheep herd from me. I have all the justice in Kent—to render or to delegate—the high, the middle, and the low."

Rolph's face turned a fearful color. He gave a signal. His troop turned, scattering all who stood by. So he led his men at a furious gallop out of the gate and off and away into Blean wood. But as they went, and the reeve with them, Turold saw that the black knight came so close to Harold that their knees touched. Lingering behind his friends, he spoke low and clear. "The boy is a singer, not a farmer. But Saxons cannot help being dull! You give good justice, my lord! To half of England, did you say? Did you ever hope to rule over the whole?"

Turold saw a strange pallor drain the life from Harold's ruddy face. With stiff lips he said, "You are very brave . . . sir Norman."

"There are some things it is best to see with one's own eyes."

"Do you not fear that I will hold you as you held me?"

The stranger laughed. "Well? Here are, as you say, a thousand men within your call. Is it not enough? I will bide quiet while you send for more."

Harold pressed his lips together.

Said the other softly, "I see that you still wear the Norman sword, the gift, it is said, of a—friend. Yet you know, by the rules of chivalry, the taking of arms at the hand of another renders you his vassal."

"No matter how it is given?"

"No matter how it is given," assented the stranger. "But now perhaps, you will send to that—friend—a pledge.

He wishes to hear the young Saxon singer at court."

"There are already too many—pledges—at Rouen. My younger brother—others. No, the young singer shall not go. We need such here ourselves."

"Then why do you use him like a churl? And you have not the ear for his great song. 'Tis of Rollant, Charlemagne's paladin, dying in the pass of Roncevalles, to save his lord. That was great vassalage!"

"It was the greatest folly and failure ever chanced in Christendom. In Normandy—they do not love failures!"

The stranger shook his head. "You have not the true knightly spirit. It is a tale of such sweet vassalage—it might spur a whole dukedom to mighty deeds."

With something of his old bantering manner, Harold asked the Norman, "Did you come to Kent to steal away our minstrels?"

Sharp as a whiplash came the answer. "I came to see if a Saxon will keep faith!"

Cerdic gripped Turold's arm. "Who is that man?"

Turold shook his head, for the earl was answering swift and hot, "You know my oath—a forced oath—can never bind this people."

"So be it!" cried the Norman, and he wheeled his horse. He rode close to Turold and Cerdic, leaned down, and looking into Turold's eyes, he said, "You will come. It is a symbol to me. To Roncevalles we go." And he pressed into Turold's hand a belt knife, saying, "Accept this at my hand!"

And when Turold took it the dark eyes seemed to smile.

The Norman rode toward the gate, first saluting the

earl, then with mocking gesture the Dragon banner where it swung by the hall. So he went slowly through the gate and out and down into Blean wood, and they could hear him singing in mocking shout as he rode, "To Roncevalles we go!"

HE earl spoke to Engelric, "You have life-right and death-right over your own. Yet I have sworn that both your sons are my men, and so they must be. We will talk of it in hall at meat."

The winter dusk was winter night now. Over the wall many fires blossomed against the gloom. There was laughter and the happy stir of men eating by the pits, and under all the rhythm of a thousand horses champing and stamping in the frosty air.

The churl sent to summon Turold to the hall found him with Cerdic, examining the horses of the house-carls.

Turold was downcast. "This I never planned. What . . . what am I going to do?"

Cerdic took him by the shoulders. "Man alive—now we'll be together!"

Turold made no answer.

Cerdic pleaded, "It will be glorious! We will carry our grandam's banner before our lord. All London turns out when Harold rides through. At dawn tomorrow we'll ride through the gate of Gytha's house in Southwark, and feast in the hall. Harold always uses his mother's house in London."

Turold kept his head turned, but Cerdic went on, "Three pages in scarlet velvet tabards will go before us

57

on white jennets blowing silver trumpets; one of us will bear the Dragon banner. After us the kingly three, Harold and his brothers, Gyrth and Leofwine, always by his side. A company of carls a hundred strong will follow us, and we sing as we go, over London bridge where great ships lie in the stream and through the city to have audience with the king. Oh, it is a fair town with walls, churches, bells, towers, palaces. Next to Winchester, our old royal city, it is the noblest in all the dear realm of England."

"It might be the noblest in all Christendom—and I would not speak it fair!" burst out Turold. "You do not ken!"

"It is plain that this Norman is William's spy!" Cerdic's voice was harsh.

Turold straightened his shoulders and looked his brother eye to eye. But Cerdic would not yield. "It will come to war soon. William has been building ships—hundreds of ships!" He turned his back on Turold and started to walk away.

"No! Wait!" Turold took his arm. "I will be Harold's man," he said.

In the hall he knelt to the Earl Harold. The earl looked earnestly at him. "We have spoken together of thee, Engelric who is just and Adela who is tender. And I have said that I will deal well with thee, a carl with Cerdic. But thou must be my man in very truth, as I have said before many witnesses."

Turold looked into his lord's eyes, for he wished to see what manner of man he would swear to. And as he stared, it seemed that the long hall swam away in a mist and he saw a long road with all England marching, shouting, singing—going down to some great and awful event. And Harold rode before, the Dragon swaying over him, unafraid, into the dark place with his people.

Aye, Turold thought, here is very king! And I am of these folk, and with them I must live and die. And the longing for what he had thought upon so long but never known died away, and he felt peace.

As Harold bent down to him, smiling, Turold looked up and said, "I will be your man, lord."

He put his hands into Harold's hands and swore to be his man, to render him good fealty and true vassalage, in life and in death. He looked into Harold's face and forgot all but what manner of man this was.

When he rose to his feet, one of the witnesses, an aged thane from the Sussex coast, Mannig by name, led him away into the bower where his grandam girded him with jewelled belt for his sword, over a red cloak such as was always set upon a young Saxon knight upon his first going forth.

When they went out, there was a great commotion in the close, for the order to ride had been passed. Snow was falling lightly on the mounted carls, horses shaking their heads and stamping. When Turold swung into the saddle, White Boy pranced as if he knew he bore a Kentish carl.

Then came Adela to Turold's stirrup in the press of riders, bearing the banner well wrapped, and he tied it to his saddle. Turold could never after remember what she said to him, only that she looked up and smiled. And Black Jarn came with a pair of fine spurs, "For the honor o' Farthingwold, lad!"

An old carl who had known their grandsire—Eadnoth

by name—shouted, "A wild night—fifteen leagues to London, yet we'll scarce draw rein till the gate swing for us at Southwark."

At the gate Ulfnoth raised his face with tears falling on his wrinkled cheeks. The horses sprang eagerly up the slope, and Turold could still sense the home smell, could almost taste it: byre and forge, roast meat and wood-smoke. Turning to look back, he saw the snow falling softly on frosted roofs, the familiar plume of smoke over the hall, a rosy light shining from the chapel. So he knew that Adela knelt there before the seven-branched candlestick.

White Boy plunged into Blean wood, and Turold leaned against his neck. Flare of torches in the snow, jingle of bridles, creak of leather, the throb and thunder of a thousand horsemen. Something swelled in Turold's throat; he galloped to catch up with Cerdic.

Now they were turning into the Way, passing westward of the old beech, its cross silvered with snow. Cerdic looked back, flourished his lance, and pointed ahead. Turold answered with a shout, and so he rode up the hill and out of Scray.

London was just as Cerdic had said it would be—grand and dirty, exciting and noisy. The best part for Turold was the praise he won for his songs, for he often sang the old lays to Harold and his household.

In a week or so came the festivity of the Christ-mass, feasting and merriment and crowds in the churches. Turold saw the king for the first and last time when he showed himself to the people. Right kingly he looked in his glittering crown and robes, though slow and feeble were his steps.

60

As the carls were leaving the palace one day, someone rode up shouting, "Turold! Where is Turold, son of Engelric, of Farthingwold-under-Blean, lathe of Scray?"

Men pointed, and a troop of richly dressed horsemen pressed through to Turold's side. The foremost was Rolph of the Tower, and behind him was Roger, brave in a new suit of mail.

Roger said little; it was his father who talked, showing with polished phrases of flattery that all was changed, that now he wished the friendship of Turold and Cerdic. His parting words were a message from Lucy. She was in their town house and wished to see them; it was near the bridge. She would be at home this afternoon. Then he gave them "adieu" and rode away with his men. Smiling, Roger gave them the old "good hunting" signal and spurred after his father.

Turold and Cerdic stared at each other, then burst into laughter. "So now he fawns on us. I wonder what he wants."

Turold laughed again. "Never mind! But let's go." He made a wry face. "It will be a little comic, in contrast to our last meeting when he wanted to hang me!"

"Not that you want to see Lucy, of course . . . . But you might not want to face that French captain—did you see him but now? He might tread on our toes; we'd best stay in Southwark."

"Well then, stay!"

Cerdic cried in mock alarm, "If you go, so do I. You might forget your sword. Besides, I mean to learn how to make pretty speeches to a maid. I might need to know someday."

"Go on! Brunhilda doesn't care for speeches; she only has to look at you, you're so beautiful." And dodging the expected blow, he almost fell off his horse.

They found Lucy sitting before the fire in the "little" hall of Rolph's house. Turold felt most awkward and strange. Was this the girl who had romped with him on the downs? He found it hard to look at her after the first glance. She wore a gown of some soft green stuff, and her curls were combed so that a long cluster fell over her shoulder. In the old days they had fought like brothers. Yet slowly he had built in his heart a dream of her as things might be when he returned with gold and fame. But he had not, alas, even made start on that far journey. Now for the first time he understood that the old carefree days could never come again.

Noting that Cerdic and Roger had left him alone with her, his tongue stuck in his mouth. But she was chattering away as though this unhappy change had not come about. He looked at her and suddenly heard what she was saying, ". . . and of course your earl is noble, and I have seen how the rabble shout after him in the streets. Yet only an earl can he be! For all men agree that William is the rightful heir to the throne."

His head cleared. He thought, of course, all your friends think so! But he said, "Why bother your pretty head about such matters?"

She pouted. "That is most unmannerly, I declare. You know that Harold is unworthy to be king."

"And why, pray?"

"Well," Lucy counted on her fingers, "he is not a true Christian, he hath a wife without Church's blessing—

and he hath given most solemn oath to help William to the crown!"

Turold shook his head. "We English folk are not much for many masses and a great scouring after relics such as yours. Yet I trust we are none the worse Christians for all that and keep the saints' days as well as other men. Harold has built a splendid abbey at Waltham, and above all others he adores that Holy Cross by which he swears. As for Edith Swanneshalls, I've heard that William had Matilda some years before the church gave consent, but let that pass."

But Lucy would not give in. "His oath to William should be sacred."

"The oath of no man can bind our people," Turold told her. "The crown is theirs alone to give."

"Poor boy!" Her eyes were merry. "How little you know of these matters. Yet I haven't the slightest wish to quarrel with you, Turold. Tell me, how do you like being a house-carl? And have you any new songs?"

He told her how he sang every night for the earl. "All the old lays—sometimes a Norman ballad. Perhaps you can teach me more of them."

She took her little harp, and they drew to the fire while she played for him. He looked at the firelight on her hair, and all the recent contentment was gone. The old longing for far places rushed back in him, and he dreamed again of Normandy.

Lucy leaned to him as if she read his thoughts and whispered softly, "It may not be long, it may be soon, oh, soon!"

"What do you mean?"

She shook her head. "I may not tell you. But that dagger you wear—you are in high favor . . . something wonderful is going to happen . . . oh, I can't say more! But you know my father! Why do you think he went to the trouble to seek you out?"

He looked at her, and they laughed.

The little hall, or the parlor, as the Normans called it, opened directly off the great hall, and when the door opened, Turold was surprised to see that French knight he had unhorsed on the moor come into the room without ceremony and drop onto a bench by them. He stretched out his muddy boots and curtly ordered Lucy to pull them off.

Astonished at the man's insolence, Turold said, "She'll not touch them!" He looked at Lucy and saw that she was trembling. Certain it was that this man had too much freedom.

Calmly Lucy spoke. "You may call a page, sir knight, to get off your boots."

The French captain laughed. "The service is made noble by the beauty of the maid who gives it." He added, "On the other hand, a man of France would feel his boots defiled by the touch of a Saxon plowboy. I wonder that your father permits the fellow in the house, mistress!"

It was Turold's turn to laugh. "Better a Saxon plowboy than a swaggering French knight who can't stay on his horse!"

The captain jumped up, and Lucy was gasping "Turold!" when there came a tumult in the great hall, men running and shouting. Roger flung open the door and stood looking at them most strangely. Turold went to the door

64

and looked in at the crowd in the great hall.

A rider, spurred and muddy, stood on the table with Rolph and his men about him listening.

"When the new minster is hallowed—only two days hence—" cried this man, "then our lord Edward the king will not be there. Our beloved cousin, on his return from Mass today, took to his bed. He has turned his face to the wall as if to say, 'It is done!'"

Roger said quickly, "Turold, do not look so! All know this is the end. He cannot keep up for the blessing of his glorious minster that he spent his last years in building!"

And now, shouts and cheers swelled in the hall. The Normans were lifting their swords, crying out.

They were crying, "Long live the king!"

But what king they meant was in doubt.

The next day London rang with terrible news. Harold's brother, the traitorous Tostig, had ravaged the Kentish coast, burning villages, looting, carrying off men and women. Some people said it was the Danes who helped him, some said it was the French. Before men could rally to go out against him, Tostig and his raiders were gone like mist before the morning sun.

It was a terrible, a shocking blow to Harold, to all England. That one of the sons of their good old earl, Godwine of hallowed memory, should ravage among his own people was the last word in treachery. Men felt that after that anything was possible.

Turold and Cerdic had their own good reasons for horror at the event. They heard that Black Jarn had been caught in the raid. He had been at a coast village selling sheep for Engelric when the raiders came suddenly upon them in the night. Black Jarn was gone, no one knew where.

That night Earl Harold sent out heralds offering a great reward for the capture of Tostig—alive.

ING Edward lay a-dying. The heavy crown rested in the carved chest in the royal bedchamber, and all England knew that soon it must go to another. The beautiful new minster had been hallowed with ceremony and solemnity, but the queen, the Lady Edith, had stood in Edward's place.

Day after day now Cerdic and Turold rode out with the Earl Harold to attend the king, to the palace where he lay. Over the bridge, through the teeming city, by ways so narrow that men on foot must press against the house walls to let them pass, they rode each morning. The streets were strangely hushed and many looked up as if in prayer to the Dragon banner, a thing of pale fire in the winter sunlight.

To the carls that ride was the only good part of those tedious days, for they must wait long hours for their lord in the chill waiting room outside the king's apartment.

On Twelfth Night, which was on Thor's day, they waited all night, for it was known in the palace that Edward's last hours were at hand, and many of the great in church and state waited silently in that outer room.

Turold went to the window and looked down upon the mass of people standing in the snow with upturned faces, calling on the saints, murmuring prayers.

67

Hour by hour the crush inside the palace became greater, of men gathering to attend Witan, for when the soul of the king passed, the voice of England must be ready to speak.

Within the anteroom they met the northern earls, Edwin and Morcar, who bowed coldly to Harold and he to them as he passed within. Cerdic whispered to Turold that this showed the one weak spot for Harold; the northern earls might not support him.

"But does the North Country matter so much?" asked Turold. "It's far away—a hundred leagues. South, east, west, are strongly with our lord. Does he need the north?"

Cerdic shook his head. "There might be a raid on the north coast. The Norse king, Harald Hardrada, is a bold sea rover looking for conquest, they say. And Edward has let the defenses fall into ruin."

Now voices were hushed, a weight pressed down on men's minds, a terrible expectancy hung over them. A wind blew along the passages, door hangings waved, and there was a moaning round the eaves.

Then it was known that the king had roused from his two-day stupor and was speaking to those who stood about his bed. Now the watchers waited for the moment when he would name his successor. Harold and the Bishop Stigand were there; Robert the Staller, a Norman favorite, and others. The Lady Edith had been crouching on the stone floor all night, warming her lord's feet in her bosom.

The king was speaking his last words on earth!

In the anteroom the hush deepened. Would the king name his successor?

It seemed that time was nothing in that hush, when

68

there sounded an outcry, distant, muffled, yet piercing. All stirred and a sigh went up as from one body.

The king was dead.

Then came one and spoke, saying that Edward had passed with holy words on his lips and that he had named Harold as his successor. A monk, making the sign of the cross, cried, "Ah, holy Edward, a saint thyself, thou art now among the blessed ones!" And an old woman added, "Clean and mild and ever blithe," the tears falling down her withered cheeks.

All at once the crowd slipped away, only a few women and Harold's folk remaining. Then came the earl, pale under the sun-hardened red of his cheeks, and bade Turold to fetch Gyrth and Leofwine to him, for they were gone to break their fast. Below it was found that no one in the palace had eaten, for the very cooks waited, spoon in hand, for the moment of death. As Turold was speaking to the earl's brothers, somewhere a great bell tolled, and then a myriad of lesser bells answered throughout the city. There was a vast murmur from the thousands who stood outside.

Then the passages of the palace were choked with hurrying folk; all men rushed to the hall where the Witan was about to sit. For now the voice of England must speak the name of its new king. And Harold—named by Edward in his last hour—he surely would be the people's choice.

Turold and Gyrth and Leofwine made their way back to Harold. When they entered the anteroom, one was speaking there, burning words, terrible words. The king, he said, just before the end had seen a vision and the

vision was God's curse upon England.

This man cried, "England is to be slaughtered in her sins and for them. We forget God and the saints. We worship idols, we do dark things, for fear of the gods that never were . . ." and he went out and left them gaping.

As Harold's brothers went down to give the Witan the formal news of the king's death, they could hear the cries echoing everywhere, "The king is dead, the king is dead!"

It seemed terrible to Turold, that time of waiting, as many came to ask favors of the new king before he was even named. He kept them in the outer room and only let them in to Harold as he was bidden. While they waited, friends brought the Lady Edith from the king's room. Wrapped in a great cloak she was, and Turold could not see her face. She walked past with bent head, and they took her away. Now she was the Old Lady, and must retire to her dower city of Winchester.

Suddenly there came a great shout and a tumult indescribable. Said Cerdic, "It is done! When they clash swords on shields, that is their sign to the archbishop."

A page came running. Gyrth and Leofwine were on their way; let Harold stand now to receive the word from the Witan. So Turold and Cerdic cleared the room, and their lord came out and stood under the Dragon, which Cerdic held over against the wall. To Turold Harold said, "Now my great ax—that I must hold when they come," and to Cerdic, "Hold the Dragon high."

Soon came the procession, the great men of the realm, the bishops, and Gyrth and Leofwine. These great ones made a lane to Harold, and Gyrth walked slowly in it, bearing in his hand a two-handed sword. And behind him came Leofwine with the crown of England on a pillow. So his brothers stood and held to him the sword and the crown, declaring them to be the gift of the people by the voice of the Witan that very hour.

Harold stood a long time before he answered. Overlong, Turold thought.

At last the earl spoke. His voice rang in the crowded chamber with a strange huskiness. He accepted the crown, he swore to give good law to all men alike, and with God's help, he would defend the dear realm of England from all enemies.

Then men spoke of the crowning, which must be held soon because of the unsettled state of the times. Edward could be laid at rest the next day very early, and then should Harold be crowned, with the voice of the Witan again crying its assent. All would be done in order, though faster than had been the custom.

Now Harold went into the inner room with his brothers and Bishop Ealdred. Among many visitors pleading urgent business came Rolph and Roger. They were with the earl some little time. When they came out, Harold was with them. He said, "Go then and make ready. I will send the one you spoke of." He bade them Godspeed and beckoned to Turold to come inside.

The earl sat down heavily on a bench and seemed lost in thought. When he looked up, he smiled ruefully. There were new lines about his mouth. He said, "Come here, lad." He looked up into Turold's face and spoke gently.

"I think," he said, "that you love me well."

73

Turold answered quickly, "You are the glory of this land!"

The earl shook his head. "I am not sure that was an answer. Now tell me, have you ever had knightly exercise?"

Turold nodded. "With Roger. The knight who trained him needed a young opponent. We used to go on the moors."

"Good! The Saxon who goes to William must be no churl. Yet I forget—William will welcome you—you of all Saxons. Listen well now. Rolph sends Roger overseas this night that his liege lord in Normandy may know that which has taken place in England today. How a man can hold to two lords I know not. Yet all these Normans who hold English land from an English king are now true men to William."

Harold paused, and Turold felt a chill. What was Harold talking about? . . . *William will welcome you* . . .

The earl's face darkened. "It pleases me to give Roger this help—a ship will be at his service at Dover. And I would like to have you go with him. But first hear my plan." He began pacing about the room. "I am sending you to William that you may serve me there. It's sure he means to claim the crown of England and that he will try to raise men against us with false reasons. Do you understand? I am asking you to be spy for England. You will be alone, among our enemies. They are wily and subtle.

"There is LanFranc, the monk, his advisor; Bishop Odo, his half-brother, and that sturdy old soldier, William Fitz-Osbern, who brought William alive through the perils that beset his boyhood. Your task is not simple! I want

74

you to win your way into William's heart with your songs.

"If they suspect you, you will be silenced. I am asking you to play a double part for me and for England. I will not blame you if you refuse. And I remember . . . William can be, if he wishes, so amiable, and so fascinating. Can you keep your head in all this?"

He stopped in front of Turold. "Will you go?"

Turold answered frankly, "It was long my wish to go to the Norman court—once I thought I was really going!"

A wry smile lighted Harold's face. "I remember that day."

Turold hesitated. "You were right, my lord, when you said that I love you. And yet I am almost Norman myself in hating some of the dull Saxon ways. I hate almost to go thus . . ." But suddenly he burst out, "I will go, I will go!"

The earl called Cerdic and Gyrth and gave them orders to prepare Turold for the long journey. At Gytha's house he must be dressed in warm wool and soft leather with no armor save some light chain and a sword, for they must ride in haste. At Rolph's house they would meet with Roger and his train. Turold must pick up a sober carl to attend him, and there would be good mounts and sumpter horses with splendid changes of raiment, and presents— all things needful. But they would come after, for at Dover, Turold and Roger must take swift ship, going alone into Normandy. Their train would catch up in two or three days, if the wind held favorable.

Then Harold called Turold aside and gave him a massive ring carved with the dragon emblem. "Be wary!

Some day a messenger will come to you with a ring like this. You must do all he bids you.

"Tomorrow, when I stand in the new minster and the bishop asks of the people, 'Sirs, I here present to you Harold, your king, the undoubted king of this realm; king of the Angles and Saxons, emperor of Albion, wherefor all you who have come together here this day to do him homage, are you willing to do the same?'

"And when they answer with great tumult, as I hope they will, wishing only to serve this England which I love, you will not be there to see it, lad. Swords will clash against shields, and the people will shout, but you will be far away. I shall miss my sweet singer of nights. . . . I wish that I need not give you too to William!" Then Harold drew out his sword.

Turold knelt, bowing his head. Had Harold forgotten that he had knighted him at Farthingwold? Yet there was something special about this, for he was truly Harold's man now. On the morrow his lord would be crowned king of the English in the West Minster, and he would not be there to see.

Said the earl softly, touching him lightly with the sword, "May the saints keep you! It may be you can be of service to this England. Rise, Sir Turold!"

SO Turold rode to Dover in the night, carrying the slender rod with the royal emblem, for now he was king's bode.

What a wild ride through London! Clattering through the narrow lanes, horses' feet throwing mud, folk running into doorways. An old man in a baker's cap ran out into the path of Turold's horse so that it reared. Fast to Turold's cloak he clung, crying, "How went it—how spoke the Witan? 'Tis rumored the Normans cried out for their duke to rule over us!"

Turold yelled, "Their voices were but weak among the men of England!"

"Then Harold will be crowned?"

"Aye, aye!"

"Praise be the lord!"

They saluted the old man and swept on. At Gytha's house, they packed in great haste, mounted fresh horses, and rushed off again, this time to Rolph's house to pick up Roger.

In the midst of the commotion in Rolph's yard, they dismounted and found Lucy in the hall. Turold noted how pale and nervous she seemed. "Come into the parlor," she said, but Turold and the rest said they hadn't time, and wasn't Roger ready?

"I wanted to give you a journey posset," she faltered. Turold stared. What ailed the lass? In a moment color came again to her cheeks, and she tossed her head. "As you are a true-born Saxon, I have a wager to make with you!"

"A wager?"

"Yes, yes!" She took him by the arm, glancing roguishly at the others. "But first you must come into the parlor, and I'll send for your stirrup cups."

Sure that she had some wild joke to play on them, Turold refused to leave the hall. "I think we'd best keep an eye on the horses," he said, glancing out the door. She came white as milk again all in an instant.

"The wager, the wager!" she cried. "A new sword against a brocade gown that you will fall under William's spell, that before you touch English soil again you will be his man!"

But Turold did not smile. "Mistress, you make sport of that which is sacred."

"La! There speaks my good solid Saxon. Men swear to two or three lords every day. But . . . I know William. You dare not!"

Turold flushed. "I take the wager," he told her. But even as he spoke he saw the face of Harold, lined and weary after his vigil with the dying king, and his perilous taking of the crown. "It may be months before I see you again," he told her.

Lucy looked down, and her foot stirred the edge of her gown.

"And London is full of young knights . . ."

But she would not help, only her foot stirred the velvet. There was a silence, broken by the sudden coming

78

into the hall of men, heavy with mail, walking purpose-fully—and silently, to the courtyard door.

"I forgot your possets . . . oh, come along. . ." Lucy's voice was strained, shrill.

But Turold was staring at the one who led these men through Rolph's hall. He was just slipping the visor of his helmet down—a strange action in a peaceful house. Gyrth was laughing at Lucy's antics but turned just as these men went through the door and mounted. The sound of their going echoed in the hall, then the beat of galloping hoofs.

Turold saw that Gyrth and Cerdic looked at each other most strangely. Who was that man—a dozen armed strangers at his back—who stalked through Rolph's hall?

Turold looked at Lucy. He thought she was going to swoon, but she only looked at him with wide eyes and said faintly, "God be wi' ye!" for Roger came in haste. They went quickly out, mounted, and the housefolk show-ered blessings on them as they moved toward the gate. Turold looked back, wishing he had not been such a fool, wishing he had kissed her.

But suddenly a window above was flung open, and Lucy appeared, laughing as always, her hair falling round her face. She tossed out a scarf of sheerest silk. Gyrth tried to get it, but Turold sidestepped his horse and caught it. Lucy's eyes were bright as she flung up her hand. Turold wrapped the scarf around his arm, saluted her, and rode on.

Now they could make haste, and the echo of their galloping mounts rang through the sleeping town. It was midnight when they passed the first gate of London Bridge, and the gateward grumbled when he opened to them. How many bodes did the new king send out tonight? was his question.

"What do you mean, old man?" asked Gyrth.

"Why, those others—the big fellow with the banderole of bode, and dozen men with him. And now you. Be ye true bodes all?"

"True bodes we," answered Gyrth, but Turold saw him give Cerdic that strange hard look again.

Galloping after Gyrth, who seemed to have the devil at his heels, they passed between the huts and stalls along the bridge. The wind brought the lonely cry of the watch on the walls, "Almost to midnight . . . wind's east . . . all's well!"

At the outer gatehouse, Gyrth stopped to question the warder. The fellow told them that a large party with a king's bode leading them had just gone through. They'd gone down to the river landing. They had a boat there, and were bent on king's business.

"The king's business indeed!" cried Gyrth. They listened and heard faint sounds over the wash of the current. A scraping sound, grunts, oars working in locks not too well muffled.

"God bless them in the king's business," said Gyrth. "We can never catch them now."

"Is anything wrong, my lord?" asked the warder.

"Aye. That big man . . . the king would have paid you five thousand florins for that man—alive."

The warder's eyes popped, he opened his mouth, trying to mouth one word. Turold thought he knew what that word was.

80

Tostig!

And he thought, Lucy, Lucy . . . that man was in your hall . . . your father gave shelter and aid to that renegade. She had been in mortal terror of bloodshed. She had been trying to protect him and Cerdic. Still, to help the man whose hands were red with the blood of Kentish men, maybe Black Jarn!

Soon came the corner where they must bid farewell to Gyrth and Cerdic. The king's brother took Roger's hand and said, "I believe that you knew nothing of this matter."

Roger was fuming for haste. "Let's be off; we'll never get there ambling along like damsels." To his men he said, "Mind now—the first ship you can get at Dover and ride straight to Rouen. We shall be weary and muddy and in want of fresh linen and our arms."

Turold was not riding White Boy; Eadnoth was bringing him with the remounts and baggage, for they must kill their horses under them this night if need be. There were ten in the company: Turold and Eadnoth his squire with two hostlers for the pack horses; Roger and his squire with two hostlers and two men-at-arms from his father's hall. And besides pack horses and six extra mounts, they took among other presents three fine horses for the duke. So they were a numerous company.

Eadnoth said to Turold, "Master, let us ride with you till you be past Gallows Hill. What traveler ever went this way in the night and did not meet with robbers there?"

Turold and Roger shouted with laughter. "Let them stop us!" they cried and put spurs to their horses and looking back shouted, "See you in Rouen!"

It made a kind of song with the hoofbeats as they went, "At Rouen, at Rouen."

Yet they made poor progress, push the horses as they might, for the Way was in fearful condition. Thaws had softened the ground, and there were sloughs deep as hell itself. And on Gallows Hill they were waylaid. Three stout rogues sprang up, but before they could hang onto their bridles, with whip and spur and a reckless joy that drove them on, they were off and away, over and down the rutted hill. And there they must pick their way with care, for the bridge had fallen in and the ford was uncertain in the dark.

Roger grumbled about the road and the bridges.

Turold told him, "What d'ye expect? It was always so."

Roger shook his head and muttered of the Norman roads. "Soon I will show you—you poor dumb Saxon. Where we are going, things are different."

The road hammered backwards under them, the night, windy and star-shot, rolled over them. They won past Rochester at last, on through sleeping hamlets, rousing the dogs to bark at them, shouting their great news where any ran to listen as they passed. And finally, with one relief of horses they entered the dark stretch of the Blean and so on to Sittingbourne, Bilmansbloke, and steep Boughton Hill where the wood pressed thick against the Way. How good, Turold felt, to be In Blean again, how wonderfully sweet the wood smells after London's foul air. And where lies Boughton herd tonight?

So at gray dawn they won at last to Beech of the Rood and Brothercrosse and with stumbling mounts turned up the lane that led to the gate of Farthingwold.

Ulfnoth gaped to see young master covered with mud and bearing banderole of king's bode. Turold said, "There be great news for all true men. Edward is gone to his rest, and Harold is raised to the kingdom!"

Soon folk came running, the bell began to ring, the outcries were merry and shrill, for this news meant a holiday for all. Then Turold was into the hall, Adela was in his arms, and he was asking for Black Jarn.

She led him to a pallet by the hearthside. Jarn's face was pale above his beard, but he opened his eyes when Turold bent over him and grinned sheepishly.

"Me lyin' here like a hurt lass! But I didn't get this cracked head making merry at Yule feast, ye know. I was over to Ebney-on-the-bay, trading our mutton for salt fish, that night he came!"

Turold answered soberly, "We heard you'd been carried off."

"Well, I was, lad, I was! But I made such a ruckus they dumped me on the beach, and some boys found me. I'm really sound as a nut right now, but your grandam . . ."

"You'll keep right on lying there for awhile," Adela told him crossly.

They listened to the story of the raid as they broke fast. Turold soon cut it off, as he could see how Roger felt. The raid had been brutal and useless, and Tostig's only motive to embarrass Harold. Adela understood and changed the subject.

Some months before, she told Turold, she had asked Otto, the armorer at Canterbury, to make two suits of mail, one for Cerdic and one for Turold. "Of exact likeness," she said, "except that one has bars of red and one has bars of black. I will have your men stop to pick up yours on their way to Dover."

"That is a great gift," he said. "Now I ask for another."

"Ask," she said.

"No listening to the night wind."

"I have already made that gift."

They galloped through Canterbury without stopping, only that they waved their banderoles and shouted the news to the people, who put food into their hands as they passed. At the earl's post they changed horses again and galloped on to the sea, with banners waving and folk in the villages running to hear their news.

At Dover as the sun dipped there was a ship ready as always for the earl's business. The weather was fair, the wind easterly. They weighed anchors at once, the sail was raised and sheeted home, and Turold leaned on the stern rail watching the land, the white cliffs, fall away. It was curious about the sea. It was like Blean wood, with a climate, a speech, and men, birds and beasts of its own. He saw the foam dashing up, falling again, from the cliffs. He saw the seabirds spreading their wings, dipping into the gray waves. He heard the cries of the gannets and the calling of the mews. Then the stars began to come out as the shore faded away. There was a glorious motion in a ship at sea; it was like a fast horse, like a great wind, if one could ride such. There was a stinging salt on his lips and spray on cheeks and roar of water. In the dark now it was wonderful to see the master of the ship lean against the steer-board and look up at the stars.

There were no tracks here as there were in Blean wood. The waters took no marks, but hissed and shouted under the planks while they rushed on to an unknown shore. Rushing on dark waters to something strange—it might be, terrible.

Turold was not looking backward now but forward to the Normandy shore. If they could make the mouth of the Seine by dawn, they would have the day to ride in like true bodes. Some twelve leagues up the river to Rouen it was. His breath quickened, thinking of that ride.

Twelve leagues to Rouen! Turold hoped that the duke's posts were close together and the horses fresh and strong.

Only once again did he look back. A star of great brilliance was setting over the far unseen line of the Saxon shore. It was glorious in beauty for a brief moment, then clouds covered it.

HE duke's first post on Seine road was kept by a man named Haimo, who was innkeeper, owner of a fleet of fishing vessels, and fat man extraordinary. He held his rights of the monks in the abbey on the hill. He bullied the fishermen, kept order, and served food that was famed from St. Michael to Guitsand. The coast prospered, and the monks were glad to leave these cares to Haimo, for they had troubles of their own, thousands of serfs in nine villages, who tilled grainfields along the river.

When their ship swung in to shore in the early morning, Turold and Roger, still carrying their banderoles, leaped to the stone jetty and ran up the bank to the inn.

Said Roger to his friend, "There's a strange man here—wait till you see him!"

"I only hope there's something to eat. I'm famished," was the reply.

Roger shook his head. "Maybe some bread and cheese. There will be food at Rouen after we have reached the duke."

So they ran into the guest room and brought up before that great fellow, Haimo, who was settled there on an oversize bench. His face was like a big bowl of dough, his body like a feather bed. His white hair hung but

86

sparsely on his big head, and two sheets would hardly have made his apron. His breeches held up his belly, but his feet were quite out of sight.

Now he appeared to be asleep. His eyes were shut, his thumbs tucked into pockets in his vast apron.

Roger poked him gently, "Your best horses, Haimo; we go with speed to Rouen."

The mountain-man quivered, then opened its eyes. They searched Roger and Turold like twin eagles astride the arched beak of his nose.

"Day after Epiphany," whispered the vast man. "Yesterday was holy day, tomorrow will be holy day. Take your time. It's four hours yet to dinner. It takes that long to prepare the best fish stew in France—and the best mutton and chickens in Normandy. Give order to the boy."

"Four hours!" shouted Roger. "Get us horses! See, here's the duke's seal, we must make haste!"

"Go faster after proper food. Wait. Horses later."

"Do you honor the duke's seal, or do you not?" Roger's face was red now, but Turold wanted to laugh. Himself, he favored the idea of a good meal. Now that he reckoned it, they'd scarcely eaten for two days, and it was still a long ride to Rouen.

But Roger shouted, "The horses, Haimo, the horses!"

The mountain shook with silent laughter. It whispered, "Horses, the best horses, Roger, son of Rolph of the Tower in Kent. And great haste. And with this Saxon! What news do you bear?"

Roger stiffened. "We be bodes!" There was suddenly a heavenly fragrance of food in the room, and he turned, then whirled back crying, "Oh, this is good! You old rogue, you scurvy fisherman, you monstrous sea-hog! Come quickly, Turold!"

For on the table two servants had set down smoking meats—hot pasties, drinks, comfits. And two bowls of steaming creamy soup, swimming with sweet clams and fish. Turold said not a word. Standing they ate and drank, standing they wiped their mouths, standing they tossed coins of good value to a maid. For now they heard horses being led to the door.

As for Haimo—he could not rub his hands together for they no longer met, except under his chin. And Haimo was ever mindful of dignity. But he closed his eyes and sat—and it seemed that he felt pleased about something.

But as the money was tossed to the maid, he came to life. His great bulk quivered and not with laughter. Trembling, the maid sidled to him, reaching out the coins. He snatched them, fumbled for a pocket, whispered, "Poorer every day. The good fathers are close with me, the fishing's bad, the . . ."

He suddenly pointed a finger at Roger, and Turold shivered in spite of himself. How could he have thought this gross fellow the soul of geniality!

Haimo whispered, "When is Harold crowned?"

Roger stammered, "Why, right after the burial . . . that is . . . no, no! I have not said it, I told you nothing! This news is for—by all the saints! How you had food ready for us, I do not know. I give you thanks for it—and good day."

So they hurried out. But Haimo's whisper, vast as his body, came after them. "I have had such a meal ready every morning and every evening these three weeks. I knew you were coming. Ah—I am but a poor man. Do not forget poor Haimo. I shall be ruined! The times are bad . . . the fishing . . ."

As they swung into the saddle Roger spoke to the hostler. "Your master takes great care of the duke's post. Yet what is his interest?"

The hostler looked over his shoulder. "He casts his eyes high, wants to lord it with a manor or maybe some day a castle. He and the monks—they've been laying up extra grain—and fattening kine and pigs."

Then they used whip and spur, the horses jumped ahead, and they were off, riding, galloping, laughing, singing, with the long road before them and Haimo's good dinner under their belts.

A feeling like nothing he had ever known swept over Turold. It was joy, it was madness. He was free now and riding to meet Duke William. Let kings die, and kings be crowned, let them fight and murder and marry, play bold and play craven; it all made songs to shout and to rollick with, riding up to Rouen.

He rushed on as in a dream. He saw, but scarce noted, the rich valley up which they rode, sparkling with a light snowfall. The castles, the abbey on the hill, the well-kept forests, the widespread orchards on the slopes. It was like a vast garden, a safe-walled demesne, and compared to it, Kent was a wilderness. He saw that the villages were very close with crowds of gaping serfs, but it meant nothing to him—only that he could shout and sing the louder to scatter them from his way.

This was Normandy, the golden land!

The road was well kept, the bridges mostly in repair,

and they swept on and on. Turold sang of Rollant in the pass of Roncevalles, making his last stand with deeds of great vassalage, winding his jewelled horn, his oliphant, that the emperor might hear and turn back and avenge them on the Sarrazins.

> *"High were the peaks, and shadowy and grand,*
> *The valleys deep, the rivers swiftly ran . . ."*

Now they saw ahead of them the walls and towers of Rouen and urged their horses still faster, and the great song still went with them the last league of the way.

> *"If Rollant be struck, will not one soul remain.*
> *God! Sixty men are all now in his train!*
> *Never a king had better capitains . . ."*

At the bridge which led over Seine to the hermitage of Grandmont and the ducal chase of Quevilty, they reined in to ask their way of a priest, and when he answered that the duke was gone over river to the chase, they bent their whips again and galloped over the bridge.

As they turned through a park gate, they saw a great crowd of folk with dogs baying, beaters shouting. And beyond, in a space by himself, a thickset man was holding a great bow. Now their ride was done, and a few words to William would fulfill their duty.

They slid from their horses and pressed forward, running away from hands held to stay them, crying out, "News from England! News for the duke!"

Turold they held, but Roger slipped through, reached the man with the bow, and gasped out his message. And Turold, leaning wearily against a tree, knew that Roger

90

said, "King Edward has ended his days, and the Earl Harold is raised to the kingdom."

Afterward, Turold was puzzled, wondering what he had expected. For William bent down his head, concealed by a hood, motionless for a long time. His people began to stir and whisper and to look strangely at the bodes. William went apart under a tree, dropped his head on his breast and with nervous fingers laced and unlaced his mantle. Turold could not see his face.

Roger came to him, and they stood with the courtiers in a tense silence, for William seemed lost to everything but his own thoughts. Turold heard the rustle of dry leaves and the restless whimpering of the hounds.

Suddenly the duke walked to the page who held his bow and spoke a word; a knight brought him a horse. He swung into the saddle and without any word, pulling the hood still lower over his face and whipping and rowelling the horse sharply, he rode swiftly through the gateway and down the road to the bridge. Quickly the company got their mounts and made off after him. In a scattering of dirt and leaves, all were gone, and Turold and Roger were left alone in the park.

But now a grizzled knight came out of the lodge and looked about and hailing them asked what had happened, for only a few minutes before the duke had been set for the hunting.

Answered Roger, "My lord, we brought news from overseas, from England, and it is this news which has upset the duke and sent him back to Rouen in the greatest haste."

"News from England!" exclaimed the old knight.

"And may I ask the nature of this news?"

Roger hesitated.

"I see!" The knight smiled. "It is of the highest importance—only for the ears of William himself, eh? Put your mind at rest, for I am that Fitz-Osbern the seneschal, and I will know soon."

Roger flushed. "All will know soon, it is true, and you, my lord, before any. For Edward is dead, and Harold has the crown."

Fitz-Osbern showed no surprise. "Your name, lad?"

"I am Roger, son of Rolph, now of Kent, and this is my brother bode, Turold, of Farthingwold-under-Blean."

Fitz-Osbern saluted them. "You have had a hard ride. Welcome to Rouen! I well remember your father, Roger. He was one of those who went into England with Edward when he became king."

"Aye, my lord!"

"The court have followed the duke. Mount now; we must ride after them."

The knight's friendliness loosened their tongues, and before they clattered up the incline to the castle bridge Fitz-Osbern the seneschal had seen well into the minds of both young bodes.

Across the cobbled courtyard he led them, under an arched gateway, high and strong such as Turold had never seen the like, no, not even in London. Indeed, this great fortified place was so massively built, so cleverly planned, so tirelessly guarded, that he saw with a leaping heart, here was something far ahead of the Saxon way. Now they stood in the great hall—it would hold a half dozen of the rooms they called halls at home. It was a sort of promenade for the castle folk, with a great fire at each end roaring up into the mouth of a channel built to receive it. And that was the finest thing of all. It gave much better outlet for the smoke than the Saxon roof-openings, keeping the air fresh and sweet, saving the walls from soot. Indeed, it would have been sad case had they been blackened, for to lend warmth the high stone partitions were hung with rugs and bright embroideries.

As they passed along Turold saw that many looked at them strangely, muddied and unkempt as they were from their ride. Now they saw the duke, sitting apart from his people, leaning his head against a pillar. And still, as he had done in the chase, his fingers plucked at the strings of the hood which covered his face.

The seneschal, who had been humming a tune as he walked, stopped as several came to him, asking what news so disturbed their lord. Then Fitz-Osbern halted and spoke loudly to the duke so that all in the hall might hear him.

"Rise up, my lord!" he cried in a ringing voice. "It is in vain to try to hide these tidings, for it is already blazoned abroad. Soon everyone must know that Edward be dead and Harold holds the kingdom of England."

Answered William in a low voice, raising his head, but turning it partly away, "It is this news indeed which grieves me, and none could grieve me more. I sorrow alike for the death of my cousin, and for the wrong done me by Harold."

Fitz-Osbern planted his feet squarely, and his words were harsh. "My lord! When you are wronged, do you mourn and mope like a puling boy? Or do you act? Are you the lord whose fame has gone through all Christendom! Do you sit here, bowed beneath this cruel wrong—or do you show what William of Normandy does when one fails in faith with him? Begin, my lord, to make good your vengeance! And having begun, carry your purpose through with a strong and bold arm.

"In a word—cross the sea and wrest the kingdom which is rightfully yours from the usurper!"

There was a shocked silence through the length of the great hall.

Then William sprang to his feet and shouted, "By the splendor of God!" He tore off his hood and the hot color came into his face; his hand played with his sword as if he would strike down the man who spoke to him such words.

But instead, all in an instant, he shifted his sword belt, threw back his head, and let out a great roar of laughter.

The duke's people were crying out, shouting at him.

Turold was wrapped in silence. He was back again in the beech wood, babbling secrets, singing—to this man who was the great duke, the greatest man in all France. He was helping him to lead the wounded Taillefer out of the wood. He was taking from him, in his father's close, the leopard dagger. Turold put his hand on it; it was cold under his fingers.

As in a dream, Turold knew that Roger was speaking to him, that Fitz-Osbern was leading them forward, that he was kneeling to the duke.

94

William was smiling, saying gently, "So you came after all, my sweet singer. I knew you must."

Turold, looking up at him, answered simply, "To Roncevalles, my lord! To Roncevalles I came!"

F Turold had met Merlin of the Old Time on Seine road as he sped to Rouen, he could not have been under greater enchantment than that which the castle, the people, the duke and his duchess laid upon him. There was an order, a beauty, a discipline that fulfilled all his dreams. And William's favor was already his, for that strange day In Blean when he had talked with William, not knowing who he was, had given him such an insight as few ever shared with the great lord of Normandy.

And soon Turold had won William's people.

After he and Roger had slept a day and a night, had bathed and clothed themselves in fresh garments sent by the Duchess Matilda, and had eaten the supper she sent them, then they waited upon the duke in the great hall just as meat was being served.

The duke saw them coming and stood up in his place at the raised table, shouting, "A new singer for us, a great new singer!"

Turold was astonished when all the folk in hall rose in their places and cheered him. He stood abashed a moment. Then friendly hands pulled him forward to a place by the duke, and someone brought him a harp.

When they sat down again and the hall was quiet, Turold turned away from the table and looking up into the vaulted roof, he sang for them.

His song was first of the glories of the Northmen of old, from whom these Normans had sprung. He showed them the isles, the northern shores with the storms buffeting the rocky cliffs, while the terns with icy plumage gave answer. He sang of the Norsemen in their nail-studded ships with reddened stripes, crimson shields, tarred oars, and foam-sprinkled awnings. He showed them those resolute princes who must drink their Yule on the tossing sea, scorning warm firesides and soft bowers. He showed the victorious warriors, enriched with money and splendid swords, jewelled and of the metal of Hunaland. They wore cloaks of scarlet, coats of woven mail, gilded baldrics, graven helms, and flashing arm rings.

There had been great vassalage too in those days; men loved their lords, and lords were lavish and hospitable to their lieges. Despising their inheritance in the homelands, they had sought a greater upon far strange shores. So they came to France and in great strife won them land upon the coast and all those fertile valleys where now their castles stood.

Then with the night deepening and the torches guttering against the walls, he sang again of Rollo and his son William Longsword, of the day of battle and carnage shared by the black raven with dusky plumage and hooked beak and that gray beast, the wolf of the forest. Then many brave men left their bonehouses, lost their life-joys, as the sons of Edward cleaved the serried bucklers with their hammered blades, hacking at the shields of linden wood. No need then had their enemies to gloat when the standards came into collision, when spear met spear, man encountered man, and blade was crossed with blade.

So they conquered and so they came, the old sea rovers, home again from the sea with their minds set upon the mead cups.

Turold sat silent with bowed head, and the hall rang with shouts and men tossed coins and arm rings on the floor at his feet. Then the bearers went round and filled all the cups again. William stood up, shouting, "To a great minstrel!" and raised the golden cup and tossed the liquid down. And his men all down the long table answered, "A great minstrel!" But some, laughing, declared that they did not love the cup as did their wild forefathers, and after this one would drink no more that night.

And when they brought a holly wreath, they gave it to Taillefer. Bent and gray, he went to Turold and placed it on his head; then he stroked his clothes, peered into his face, and stroked cheeks and hair. Although some exclaimed that the old man was fey, Turold suffered this familiarity. As he looked up at his face, he felt that Taillefer looked like someone he knew if he could only remember.

There was a stir, then an angry murmur through the hall, and he turned and looked up into the dark and bitter face of Tostig the traitor. The man swept him a mocking bow and turned to William.

"My lord duke! Here be Saxon spies, the lieges of my noble brother in Kent. What are they doing here? Beguiling you with flattering tales—and sending word to England of all our plans?"

He took a step and raised his arm as if to sweep Turold and Taillefer aside, but William spoke a word, and Tostig stepped back.

"I know these men, my lord!" he protested. "The old man, the mad singer, and the younger one are both of the same family, of a manor in Scray—I forget the names— we'd count them churls at home, not throw them gold! My lord, have them both laid up in irons where they can do us no harm."

"Harm!" shouted William. "They do us great good, helping to beguile the dreary winter."

Tostig dropped his eyes as William's men raised a clamor in praise of Turold. "My lord . . ." he stammered.

But William was laughing now. "You see, the night is young. The Saxon lad shall sing on for our amusement. Turold, give my lord Tostig a tale. A veritable tale of traitors!"

Turold was staring at Taillefer. Aye, Tostig had given him the key, for Taillefer was that lost Turold for whom Adela had waited so long. . . . Now William's voice came, urging him to sing of traitors. To Tostig, brother of Harold, he was bidden to sing of traitors!

The slow red crept over Turold's face. Suddenly he laughed, looked at William, and set the harp in position.

Now he sang to them of fair Albion Isle, of England, set like a jewel in a silver sea. So fair a land it was, he said, that for a thousand years many tribes had come to conquer it. They came, but in the end the island conquered them.

He told them of Cerdic and Cynric, of Uther and Arthur, and of the Danes and their raids. Then he opened to them the glory and sorrow of the conquests of Canute the Dane and of the resistance of the Saxons led by the prince, Edmund Ironside. The king of that time, Ethelred,

99

was ever Unready. But the Ironside was peerless in knighthood, in deeds to free his people from the ravagers of England.

During many battles he had harried Canute till at last he met him at Ashingdon, and there the Saxon ranks pushed the Danes hard, making great slaughter. Feeling they must be victorious, Edmund pressed on, found Canute, and forced him to give combat.

How the Saxons shouted, how they gloried that England should at last be free!

Yet there was a traitor among them, Edric the renegade. He turned against the Ironside, with his lieges he turned, pressed back against his own people, took them on the flank, drove them bewildered, seeing their own blood turn against them.

There was a deep hush in the hall now, and the Normans looked sideways at Tostig, and those near him moved away along the bench.

Turold let the pause ripen in men's minds. Then he suddenly began to sing of the end of that day of terror at Ashingdon. The day, the battle, the kingdom lost to Edmund. The land divided by consent between the two great lords.

Not for long, not for long! Soon an outlaw's knife lay in the heart of the Ironside and all fell to Canute. They hung the crown of the young king, all blazing with jewels as it was, over the high altar of the priory of St. Swithin.

Turold paused again. Then in a voice so low men leaned closer to hear, he sang, so the kingdom was lost because of a traitor!

It was late now, almost to morning. Turold laid down

the harp, men stirred and sighed. Taillefer took the wreath and put it again on Turold's head, and all the castle folk made a procession in honor of their new minstrel, leading him to his room in the little tower.

As they unlaced their points and put out the torch, Roger said, "I am so glad, Turold, that you have found your lost uncle. Let Tostig sneer as he likes, I'd be proud to have Taillefer, bemused as he is, in my family. Strange that he lost all memory of his family. It was that head injury, I suppose."

Turold answered "Aye," with dry throat. Roger meant well, but he wished he would not speak of these things. There was too much to think of as it was. As he fell asleep, he recalled how Tostig had looked, sitting alone there when they had all trooped out to escort him to bed. For he had looked back, and Tostig, bowed and sullen, had given Taillefer a dark look.

He was not surprised the next day when passing through the guard-hall court to find that Taillefer was being hectored by a crowd of serving men—led on by Tostig. He pushed his way into the crowd, took his uncle by the arm, and hurried him away. But the incident troubled him. Tostig must feel very sure of his standing with William to dare such venting of his spleen. Aye, William would use Tostig as Black Jarn at home used the stupid oxen to plow the fields. But would Tostig plow in a field already waiting for another man's grain? That night Turold went to Taillefer's quarters in a little tower carrying the old harp from Adela's bower. The old man stroked it, then played some songs, old songs. Aye, this man was indeed the elder Turold, brother to Engelric.

The next day Taillefer escorted Turold to the hall and after that was always by him. When there were calls for a song, when William in the hall or Matilda in the bower asked for a glee, then they took turn as friendly rivals. And soon the sullen face of Tostig shadowed them no more, for he was gone on some mysterious errand. To the Danish king, some said, to get help to invade England from the north and recover his lost earldom. An invasion from the north? God help England!

William gathered his barons for a council, men poured in from all quarters, and the castle hummed. Attending daily upon the duke, Turold began to know many of these lords, and gold and ornaments were heaped upon him for his singing.

One day orders went out for a great meeting of all loyal vassals at a place called Lillebonne, and as they rode down in a great company to this place, the duke had Turold ride by his side. "Lad," he said, "you sing of great vassalage. We go to Lillebonne to see how many good vassals we have, and you shall sing to them there."

Turold's hands tightened on the reins. "Of what shall I sing, my lord?"

"Not of treachery!" William leaned to him, gave him the look that, as Turold had seen, made men eager for anything the duke might ask of them. "You shall sing of Rollant, of Roncevalles! Your great song was made for such a time as this."

But at Lillebonne things did not go as William wished. For he let Fitz-Osbern lead the barons' meeting, staying away himself. And Fitz-Osbern unfolded to them William's plan to invade England. And asked, in an excess of zeal that each give twice what he owed to the duke's services. If they gave as their due six knights' service, to give him twelve, and two ships if they owed him one. Each according to his strength.

At that there were murmurings and dissension. The lords demurred, saying loudly that they were never bound to serve overseas, neither would they give double, lest it be held of them as their due and asked of their sons in time to come.

When this word was brought to William, who for reasons of policy had not been present at the meeting, he only smiled. And soon there was a constant stream of his vassals going to his private chambers, one by one. And William so persuaded them that they came away pledged to give him, not as a right, but as a favor, the men and ships he asked in order to assert his claim to the English crown.

That night William gave a great feast in Lillebonne, and Turold sang to the noble assembly the wonderful tale of Douce France.

It took all night for him to sing the song of Rollant, paladin of Charlemagne. And while he sang, on and on, it was as if a fire was kindled which would burn on to white heat, and Turold did not know that he had done that thing which he had promised Cerdic and himself never to do—to help bring invasion upon England.

Turold sang to them of Charles the Great, conquering the pagans of Spain, marching home to France with his victorious host; of Rollant and Oliver, the two who never left each other, who were invincible in battle. He told them of that traitor, Guenelun, who caused the emperor to set Rollant and Oliver with their twenty thousand for rear guard,

as the host made its way through the high black passes home to France. He showed them Rollant facing the pagans, a hundred thousand strong, pouring down off the heights; and Oliver who begged Rollant to sound his horn, his oliphant, that Charles return to aid them. And Rollant, proud and eager to fight for his lord, refusing.

And he sang of the great combats between the mighty knights of each side, and of the Franks' grief when their friends fell. When the pagan Valdabron struck the duke, Sanson, dead from his saddle, *God!* say the Franks, *Grief for a brave baron!*

And when Climborins of the Sarrazins killed Engilier of Gascune, *God!* say the Franks, *Grief such a man to lose!* Turold sang on and the night waned and the fires fell ashy, yet men forgot where they were and saw only the pass of Roncevalles.

> *"The count Rollant, he canters through the field,*
> *Holds Durendal, he well can thrust and wield,*
> *Right great damage he's done the Sarrazins.*
> *Through all that place their blood was flowing*
> *   clear!*
> *Says the archbishop; 'Good baronage indeed!'*

> *"And Rollant says:*
> *'Felon he's named that sells his body cheap!*
> *Strike on my lords with burnished swords and*
> *   keen;*
> *Contest each inch your life and death between,*
> *That ne'er by us Douce France in shame be*
> *   steeped!'*

"Says Oliver, 'Who holds back is condemned!'

The count Rollant has never loved cowards,
Nor arrogant nor men of evil heart,
Nor chevalier that was not good vassal . . .

Now through the press he goes their line to
meet!"

All through the long night, Turold held them there
at Lillebonne. They saw the rear guard, the twenty thousand Franks, die in the pass, making as they did so great
slaughter of the pagans to protect their king. They saw
the death of Oliver, beloved of Rollant. They saw Rollant,
mortally wounded, the last of the Franks alive. On the
four marble terraces he stood, trying to break his sword—
and it would not break. In the golden hilt were precious
relics: Saint Peter's tooth, the blood of St. Basile, a piece
of the robe of St. Mary.

At last on a peak under a high pine Rollant lay down
upon his sword and his oliphant with his face towards
Spain . . .

"That Charles, finding him, might say . . .
'Ah gentle count, conquering he was slain!'"

So Rollant asked God's blessing and forgiveness for
all his sins:

"His right-hand glove, to God he offers it.
Saint Gabriel from's hand hath taken it.

107

God sent down His angel cherubim,
And Saint Michael, we worship in peril;
So the count's soul they bare to Paradis.

"Rollant is dead, his soul to Heaven God bare.
That Emperor to Roncevalles doth fare.
There was no path nor passage anywhere
Without a Frank or pagan lying there . . .

" 'God!' says the King, 'Now well I may despair,
I was not here the first assault to share!' "

And the great song says that the sun stood still in its going down while Charles took vengeance on the fleeing pagans in the pass. And the standard of the pagans was a dragon banner, of great magic, yet it availed them naught before the vengeance of the Christians.

Now the tale was told. Slowly, William and his men came back to Lillebonne; the fires were out, the winds moved in the hall, the night was almost to morning.

Turold sat with drooping head. It was hard for him to come back from Roncevalles.

William touched his arm. "Singer—did you note—it was the pagans who bore a dragon banner?"

"Yet Alfred of old, and the Ironside, thought it no shame to fight under the dragon."

William smiled. "There was great vassalage in the days of Charles."

Turold said gently, "To a great lord, great vassals!"

And William seemed satisfied.

Yet when Turold was alone he looked long at the dragon ring which Harold had put on his finger.

108

N an April evening of high winds and scudding clouds Turold rode back to the castle by a lane which wound across the orchard-covered slopes. The trees were bursting into bloom about him and a multitude of birds, tossed in the wind, soared and sang above. The smells troubled him the most, the blossoms, the wind, the plowed ground. The same advance of spring-tide must be warm and sweet upon England too. He had not forgotten that at home the manor roofs sagged, that the Saxons did not work to single ends as did the Nor-mans, but resisted change as they would the devil. Yet spring in Kent was something to see, and he longed for Farthingwold and Blean wood, for Lucy and Adela. Had Black Jarn brought the cattle safely through the winter? How had the lambing gone? How many farrows of pigs did Pig-Boy have?

He thought of his true lord, Harold, how he had taken the sword of kingly office from the hand of his brother, the sadness in his voice as he sent him on the Norman mission, saying, "I think you love me well."

Aye, Harold was his lord and England his mother-land. All this great gathering of invaders must bring her sorrow. Normandy—nay, all of France—was on the march. They knew that England lay defenseless before them,

109

knew that the fortresses were decayed, the fleet of three thousand ships which had guarded the Saxon shores in the time of Edgar was scattered and lost. And Tostig had gone to the Norse king with rich gifts and promises of land in England if he would invade the northeast coast at the same time that William attacked from the south. It was a clever scheme, if the Norsemen could get ready in time. And that wily monk, LanFranc, had gone to Rome to get the pope's blessing upon the great emprise.

Sorrowing for England, Turold knew that he himself was Norman too, both in blood and feeling. He owed love and devoir to two different ways of life. But honor and great vassalage never came from double duty. The greatest virtue for any man, high or low, was loyalty to one worthy lord. He therefore was no true man. He twisted the heavy ring on his finger.

The first stars were showing through clouds across the river to the west. There was a glow there that made Turold wonder, and he reined in White Boy to see what it was. Suddenly the clouds opened, a space in the sky was clear and there appeared a marvel, a thing of splendor, a great blazing star like a dragon in the sky.

Turold lifted his face to it for a long time. Then he raced back to the castle and found the duke and his people all outside gazing into the sky. The new star had a head like a torch and a fiery tail streaming out behind, and it cast an awesome glow across sky and earth. The duke's people were on their knees, crossing themselves, and there were doleful cries to the saints and the telling of beads. Turold knelt close to William, saw his hand clasp his reliquary. Then William raised his face to the star with a look of triumph, as if he saw in it a sign from Heaven.

While the duke's folk still cried out in terror, there came a clatter of horsemen into the court, with LanFranc at their head, he who had gone to Rome. He stood up in his stirrups and shouted, "You great fools! The star is blessing, not cursing, for Normandy and all we do this year. And look! From Rome! A banner—blessed by the Holy Father for us. Hail to William! He shall carry it in triumph through England!"

The people hushed, trembling, staring up at the banner, then back at the star. It seemed to Turold that they gave a shuddering sigh as of relief from terror before they began to shout. Then the joyful clamor rang—acclamation for William, the banner, and the great adventure. Thus LanFranc used the advent of the star to turn Normandy to triumphant expectation of victory which would increase the pace of preparation to incredible activity.

Turold turned away as the crowd followed LanFranc into the hall, and went back to the postern gate to tend to White Boy. The old warder there was his special friend, by order of the duke. When he had first come to the castle and wanted to slip out for a ride one evening, the old man nodded and winked.

"I'm to wink at ye, lad, thus. By the duke's orders. Duke says, very self to me he says, 'My singer with hair like gold, be he armed or unarmed, mailed or unmailed, give him the little door swinging as he will. Wink at him,' says the duke. 'Aye, if ye see double and there be two of him, let them by. The more we have o' such lads the better!'" The old man grinned. "Hast a lass in the village?"

Turold had laughed. William must have his fun.

III

Now he winked at the old man, and the warder winked back, then beckoned to him. "Your horse white as snow is safe tied to the wall," he said. "But right after ye ran in a little lad came and left this for you." He slipped something into Turold's hand.

Turold swung about, looking at it by the light of the torch. It was a ring made like a dragon, exactly like the one he wore.

He turned back to the warder. "You say it was a little lad? No one else?"

The old man shook his head. "I looked out. I thought, maybe there's a pretty lass just over yonder in the lane, riding a little palfrey, with veil flying, as the songs say. Eh—she sends you a great heavy ring—for a lady." The old man's eyes narrowed. "Or by chance you've a rival, and it's a challenge."

"Aye, that's it," answered Turold slowly, "a challenge."

He mounted and went over the little bridge and across the wide slope of the hill, pausing often to look about. He saw no one. The light of the star made strange shadows among the blossoming trees. He kept shifting in the saddle; it was warm and windless, and his armor chafed a little. But he was duke's man now and must never ride unarmed. He took off his helm and hung it to the pommel, wishing for wind to stir his long hair. Where was the messenger who had sent the lad to the postern gate with a dragon ring for him? There was no one in sight along the hill.

He had known that someday he must expect this. Harold's words were burned into his heart. "Some day I will send you a messenger with a ring like this. Do all that he bids you."

Now this messenger was come. Now must Turold remember that he was Harold's man. Aye—now he must be false to William, who trusted him. Suddenly he pulled up White Boy. "St. Mildred! What am I to do? For I love this Norman too. He is a great lord. Must I then be false to both?"

He looked around. Where could he hide such a messenger, for here was no Blean wood. The land was covered with orchards and fields of grain. And whom had King Harold sent? Who could the messenger be?

He rode on. The lane turned left at the crest of the ridge, and he saw a horseman under the trees beyond. It was a knightly figure, dimly seen. The other horseman moved toward him through the shadows. It was as if he saw himself coming, for the stranger rode a white horse and his mail was identical with Turold's own. His helm too was on his saddle, and his hair, thick and yellow, fell down his shoulders.

Turold came knee to knee with this rider and said, "Cerdic!" And then, staring, he cried, "You must be mad . . . how could you get past them all?"

Cerdic laughed softly. "You have forgotten. I appear as the young minstrel of Rouen. Even our armor is of an exact likeness."

"The colors of the bars are different."

"Who can see that on a trotting horse?" Cerdic told him how he had come all the way up Seine road and been given great cheer all the way and even been urged to use the duke's post horses. But he had wished to keep his own horse, brother to Turold's, and had ridden leisurely along, taking two days.

When this was spoken, he seemed unable to say more. Neither could Turold speak. They turned up the river and walked their mounts, looking at each other and the star.

At last Cerdic said slowly, "This is a great people. I am not blind. I saw the great ships on the forms all along the river, I saw the swarms of workmen. I saw forges blazing on the hills last night. The roads are choked with knights and their men, with wains, with herds of all kinds of cattle driven in from far places." His voice was edged with bitterness. "At home we argue, we have no ships, we cannot get together. Our thanes spend much of their time over the mead cups boasting of victories of former days. Dear God!"

Turold answered heavily. "What can I say? I would not have you taken here as a spy. Yet I myself am a spy—and bound to send to Harold word of all he wishes to know."

Cerdic laid his hand on Turold's shoulder. "What spell does William cast over men? All these wonderful preparations—and you. Turold, Turold! You have lost your heart to this Norman."

"He is a great lord, a leader to follow, a man to love."

"He is the enemy of England. They mean to destroy us! All this great army of knights—they go to loot us."

Turold sagged in the saddle. "I am still Harold's man."

"He will release you!"

"What do you mean?" Turold reined in.

"Harold knows the spell that William can throw over men. He bade me tell you that if you wished to see him you must come to the Saxon shore during the early heat, for we shall make watch there all summer. At least we shall try to hold the Normans from landing! Come about Midsummer Night. We shall probably make the chief station at the old castle on the bluff at Pevensey. And now you must tell me two things. What allies has William bound to him—and will there be invasion from more than one side?"

Haltingly, truthfully, as far as he knew, Turold listed the alliances and explained the plottings of Tostig.

"Tostig!" Cerdic's look was grim now. "It's rumored in England that he is with Harald Hardrada offering him a slice of England to help."

Turold's face looked old under the unearthly light of the comet. "It is true. If he wins them over, Harold will be attacked from two sides at once."

They rode all night up the river and turned back as dawn was coming up the sky. They talked now of homeplace and homefolk, and Turold showed to his brother the story of Taillefer, the lost son of Adela.

Beyond sight of the postern gate, they reined in, and Turold told Cerdic what to do when he entered there. Boldness, a wink to the old man, a quip. He explained the turnings to the lower level of the stables in the third ward and how to say the right things to the grooms. Then through the passage, through the inner ward, and so on to Taillefer's tower quarters.

"Stop for no one; wave your hand and pass on. You are Turold the minstrel and do as you please."

"You have made no enemies in the castle?"

"None here now that Tostig is gone. I'm sure you'll

be all right. You can rest and eat, and when night comes I'll get you away."

"I'll be all right. How long before you can join me?"

"I must wait till I'm sure you've arrived at the little tower. I'll take White Boy to the upper level of the stables. We have hundreds of horses, and no one will ever notice that the minstrel rode in twice this morning. But it wouldn't do to have us meet on the way to Taillefer."

They laughed and touched hands. Turold watched Cerdic go down to the postern, saw it open, saw him ride through under the low-arched gate. Then he turned White Boy's head to make a circle across the hill to come out at the main gate. He heard the gate-horn blowing and knew that someone was demanding entrance. He must go in with a group if he could, so he kicked the horse into a gallop. As he turned the corner, a company of horsemen were clattering across the bridge. In a moment he was among them. They were certainly strangers, fierce looking men with long yellow beards. Norsemen from the wild North! And Tostig was with them, back to report with some of the new allies.

Turold hung back as they entered the main court; it would never do for him to come face to face with Tostig now. He turned White Boy into the forge building. Three blacksmiths were working at the great forge, and Turold dismounted and watched idly, content that the horse was under cover here. He wished that he had a cloak with him, even though it might look queer on a sunny spring morning when everyone was shedding cloaks, the pages so careless they dropped them anywhere. Still, Turold thought, it might be useful. He hunted along the benches, found one on the floor, put it on over mail and surcoat and felt safer.

When he thought enough time had passed, he mounted and turned into the inner bailey toward the passage leading to the stables. Courts and alleys were filled now with folk hurrying about the business of the day. Turold pushed to the wall to let pass a baker boy with a handcart piled with bread. As he emerged from the gloom of the passage he heard an uproar ahead—voices shouting, then a sudden silence.

It was here, if anywhere, that he would meet Cerdic, for it was through the court ahead that he must pass on the way to Taillefer's tower. But Cerdic was surely in the clear now.

He walked White Boy into the sunlight and instantly tightened the rein and pulled him back, step by step. In the protecting shadow of the passage, he bowed his head. Cerdic was at that moment standing back to the wall, on guard with flashing sword, for Tostig and three of the wild vikings pressed him close.

The sweat rolled on Turold's face. God! I was sure he would be safe!

There was no choice now, no choice at all. The rabble who looked on at this thing were the unknightly serving folk. They would yowl and gawk and snigger, and run away when Cerdic lay dead. If it should be asked why no help was given the duke's minstrel, they would know nothing. Duke's minstrel . . . nay, now there are two—and we are betrayed.

He lingered no more. There was only one thing he could do—he must save Cerdic.

Hastily he donned his helm, pulled down the visor, drew his sword and yelled at White Boy. Cerdic and his antagonists were all on foot, and he came upon them like a whirlwind. Cerdic looked up at him with a flash of his eyes, then turned back to the business of the swordplay. Someone shouted, "The guard, the guard!" Tostig was yelling for help, now that he and his friends were getting the worst of it. Then there were shouts and running feet, and Tostig and the vikings drew off; one of them had lost a hand. It was apt to be bad for anyone caught brawling if blood was shed. William kept good order.

Panting, Turold put his sword at rest, watching for a moment. But Tostig and friends were hurrying away now. Cerdic was holding to his hand which dripped red, trying to smile up at Turold.

Turold kicked one foot free of the stirrup. "Get up! Get your foot into this stirrup, lean over the saddle!"

White Boy carried them out of the court into the left-hand passage. "Just to the tower steps!" They came into the little court in the west ward, and Cerdic sagged and slipped to the ground. In an instant Turold was down, bending over him.

"I'm all right," Cerdic whispered.

Turold said, "You've got to be! The guard will be here looking for—for me. Leave it to that scurvy Tostig to tell them some story. Come on now." He lifted him, got him to the tower door. Cerdic stood up.

"I'm all right now. It's just my hand, no bones touched, I think. I'll make it . . . only four flights, did you say!" They both laughed a little, weakly. Turold urged, "Go on now, we mustn't be caught here together."

Turold watched him start up, finally disappear around the first bend. There was blood showing on every step. Many people had seen the duke's minstrel receive a wound in the hand—and Turold had no wound. He took his knife . . .

Which hand was Cerdic wounded in? He could not remember. Was it the sword arm, the right? He bethought him how Cerdic had leaned, going up the stairs. Yes, it was the right. Turold felt a sudden cherishing of his own sword hand. Could anyone know, in the heat of the encounter, which hand it was?

Now he could hear the guard coming up the passage into the west ward. The lower arm would do, just above the wrist as if the point of the blade had slipped under the edge of the mail. When blood runs, can onlookers swear where exactly the cut was?

In a moment it was done, only a scratch, really, but it stung. He tried to stanch the flow of blood.

He must get out of here—but this was a dead-end court. If the guard took him, who would look out for Cerdic? Could Taillefer be trusted? Cerdic needed help now, a barber to tend his wound, food. And then he must escape from the castle and pass again down that road choked with knights and William's messengers, get safely overseas to England.

If the guard took Turold, Cerdic would surely be found. They would be hung as spies—and he would be branded as false knight forever. But he did not flinch when, with clatter of heavy boots, an officer of the guard ran in, touched him on the shoulder, and said, "I must arrest you, Sir Turold!"

S Turold turned about to him, the officer cried, "Sir, you are wounded!"

"It is nothing!" Turold told him, but the officer insisted on making a hasty binding with a scarf, then helped him into the saddle, and led him into the inner bailey. But now a bugle was blown, and William and a dozen knights came riding up from the stable incline. At once William saw Turold and rode to him.

"Splendor of God!" he shouted. "I'll hang the man who has hurt my singer! What happened?"

The officer gave him the details; Tostig had entered a complaint that he and certain visitors from the Norse land, passing peacefully from the stables, had been wantonly attacked by the minstrel.

William cried, "Ha!" and looked at Turold a long moment. "Did you dare to do this?" he asked. "Dare to attack my allies here in peace?"

Turold looked William full in the face. "Do you take the word of such a man? Or am I allowed to speak in my own defense?"

"Speak in your own defense you shall," answered the duke. "I will hear you at table tonight." And he rode on, but turned back to say to the guard, "Take the lad to my barber—then to the duchess. Release him in her custody."

Turold stared after him. How could he face them—face Tostig with the wrong hand hurt? What a fool he was, trying to save his right hand. It was Cerdic who had to be saved!

The barber, as he dressed the wound, remarked upon Turold's pale face. "You look, sir minstrel, as if you had lost blood, yet 'tis but a scratch."

Turold grinned and assured him that he felt quite well, was in fact full of good red blood. The truth was, he was now full of worry for Cerdic. While he was having everything done for a silly scratch, Cerdic lay somewhere in the west ward, much blood lost, untended. And how was he going to hide him till the wound healed enough so he could ride?

The Duchess Matilda at this time was about thirty-five years old, the mother of a large family, but still beautiful—and very clever. She was the daughter of the count of Flanders, and her mother was sister to King Henry of France. Thus her influence in both Flanders and France had been of great help to William in strengthening his dukedom. He had in her the utmost confidence—and she shared all his plans.

When the officer led Turold into her presence this bright April morning, they found her at her embroidery frame by the fire, with three of her children romping about. A page was reading from an old Frankish romance.

She rose at once and went to Turold, exclaiming and sympathetic over his wound. When the officer gave her the duke's charge, she smiled and said, "I will keep him!" and dismissed the man.

At once she insisted that she must have off the barber's

bandage and dress the wound properly. "I wouldn't let that fellow take care of my dogs!" she said.

But Turold backed away. "Oh, no, your grace! It is not fitting. The barber did it very well and it's only a scratch anyway. Come, I'll give you a song, but first, by your leave, I'd like to take a few dainties to Taillefer. Lately his appetite flags."

He thought she smiled a little too sweetly. She said, "I myself will get a basket of things for him. We'll go together, it will be good to get a breath of spring."

Turold was very fond of the duchess, for she had been very kind to him since he came to Rouen. But now he wished she were a female of another sort. And every moment was precious—he must get away from her—go to Cerdic at once.

He said, trying not to seem too urgent, "My surcoat is soiled. Have I your grace's leave to withdraw to my room to change?"

She laughed. "Why, I have a new one for you, exactly like the others we made for our handsome young minstrel." She went to a chest, took out a surcoat, held it up. "Aren't the leopards fine?"

"They are beautiful!" He took it from her hand, knelt on one knee, kissed her hand. "I'll be back soon," he told her, and ran out before she could stop him. He hurried to one of the kitchens, where the cooks were always willing to give him something for Taillefer. They heaped up a basket with stuff and he rushed off along the passage into the west ward. There was no one in sight. He hurried up the winding stair in the tower and knocked at Taillefer's door.

There was no answer. But he was sure he heard someone breathing close to the door. He put his lips to the keyhole and said, "Let me in—it's Turold."

In a moment the bolt was drawn, and he stepped in and set basket and surcoat down. Cerdic was asleep on Taillefer's bed, looking a little white. His hurt hand was bandaged in clean linen. Taillefer shut the door, bolted it, and pointed to Cerdic with finger on lips.

Turold said, "I must wake him. I have to know what happened."

"I washed the wound," said Taillefer calmly. "Turold will be all right; he just needs sleep. Nay—you are Turold! Well, that is all right, I have always known there are two Turolds."

It was sometimes a help, Turold thought, to have your fellow conspirator bemused.

He left the food, gave Taillefer instructions as to Cerdic's care and warned him to let no one in, no one at all, even the duke. "Say you are sick, or just play stupid as you often do when you don't feel like seeing people," Turold said. The answering gleam in the old man's eyes confirmed his suspicions that a good part of his madness was feigned—to get a little peace in a too demanding world.

He showed him the new surcoat. "When he wakes, have him put it on. Then he can pass for me."

Taillefer nodded, let him out, and Turold heard the bolt shot home. Much easier now in his mind, he took the tower stairs three at a time and ran through the passages and back into the inner bailey. But he had not reached Matilda's door when he met Tostig, disputing the passage with him.

123

Tostig was laughing, swaggering. He said with relish, "You'll crow a little less loudly, my cock from Scray, when I get through with you tonight." Suddenly, his eyes popped, he pointed to Turold's wrist, was about to say something. But Turold leaped away, got around him and through Matilda's door. Behind him echoed Tostig's laugh, loud and coarse.

When at supper time a summons came from William for him to go to the hall, Matilda said quietly, "You'd better put on that new surcoat after all, Turold," and he looked down and saw he still wore the dirty one. He flushed, stammered some excuse, and rushed off again, this time to his own room where he donned a fresh garment and went down to the duke.

William, as was the custom, was holding court for the day's offenders before he dined, and he received Turold with great solemnity. Soon Tostig was ushered into the hall, and now this Saxon who was brother to Harold and kin to William launched into a tirade against Turold.

William's fingers drummed on his chair while Tostig hurled these accusations against Turold, who was, he said, a spy for Harold and no true man. "And see, my lord," he ended triumphantly, "see this one whom you nurtured in your bosom, yet he injures those who help you to your heart's desire. He attacked wantonly, we only defended ourselves. And who, may I ask, was that knight who came to his help—and on horseback too. No one has seen him since; he vanished. He robbed us of our rightful vengeance and moreover he took off by swordthrust the hand of one of the ambassadors to your court from our ally, king of the Norsemen!"

William smiled as if Tostig had said something pleasant. "True, too true, my good Tostig. It would be better far however, if when the ambassadors of the Norse king come to my court, they not be found with sword in hand against any of my people. But let that pass!" His voice rose. "Is that all?"

Tostig glared at Turold, said pointedly, "My lord! Look at the hand of the minstrel!"

All stared now at Turold. And Turold, with a pain somewhere in his middle, knew that he had no defense, for he had not talked with Cerdic. Alas, no defense at all!

Tostig was shouting, "Can't you see what this all is—there are spies here, spies from my false brother Harold. This Saxon youth, as I well know, has a—"

Turold closed his eyes. How could he have brought Cerdic to this pass. It was utterly stupid, utterly needless.

But the duke suddenly checked Tostig, commanding him sternly to be silent. Tostig stopped in mid-sentence, mouth open. His face was, if possible, even redder than before.

William said, "This is all very interesting. The truth is, it was four against one—till the strange knight came. I cannot see that you have any case, Sir Tostig. Come, I have hunger!"

All through dinner, sitting at the duke's left hand, Turold tried to hide his hands. Yet he could not let it be too apparent; that would be worse than anything. Toward the end of the meal, a page came and whispered in the duke's ear—one of Matilda's people, by his livery. It made Turold nervous to see how the duke whispered with this lad, and smiled and nodded. He suddenly felt that his position was past all bearing. Something must be done!

He leaned on his hands, groaned, and when the duke turned to him, he said, "I feel ill, my lord. Have I your leave to withdraw?"

"Poor lad," replied William. "Go, by all means. Go to Matilda; she will give you some physic."

Turold hurried off. Matilda, always Matilda! First he must go again to the tower and see that all was well, then report to the duchess as the duke commanded. He was not deceived; William might be kind—yet trouble still lurk. He was quite out of breath when at last he knocked on Taillefer's door. The old man opened to him at once and stood blinking. He pushed by and looked around. The place was empty.

Cerdic was gone.

Turold took Taillefer roughly by the shoulders. "Where is he? Oh, you poor fool! Why did you let them in? Who took him. . . where . . ." Then he left off; it was no use talking, the old man was in one of his blank spells. He sat down on the bed-place.

But Taillefer suddenly revived. He said, "But you yourself went with her! She is always so good to us . . ." He lapsed into silence.

"She is always so good to us." It was Matilda, always the duchess. Much too clever for a simple Saxon. There was one thing left. He would go to her, yes, he would throw their fate into her hands!

Suddenly there was a tremendous racket below, shouting, feet on the stairs, laughter. The duke's voice boomed up the stairwell; then he was before the door. More mischief by Tostig? It might as well be faced at once.

Turold flung back the door. He made his face smile, he bowed before the duke. Men crowded behind, and among them Tostig's red face glowered in the light of the torches. Well, let them come in. Cerdic was somewhere else. Maybe soon to come to disaster. But at least he was not here!

Turold bowed his lord into the little room. William came in and stood with arms akimbo, and his eyes were merry as he roared at Tostig, "Well, I win the wager! You see, there is only one lad here. If you did not drink so much sack you wouldn't see double all the time. And now you owe me the finest Flanders mare from your wife's stables!"

It was Tostig again, yet suddenly Turold felt an easing of the tightness in his breast. Somewhere, Cerdic was safe.

Tostig was glaring, but Turold laughed in his face. He bowed mockingly. "Your servant, Sir Tostig! Welcome to this humble room. May I present to you my uncle, the minstrel Taillefer?"

Tostig bowed. He said, "Did you know that my brother, now he has the crown, has shrugged off his Saxon wife, Edith of the Swan Neck, as one would drop an old shoe. He hath wedded a woman who can further his ambitions."

Turold turned away that Tostig might not see his face. It could not be true. Harold would not disown his splendid sons by Edith—Godwine, Edmund, Magnus. Yet he knew that Edith was dane-wife. That she had refused to go to churching with Harold so that some day he might wed for the kingdom if the Witan so wished.

Tostig uttered more of the same but William silenced him. "Be still! You lost the wager. Now we'll go back, and Turold shall sing to us. I'll have someone pluck the harp for him, but he shall sing. Lad, go first to Matilda, then report to the hall."

Turold felt very weary. He had run about all day, dodging, and he had not slept the night before, riding with Cerdic, talking, looking at the star. But he hurried to Matilda.

She was standing before the leaping fire, warming night covers for her children. Now she turned and exclaimed, "Back so soon? But I just sent you off again to be with duke in hall, after bandaging your arm. Did it slip? Or maybe it's too tight."

Turold put his hands behind his back. He felt quite weak. So Cerdic had been here then, and she had fixed his dressings. He put his hand to his head. Someone was playing a very bad jest. Cerdic was now in hall with William, and Cerdic could not sing a note. Matilda was concerned. "Turold! You are weary after this hard day. Sit here and rest awhile."

He sank down on a bench and leaned his head against the wall. How wonderful just to rest, not to think, not to think of anything at all.

Almost at once it seemed, the door to the bower burst open, and William stood there roaring. He was, it seemed, roaring at Turold and Turold opened his tired eyes and looked at his lord. "I thought I sent you back to Taillefer's tower," William shouted. "Matilda, look at the lad! He fainted but now in hall when I asked for a song, so I commanded that he go at once to the tower and get a good rest. But this is the kind of obedience I get. Does he go to the tower? No, he comes here."

Turold rose. "Lord, could I but go now to my own room."

Then came the final horror, a nightmare, for William declared that he himself would escort him to the tower, for there, he vowed, the air was better and would heal him of all his troubles. Aye, it was nightmare all the way into the west ward and on the weary climb to Taillefer's door.

Now was the end, and he waited for William to have door opened and to make discovery of Cerdic, as like to Turold as one pea to another. But William only bade him a curt "Good night!" and hurried down the steps.

Utterly spent, Turold dropped onto the bed-place. This night the two of them would be in the same place and Tostig proved right if he only knew it. He sank into sleep and waked to see the morning sun streaming in through a high slit in the wall. Taillefer and Cerdic were still asleep. He went to the narrow window and looked down into the court. Two men lounged there. As he looked someone came into the court and tried to approach the stair, but the two men came to attention, challenged the newcomer, had words with him, and in the end barred his way with their halberds. The man turned away, roundly cursing the men-at-arms. Turold had a good look at him. It was Tostig.

The two men on guard were by their livery of William's bodyguard. Turold took a deep breath. Duke's men below on watch. Guarding him and Cerdic? Turning away Tostig?

For four more days Turold and Cerdic played hide and seek with Tostig, William and Matilda. Turold changed his bandage to his right hand, for the scratch was practically healed, the scar hidden by his sleeve. And every day Turold went into the hall to sing, and Cerdic went to Matilda and had his wound tended. Every night the two men stood guard at the foot of the tower stair.

On the fourth night William spoke to Turold. "I have just remembered that you are not sworn to me. You must not be masterless man. Come, we shall knight you after the Norman custom. Now give me your hands."

What did this mean? William heard Harold claim me as his man at Farthingwold. He knows that I am bound to Harold as the falcon is bound to the wrist of its master, to whom it must return. Is this too part of the jest?

William leaned forward and commanded, "Come, Turold, give me your hands!"

"My lord," Turold stammered, "I will serve you as best I may. But not yet can I be your man."

The duke smiled. "Your scruples are those of a boy. Harold himself is my man. He took full armor from me, swore to me, went to war as my liege. And on a certain day in Kent, I gave you a dagger. You already are my man, Turold."

Turold looked him boldly in the eye. "Begging your grace's pardon, sire, but how could I have then been your man when I did not know who you were?"

The duke glared, then laughed.

Turold stood head up, unyielding. Stubbornly he felt that he must win release from Harold before he could lay his head on William's knee. Then many things came surging back from his memory, overwhelming him. He bowed his head.

The duke spoke softly then. "Turold, tell me one thing."

"My lord!"

"Do you love me?"

Slowly Turold went down on one knee to William and looked up at him. "Yes, lord. Yes."

William smiled. "Then I am content, for this time. Now, Tostig is leaving in the morning, early I hope. I am sending him down river under guard to avoid brawls. But you need a change, lad. Do you ride out soon, take two days or more. Ride up river or down—does it matter which way you go? Go both ways if you wish. Aye, you shall have release from your duties and be free. You can leave by the postern—or by the main gate—or by both. Ha! Lad, there really should be two of you, as Tostig declares." William was laughing now.

Turold took a deep breath. "Thank you, my lord. I will go. It will be good for me."

What did William mean? Was it a trap? But he would have to take this chance to get Cerdic away.

The next night Turold got Cerdic's horse from the stables, rode him to the foot of Taillefer's stair, leaving Eadnoth to keep watch. Cerdic was waiting in full armor. It was odd about Saxons, Turold thought. Frankish men at such a moment would be kissing and weeping. But he and Cerdic did not even touch hands. Turold's heart was bursting, he knew Cerdic felt the same; therefore they only looked at each other a moment, saluted. Then Cerdic went out and down the stair. Turold went to the window and looked out where the late moon was shining across the orchards and the fields of grain.

It seemed to him that he stood there a long time. Surely the old warder at the postern gate would let Cerdic through without question, surely Cerdic would remember to say, "The duke sends me away for two days this time— to catch a little fish!" To wink. And then the old man would let him through.

At last, when Turold was ready to rush down and go to the postern gate himself, he saw something moving among the trees. Then he saw the white horse cross an open place and gallop from sight on the curve of the hill. Turold took a deep breath. God grant he meet not Tostig on the road!

Early the next morning he rode White Boy out through the main gateway and thought that all must be well when he returned the second night and the warder let him through the postern with much joking about fishing and maidens and rivals and such romancing. It was sure that none of the duke's people knew that Cerdic had been in the castle.

Yet later he was not so sure, at least that William himself and Matilda did not know. For sometimes they made merry over Tostig's delusion of thinking that there were two Saxon minstrels.

HE spring overflowed into summer; the green of the crops rose like a tide in the valleys. And now came such a gathering of men to the duke as had never been seen in the land before. All the castles, all the hamlets swarmed with men.

Before this time Roger had gone into England and Turold was left with no friend save Eadnoth the old carl. But when the time came for the great rendezvous of men and ships at the mouth of the Dives, then Turold lay sick of a fever. That is, Matilda called it a fever, but Turold could have told her that it was a storm in him: a battle between two songs, home song and war song. So he tossed miserably on his pallet and spoke many strange things, and Matilda went to her lord saying that it was sure the young minstrel had the sickness for his homeland.

In a few days when his head was clearer and he was stronger, she gave him a purse of gold and bade him make journey to England to see his people. "See all of them, lad; set your heart at rest. If there be anything that troubles you, anything you wish to arrange, then do it and come to us merry and blithe as you were. For we need your songs to lighten the press of this grave business upon my lord."

Early one morning Turold and Eadnoth rode out of

the castle and took the road to the coast. Turold was thinking that it would soon be Midsummer Eve in England. There would be merrymaking, pranks among men and maids. Here the tillers of the soil were like dumb beasts; there they were sturdy men and women. Here only the lord's will might speak; in England were many voices, many wills, much confusion. After all, at home they could never have got such an expedition together in five short months.

But here the whole land was ringing with William's purpose. In every backwater the clang of tools showed where men worked night and day to finish ships. Everywhere smiths and artisans toiled, fashioning suits of mail, swords, lances, horse furniture. They passed droves of cattle in the roads, horses in the fields, women sewing in doorways. Huge ovens smoked all day, meats cooked in the open. Always, day and night, the pounding of iron on iron in the smithies never ceased ringing.

They rode all day and into the summer twilight and came at last to the inn of Haimo.

In the light of torches they saw something strange. On a raised platform framed up of sturdy timbers sat that great fellow Haimo as if on a throne. With one eye he watched his little ships along the shore, with the other he looked into his inn through the top of a wind-door and told the cooks how to make the stew and watched the count of the coins his servants took in. Turold and Eadnoth drew rein beside him, and Turold looked up at the mountain-man and asked most civilly, "Sir host, have you been keeping my supper ready for me these three weeks?"

Haimo gave him the benefit of part of one eye. "Two of you have gone up," he said, "and now two of you have come down. Supper, young master?" The great creature fluttered his hands. "We starve, we famish. We are almost ruined!"

Turold could not keep the amusement from his voice. "Why, the country is full to bursting!"

Said Haimo, wiping the sweat from his face with a huge kerchief, "All is under charge to the duke's agents to feed the army. Not so much as a pig's eyebrow may be used for common folk. Fish too. All we get is the scales." He turned away to take money from some workmen who came out of the inn picking their teeth. They reached up to him, and he put the coins in his pocket, groaning, "It will be the ruin,"—he spared one eye while he counted the coins and returned them to his pocket—"the ruin of honest men!"

Turold laughed; he could not help it. It was a mistake that was to cost him later more than he could well lose. He cried, "I heard you are canny, Haimo, that you have been hoarding grain these many months . . ." He stopped, for it was plain something was wrong.

More than ever the gross man looked like a bag of dough. He closed one eye for a moment, then opened it and looked at Turold. "So! I have been hoarding grain? Perhaps you do not think I make an honest profit? Perhaps you would like to speak of it to the duke?"

He untied a rope, and a big dog leaped out at them. Not wishing White Boy hurt, Turold used his whip to hold the creature off. Eadnoth was just about to spear it, when Haimo spoke a word that brought the brute growling to his side.

Turold sat without speaking, for Eadnoth was shouting, "You big pudding bag, you sail-without-wind! Do you know that if you touch one hair of my master the duke will cut you into little bits and serve you to his hounds? This young knight is the great minstrel, Turold!"

Haimo did not blink. He sat.

"We want supper, and a ship to take us to the Saxon coast," urged Turold, thinking it best to ignore the matter of the dog.

But Haimo suddenly gave him both eyes, and Turold drew in his breath. Such a large man, and so full of malice!

"Two go up, one after the other," whispered Haimo. "And now two come down, one after the other. On white horses both. The duke does not love spies, nor traitors, though they be singers. He cuts them up in little bits, and he feeds them to his hounds. And I have no supper. And there are no ships."

As for the ships, it was true. They had to go to the Somme river eastward, where the monks of St. Valery found a little ship soon crossing to the English shore. After waiting four days for the south wind, they went aboard one evening with the horses and set sail for England.

When the sun rose, they saw a gray line which the mariner watched with steady eyes and turned his ship a little. Before long they saw the loom of a sandy shore, then bluffs lifted through the mist. The landfall was at Pevensey, where they wished to be.

Eadnoth had been talking of the wild tales he had heard about Harold in Normandy. "Such stories! And they reckon all Saxons heathen. And eaters of children!"

Turold laughed. "Guard-hall gossip. But you know as well as I do that there are black things done by some of our folk at dark of the moon. Many still fear Woden, and even, 'tis whispered, make tree sacrifices!"

"Aye. I don't say we don't. But now we only hang to the tree some malefactor. In the old days we took our best, king's children, wise elders, or a stranger who walked in the wrong field. But it wasn't savage, master. It was holy, a sacrifice. Now we celebrate the passion of our Lord Jesus. And was he not hung on a tree as Woden was? Woden, they say, hung for nine nights, a sacrifice to himself, between earth and heaven, on the world tree."

Turold nodded. "On that tree, as it is said, 'On that tree of which no one knows from what root it springs.' Yet there are no bloody sacrifices in Jesus' name."

But Eadnoth only shook his head.

As they drew in to the beach, they saw many little huts along the shore, breakfast fires going, smoke rising everywhere, men running about, horses moving, flags on a watchtower.

Eadnoth cried joyfully, "Look what guard our folk keep!"

Yet at that moment Turold cared little about the watch on the Saxon shore. To get the earth of Wessex under his feet, to look into Cerdic's face, that would be drink after long thirst. For he had not even known if Cerdic had ever got back home!

He leaped from the ship, splashed to the shingle, shouted to some men about a fire. "Any folk from Scray hereabouts?"

The men stared. Then someone shouted, "There be folk from Canterbury way up to the fort with Mannig."

Mannig! Turold ran up the beach, up the rise to the

137

fort, pushing aside the sentry who tried to bar the door. "I be Kentish man, ye dolt! Where is Mannig?"

"Breakin' fast," growled the sentry, and Turold hurried in and found not only Mannig but Black Jarn, both stuffing themselves with sausage and black bread. Turold fell upon them with cries of joy, demanding news of Cerdic. Was Cerdic safely returned from Normandy?

Black Jarn held him off. "Wait, wait, ye go too fast. I can't tell ye where Cerdic is." At Turold's wild looks he said, "Oh, he got back all right. But right now—well, I can't rightly tell where he is."

"I knew he really did. But just the same I've been sweating. I suppose now he's bode for Harold? When will he be here again?"

Black Jarn looked at Mannig, and that one stroked his whiskers and said nothing.

"I don't know why I stand here famished when you've got all that food," laughed Turold. "Ye might ask me, did I break fast at least." Then he had a tussle with Black Jarn, who finally flung him onto a bench and began to cram sausage into him.

"Not as good as Kyndritha's, but not bad," he said when he could speak.

"Not as good—it is Kyndritha's!"

It was good to see Jarn again, but Jarn was the only one from home that he did see. Jarn and Mannig were consistently vague about Cerdic's whereabouts. Even Engelric was off on some secret errand, something they would not talk about.

Now he must find Harold and be free of his vassal's duty. Harold also was hard to find. He was up and down the shore, overseeing the watch against William's coming. But when Turold went westward after him, Harold was always just ahead out of reach. Turold marvelled at the Saxon folk. They were like boys at play, not soldiers waiting for invasion. They were farmers, not knights, and their hearts were at home with families and crops. They complained continuously because camp fare was not up to home fare; in short, they were Saxons and trenchermen, lovers of good food.

Even as he rode back along the line of watch from the Isle of Wight, still seeking Harold, he noted that the levies were shrinking by thousands. The farmers were going home to look after their crops, the trenchermen to sit at their boards.

After all, the Norman way was the best way. Let the bordars and villeins toil on the land, and let their masters look to its protection.

Thwarted in his search, he rode one evening with Eadnoth up to the Pevensey fort again and went in and found Black Jarn. Jarn's face lighted up. "Mayhap ye've come at the right time; Cerdic and Engelric are expected here tonight—" he hesitated.

"Mayhap!" shouted Turold. "I've missed Harold all along the line, and now you stand there and talk about mayhap I can see my father and brother. God! Anyone would think I was a spy or something." But suddenly he saw the key to all the mystery. Of course. Now he knew what Cerdic and Engelric were doing.

"I'll see them in spite of you," he warned Jarn.

But Jarn shook his head. "You'd better go up and get permission from Mannig. He's gone to his manor up the Hastings road. You see, Turold, no one here can forget that you have been six months with William at Rouen."

Turold wanted to protest. But he could not. He was in truth a spy and a double dealer, a traitor, to William. He was no true man, and he had not found Harold and won his release. So what could he say to Jarn? He turned away.

Jarn said slowly, "Now, Turold, you go on up and find Mannig. You'll have to anyway, if you want ship to take you back, as you say. There's one going out soon. That is, if you really mean to go back. I'd kind of hoped . . . that is, it would please your father. We thought maybe you'd stay."

Still Turold could not speak. At last he said, "Do you not ken what William is sending against you? The great ships, the thousands of knights, the trained bowmen."

Black Jarn scratched his thick hair. "Oh, yes, we've heard all that, lad! But we'll make out somehow, we'll muddle along. A storm may wreck them before they land. Or if they do, we'll drown them in the surf in their heavy armor. Oh, yes, we've been hearing about this invasion. But somehow we can't really believe it will ever come."

And that, thought Turold, was the whole trouble.

He rode for Mannig's place, up into the thickets of the Andredes Leag, and a lonely ride it was at day's end. Eadnoth had held to his bridle a moment, begging him not to go up alone. "I heard some woodsy folk talk by the fire. There be black doings up there tonight. I mistrust ye'll get into it."

He stood looking after Turold even when he was out of sight. He felt trouble in his bones and the next morning was not surprised when Mannig came in with six of his men, and one of them carrying Turold, unconscious, across his saddle. After Eadnoth had tended to his master, Mannig told what he knew. As he rode early to Pevensey, he found Turold lying hurt by the forest track. A little girl was crouched by his side, watching, but she was too terrified by what she had seen to tell anything clearly. She could only whimper over and over, "They're going to hang me on the Woden tree."

It was plain enough what had happened. Mannig found an aged oak, with the ground around all trampled. There in the night the frenzied worshippers of Woden had been trying to appease their god. If they had intended to sacrifice the child, it was plain they had found a more acceptable offering. A white horse was the most precious gift that could be given to Woden.

Aye, White Boy had been hung on the tree in place of the child as was sometimes done in olden time. Mannig told them this, then would speak of it no more.

Turold struggled back to life and sense through a fog in which he saw the face of the child, running to him, then heard the hysterical shrieks, "A white horse for Woden!"

"He will save us, he will raise a storm against them!"

He felt again the clubs and stones that had overwhelmed him, he struggled again to resist—and opened his eyes and found he was struggling with Black Jarn.

When they tried to comfort him, he brushed it aside. "I lost White Boy through my own pigheadedness. Where are my father and brother? You said they'd be here."

Black Jarn's eyes shadowed. "They came to ye, and

141

ye were unseeing of anything."

Turold got up. "I'm all right now. Let me see them."

Heavily, Jarn explained, "They could not wait!"

The next night Mannig put Turold on a little ship going to the Somme shore and bade him Godspeed. The evening shadows were closing in as they lifted sail. On shore a crazy monk was crying dole upon England.

"The destroyer shall come as the whirlwind, his horses be swifter than eagles. Our streams shall be as pitch, the land as burning pitch. In our dwellings wild beasts shall lie down, the wolf, the owl and the bat. Woe unto us, for we are laid waste!"

Then Turold had a vision, like that in his father's hall. That had been the folk going down into the place of woe and terror. Now he saw them all, marching over the night-shadowed sea: Saxons, Angles, Danes, even the ancient folk of Albion Isle, marching and singing.

But now he saw where they came out: a sunny place, leading over green hills and by fruitful valleys, on to a great sea, blue and dazzling, with spires of fabulous cities cutting purple segments from the sky. Then they were swelled by a new host.

Beyond he saw one people, a new race that carried the strength of the others. Like a mighty river carrying many lesser streams to the sea, where at last they all become one together. "For God hath made of one blood all nations of men . . ."

Yet later, when there was bitter sorrow to bear and he tried to remember these things, as if there must be comfort in them, he could not.

HERE was a time of great heat upon the land when Turold and Eadnoth rode from St. Valery to find William. The roads were thick with dust, and thirst was a torment. Halfway to Rouen they met with Fitz-Osbern riding with letters for William, who was, he told them, at the mouth of the Dives.

They turned back and rode with him.

There beside the great ships they searched. The duke was on board the *Mora*, the special gift of Matilda to her lord. It was a splendid vessel, extra large, with a frame of polished oak beams. William was just inspecting the figurehead, a boy blowing on a golden trumpet. Seeing Turold, William beckoned to him, waving back his attendants. He put his hand on the minstrel's shoulder and searched his face.

"You are well recovered of your humor? You have seen all that you wished to see?"

"I am well, and can sing again."

And strangely, it was true. For now comfort had come to him. He knew now that it did not matter that he, a Saxon by birth, had swelled the purpose of these Normans to invade his country. It was an event foreordained, inevitable.

Now he was content to serve William and leave the

end of these events to Heaven and no longer torture himself with questionings.

One day, laughing with friends over the sudden rise of Haimo of the Inn to power as sutler-extraordinary to the duke's levies, he made a jesting song about the fat man.

"There was an old pig so fat and so old,
Dressed up like a cock and thought himself bold.
He got into the barnyard and . . ."

At this point his companions stopped in midverse—and Turold looked over his shoulder. Haimo was standing behind him, dressed, as the verse hinted, most ludicrously. His vast expanse, like a field in full flower, was covered with ribbons and broideries. A hat of normal size graced his head, and there it sat like a biscuit on a boulder, the little feather waving.

Haimo whispered to his retainers, and Turold found himself dragged shamefully away to the inn where William sat at business inside, in a position he liked not before his lord.

William looked up in surprise.

Haimo whispered, "Here be traitor, lord! There be two of them, lord, Saxons as like as two peas in a pod. At my inn they passed. Two up, then two down. Traitors! Alike even to their armor!"

William asked, "Are you sure? Utterly and exactly alike?"

"Oh, 'tis sure!"

William roared with laughter. "You disappoint me, you are not as keen as you are big. No, my worthy sutler, they were not exactly alike. For I noted it as you say. If one Saxon lad makes songs of wonder and glory, why not have two such? So I too noted. Yet their armor had a slight difference. One had bars of red, one bars of black. And one of them has hair of a tinge of red, but the other's is pure gold."

Turold stared at his lord.

"Moreover," William's voice took on a keen edge, "I have just been looking at reports—and your prices are too high! And the provision gets of poorer quality every day, and sometimes we even lack that."

Haimo trembled in all his mountain of flesh. "My lord! For many leagues your army has eaten this country bare. But westward, in Picardy, my men report rich herds, much grain. And eastward by the Somme, we can still find food. But it will be hard to bring it so far."

"Bring it!" commanded the duke.

Haimo turned; it was wonderful to see him glide away on his almost invisible feet. He came close to Turold, whispering, "I hear your father has a rich manor in Kent."

Often now the fat man would whisper to him of rich English manors soon to fall to Normans. Of widows, and heiresses, who would, perforce, take to themselves Norman husbands, "if they love life!" And soon there would be many Saxon widows.

No choler rose in Turold; he went his way, privately laughing at the fat man's airs.

For there was a greater marvel to muse upon. The duke and Matilda had known all about Cerdic, his coming, the comedy in the castle, his going. Indeed they had helped him!

Where in all Christendom could be found a lord of

such greatness of mind and heart?

After a farewell visit to Matilda and his children, the duke, on the tenth day of Weed Month, August, rode to the rendezvous at the Dives.

Behind him twenty thousand knights rode down to meet their ships. Men from Maine and Anjou, from Poitou and Bretagne, from central France and southern France, from Burgundy and from Aquitaine. They choked the roads for three days.

At every hilltop as they went, Turold must thrill to see the long unending line coming on after them. The splendid knights on their great horses, winding, winding down the road with trumpets echoing, banners waving, and the flash of sunlight from myriad surfaces of polished metal. That day it was a glorious pageant, the long, long road and brave to see, with no thought of anything ugly or harmful in it.

So they came to the Dives where lay the thousand ships, and waited for a south wind.

They waited many weeks.

Every morning Turold went out and looked at the little weathercock on the stable roof, though he knew that if it changed watchers would come in haste to rouse the duke.

One morning as he came out with William, there was a commotion by the shore, and men dragged two struggling figures and flung them down at William's feet. There were cries, "Spies, kill them! Cut off their ears, tear out their tongues!"

Half-stunned, the two creatures lay at the duke's feet,

while crowds of men came running, pushing, shouting. The duke's face hardened. "Get back! Keep your hands off them. Now let them up; they be only fishermen."

"Not so," answered a sailor. "They be Saxon spies, lord duke. We found them running along the bank."

At first the two men seemed too dazed to rise. Then one, a tall youth, struggled to his feet. His cap fell off, and his long yellow hair fell on his tattered jacket. His dark skin was plainly stained, but he did smell of fish and the sea as did his companion, whom he raised to his feet. This one was older, grizzled, thick of shoulder and arms.

Shoulder to shoulder, these two ragged men stood and looked at the duke. And Turold looked at them. Straight into the eyes of Cerdic and Engelric.

William spoke. "Are you honest fishermen, or are you spies?"

Cerdic raised his head, and boldly he answered, "We be spies, my lord!"

Suddenly the duke smiled, but it was a grim smile.

He bowed mockingly to the ragged men and said, "Bodes from Harold, welcome! England must indeed be poor to send you thus. But it will give your lord great cheer to hear of our great fleet, our host assembled here, our herds of magnificent horses. Tell him of knights, of strong-armed archers, such as the crude fighting men of England cannot meet in open battle."

He called an aide and bade him show these spies through all their camp, all their fleet.

"And tell your lord that my lieges have rallied to me with many times their service due. My brothers have given one hundred and one hundred twenty ships, eighty ships

147

have I had from William of Evreux, and sixty each from the houses of my lords Fitz-Osbern, Montgomery, Beaumont, and Avranches, fifty each from Hugh of Montfort and Fulk the Lame. Also forty each from Gerald the Seneschal, Walter Gifford and Vulgin, the pious bishop of LeMans. And scores more from lesser men—all loyal, all eager to press my claim!

"Let these men miss nothing of all that we can show. And I will order a ship to take them home, with oars if need be. Aye, we will have them rowed back! I wish Harold—and all England—to know what is coming."

Taillefer, beside Turold, was staring at Cerdic and Engelric, but made no sign. Turold felt stiff as a lance. The duke had not looked at him, but of course he must have recognized Cerdic.

He had seen Cerdic before!

As the aide hurried the Saxons away, there came outcry, "The cock, the cock!"

The little wind cock had turned its tail, and still shivering a little, pointed its face into the west. Then came mariners from the ships and urged the duke to sail east up the coast to some haven nearer to the English shore.

William flung up his hand. "It will be action at last. One step eastward, one step northward!" He turned to Haimo. "Get on board my ship. You said there is fat provisioning in Somme valley. We can reach it tonight."

"Yes, lord," answered the trembling mountain.

William said to the mariners, "We shall sail! Give out the orders; we go out on the tide. Send Montgomery to me. And Fitz-Osbern, Beaumont, Fulk—get them moving!"

148

Before noon the greater part of the fleet was under sail offshore.

The west wind brought rain, and all that day and part of the night, the ships labored up the coast. Day broke at last, and with thankful hearts, they made into the mouth of the Somme. The monks of St. Valery came down to bid them welcome and to offer shelter to their lord, but William would not leave the shore till the next morning, when most of the ships were safely into haven. That night a salt-crusted sailor came quietly to William and told him that about a dozen ships were wrecked below the river mouth. The duke gave orders to have the bodies which should be cast up by the sea buried in darkness and all traces of wreckage removed. So secretly was this managed that few ever knew of these losses.

The wind went round again into the north. Now the Hailig Month, September, was come, and the duke spent much time in prayers at the abbey on the hill. After many days without change of wind, the duke made an announcement that the whole army should fast, then make generous offerings to the shrine of St. Valery. "We are asking much," he said. "Let us give much!"

For seven days the host kept a fast and made prayers to God and the saints. On the morning of the eighth day, they gathered along the hill. The monks carried out the shrine, and the vast company fell to its knees. Step by step the monks moved, till they set the holy reliquary down. A mighty prayer went up.

Then all of them from the mightiest captain to the humblest camp follower passed before the shrine and showered upon it a mass of treasure. When the last man had passed down the hill, it was buried in the heaped-up offerings.

William stood on the deck of the *Mora* and spoke. There was great news. Tostig with an army of the Northmen had already landed on the northeast coast of England, and Harold had gone to meet him.

Then he shouted, "The Saxon coast is undefended. Far away our enemies are destroying each other!"

He pointed to the abbey where the weathervane held as before stubbornly to the north.

"Let us thank God for His help. Behold the Finger of God! When He is ready for us to sail, He will show us the way."

HE watch on the Saxon shore was gone as if it had never been. William's news given out to his men at St. Valery was no jest but solemn truth. Harold, receiving the frantic messages asking for help from the men of Northumbria, had gathered all the force he could muster and was making rapid march to York. The south and east of England, so long on the alert for a foe from the south, poured out men to repel the invaders. For Harald, son of Sigurd, or Harald Hardrada as some called him, who was king of the Norsemen, with Tostig and other allies, was already landed on the northeast coast, spreading ravage and terror.

Cerdic, after his return from the Dives, had not gone north when the carls set out with Harold. Almost alone, he was keeping watch at the fort on the Pevensey shore. He had an old monk to help him and a good horse on which to take warning to London and his lord, if the wind should change and the Normans come down at last upon the coast with their great fleet.

All that long summer the gods of the winds, it seemed, had been on the side of Harold and the waiting Saxons. Certainly Cerdic had been sure of it when he saw William's host, the fleet, that day at the mouth of the Dives. Yet now he was not so sure. For if the host of William had come when the shore was well-manned, it would have met fierce resistance and might not have been able to make good its landing. Whereas now, should the wind turn at last into the south, the whole coast was open and undefended, and William might land wherever he would, save at Dover.

Day after day Cerdic watched the sea and often long into the night, too, taking snatches of rest while the holy man took his place on the wall. Cerdic was fevered in spirit, for when he was at the Dives he had seen the wind turn westward, had seen the great armada setting out eastward up the coast.

They lay now somewhere across the channel, probably in the mouth of the Somme. And there with them was his brother Turold, who served and loved the man coming with armed thousands to take by force the crown of the English.

So mused Cerdic on the day of St. Valery, that day when the host of William knelt on the hillside before the shrine. That night he looked at the wind cock which stood on a post at the corner of the stockade. It still faced north.

But when he rose again the next morning very early and looked out to sea, he saw with an uncontrollable tremor that it was facing out to sea. It was facing due south.

At St. Valery on the Somme, Turold waked early and ran out into the court of the convent. Others were tumbling from their beds too, coming to look at the vane on the tower. Surely the saint had heard them!

Turold thought, "It is true—you can do such things!

152

Like in the days of the prophets."

He gave a great shout, "The wind, the wind! It comes south, south! Rise up!"

William came running with his captains and his barons. The monks, the sailors, the knights, the men-at-arms, the cooks, all the host ran out from their tents and their beds under the hedges. The river and the hill rang with their triumphant cries.

The host did not need any orders now. Soon the camp resounded with the tumult of martial music—the sound of drums, pipes and cymbals and over all the insistent call of the trumpets: *Arise, go forth. The Lord hath sent His wind!*

The massed ranks of the ships began to show a forest of masts as the sailors stepped them into place. Sails were shaken out and furled again till all should be ready. There was a confused yet orderly medley of the cries of thousands of men urging one another to their tasks. Sometimes they cried out in an abandonment of thankfulness to God and the saints.

Aye, it must indeed be true that Heaven blessed this venture! At the camp, in the river, everywhere William's people were in a delirium of joy and frenzied activity.

The monks were bringing food to William and his aides. Turold ate, he knew not what, from the trencher that was handed to him. He was kept running with messages from the duke to his captains. The sun rose, and still the loading of the ships went on. At midday Turold went with William to the minster, where they kneeled in prayer again before the shrine.

When they came out, the day was bright and hot

under the noon sun. Everywhere men toiled with unflag-
ging zeal at their tasks. Servants carried heavy armor on
poles over their shoulders. Some yoked themselves to
heavy carts filled with spears and shields and the accoutrements of the archers. Others rolled heavy barrels and casks
into the ships. Everywhere, the great horses were led and
urged up the planks into the transports.

All along the hillside there were fires burning and the
good smell of meats roasting where men snatched food as
they passed. And now this great day, the twenty-seventh
of the Hailig Month, September, began drawing to a close.

The duke stood on the crest of the slope and looked
at the sky. The sun was about to set, the moon was already
in the sky, but clouds had begun to gather. The duke bade
Turold to call up the heralds. The trumpets spoke, and
there fell a hush over river and hill. Men rested where they
stood and looked about them.

There were no more tents, no sign of the vast camp
which had been there that morning. The fleet was ready
to sail, to set forth on that path from which there could
be no return. Turold looked at the crowded masts, the
sails blossoming on them like giant flowers. The neighing
of the restless multitudes of the horses aboard was softened
by the continuing flow of the south wind.

Again the trumpets called and the leaders of the fleet
stood before their duke, waiting. Fitz-Osbern the younger,
Montgomery and Bishop Odo, Robert of Mortmain, and
Beaumont, Avranches, Montfort, and a score of others;
they stood in their pride and heard the herald announce
William's last orders.

"There will be a beacon all night to shine from the

154

duke's vessel," announced the herald.

And as he spoke it burst into flower from the masthead of the *Mora*, a guiding star to lead them over the sea.

"Each ship must bear its own light, and all must keep together as closely as possible without running foul of one another. You must follow after the *Mora* as closely as you can, but in the dead of night you are to furl sail and rest. Signals and a trumpet from the duke's ship will direct you."

Once again, the voice of the herald asked the blessing of Heaven.

Quickly now William and those attending him passed down to the water and went on board the *Mora*. The plank was drawn in, the sail let full to the breeze, and they glided away from the shore.

Looking back, Turold saw the coast of France fall quickly away; the rolling hills, the broad estuary, melted into the shadows and mists of evening.

The *Mora* sailed beautifully; the sea was calm, and the south wind held steady. When the moon went down, then the ship blew the trumpet and furled sail, lying in the trough of the waves. Many on her slept, while the sailors kept watch. Taillefer stretched himself in his cloak and slept, and even the duke retired to his little silk tent. But Turold could not close his eyes. Normandy was behind him now, and he was remembering what he had last seen upon that shore which lay ahead of them somewhere in the darkness. All his comfort was fled.

It was understood between him and William that he would now ride always unmailed and unarmed, for in his homeland he could not play the invader. He alone, among thirty thousand knights, would go unarmed.

Many of these Normans and Franks seemed to believe that William's claim was so holy and just—and Harold so miserable a creature—that England would soon welcome their duke. If not at once, then very soon, especially when they saw this magnificent army, meaning themselves. Yet it was, Turold knew, foolish to expect that the men of England would tamely give over lands and homes to these invaders.

As the ship swung in the trough of the sea, Turold looked up at the stars and heard the two songs which troubled him. Louder and louder now came the song of Rollant, of knightly battle and great vassalage. And thin and sweet, as if from the unseen English shore, he heard the home song.

Aye, out there were those he loved: Engelric and Cerdic, Harold, Roger, Lucy. And Adela, frail and help-less.

Taillefer came and stood beside him without speaking. Turold looked up at the great light which shone at the masthead and remembered a saying of Adela's, *To a great night a great lanthorn.*

But what great light could now come to his night of sorrow?

In a brief hour the duke came from the tent and ordered signals blown for the fleet. They could now see other lights upon the sea, many behind and to each side. Now the sailors loosed the sail, the ship came to life and cut through the waves again. The spray surged back once more from the figure of the golden boy at the prow, pointing onward with his trumpet. Now Turold and Taillefer saw that the lights of the other ships were fast receding behind them. The *Mora* was outsailing them, perhaps because she was not loaded with horses as were most of the others.

Now William stood alone in the prow as if he bore the ship onward by the terrible urgency of his eagerness, as if he were more than mortal flesh—stronger even than the elements that might try to hold him back.

Day broke at last, the dawn of St. Michael's Eve, September 28, 1066. It was a glorious autumn sunrise. A long spear-shaped cloud hung like a banner over the sun as it came out of the sea to their right. It glowed with crimson and then drifted away to the north.

In all the sea behind them there was not a sail to be seen.

At a word from William, Turold climbed the mast to the peak where the great lanthorn had burned all night. But the waters were still empty, the duke had left his fleet far behind.

Anchor was cast over, and the duke ordered a noble meal to break their fast. The sun warmed them, and their lord's hearty voice was heard in all the ship bidding his men be of good heart, for their comrades would soon overtake them. The god of hosts, said William, in whose cause they had set out, was watching over them.

Once more William asked Turold to look from the masthead. Climbing up, this time he saw behind them four ships making good sail.

He called down, "Four ships in sight, sailing fast!" and heard this good news greeted with a cheer. Soon these ships were in sight to those below, but Turold still clung to the masthead looking eagerly over the sea. Then far

157

away over the edge of the world, as it seemed, there marched across the waters a forest of mastheads. Alone and unsupported, they walked the waters as if carried by pixies under the waves. Then as they came on Turold could see the sails, then the ships. And after them came more and more.

Quickly he descended the mast and ran to William. "My lord," he cried, "there be such a multitude of ships sailing to us, as their masts look like a very forest on the water."

William now knelt, and all on the ship joined him in a brief prayer of thanksgiving.

The sailors again shook out the sail, that sail made from the directions of Matilda, checked with squares of blue and gold, unlike any other in the fleet. It shone in the morning sun ahead of the oncoming ships. The south wind still blew for them, and all eyes watched ahead as the fleet pressed on.

Within two hours the shores of England rose before them.

Quickly the coast opened out, a wide haven loomed with protecting bluffs enclosing a low shore, where all the fleet might easily be drawn up.

William commanded the master mariner to sail straight in. He smiled to see the shore deserted of men. There were now no rows of Saxon shields, nor bristling of two-handed axes. On the puny watch-fort to the east, only one man stood to see them come.

Turold, at his lord's side, saw the beach where he had landed in Heat Month deserted, the huts lonely and sagging, and seabirds crying over the bluff and the one watcher there. Aye, William was come, and there was no watch on the coast to stay his landing with thirty thousand knights. Harold and his men were far away. William was indeed the favored of Heaven.

As Turold was thinking, so Cerdic on the bluff was thinking. William is the favored of Heaven.

When he first saw that the wind was gone into the south, Cerdic knew that the fleet would come. Yet he was astonished when he went out the very next morning and beheld the forest of masts rising against him, then the long ships, full of men and horses. He looked at the bright sail of the leading ship and knew that Turold must be there, close to William. He sent the monk to saddle his horse and hold it ready behind the fort, while he watched the landing of the Norman host.

Quickly the ships touched the beach, men poured from them and began to lead out the horses and hold armor for their masters. Now the knights were debarking, donning hauberks, bracing bucklers, taking bannered lances in hand and mounting all along the shore, thousands and thousands of them, a multitude! Now the archers, close shaven, dressed all alike in close kirtles, came pouring forth down upon the shingle, deploying in orderly ranks, scouting through the low sand hills behind the shore.

And William, leaping over the side of the *Mora,* slipped and fell, fell on his knees with both hands upon the ground. A loud cry went up from the host. Heaven avert this evil omen!

But the duke, springing at once to his feet, cried in a voice of thunder, "By the splendor of God! I have taken seizin of my kingdom. The earth of England is in my two hands!"

A squire started forward to a fisherman's hut close by, and plucking a handful of thatch from the roof brought it to William, crying, "And here be seizin of that which England contains."

William answered, "I accept. May God be with us."

Cerdic, where he stood, could not hear the words, but he saw what happened and understood what it meant.

So for an hour the last Saxon watcher saw the great array landing. Such order and discipline he had never seen.

Now, between the ranks of mounted knights, workmen were bringing great sections of wood from the ships. They began setting them up not far from the shore. Other workers began to dig a ditch; it was soon evident that they were putting together a small wooden castle cunningly fashioned to fit, with bolts to hold it. A clever plan, to have such a rallying point!

Cerdic saw that all the ships were being unmasted, that William had gathered a council of his captains and that a red silk tent was being set up near the wooden fort.

As the scouts ranged farther and farther, Cerdic at last left his post on the wall, and running out the rear gate, he snatched the bridle from the monk, saying, "Get out of here, father, and quickly. Spread the alarm as far as you can. Dear Christ! This island has been invaded for hundreds of years. But there has never been anything like this! Now I am off—to find the lord Harold!"

He leaped into the saddle, took his banderole from the hand of the monk, gave the horse his head, and galloped away into the hills, making a short cut to the old Rye road.

160

ATE that night, the Eve of St. Michael's, Cerdic rode into Southwark straight to Gytha's house, tossed the reins of his trembling horse to a boy and pounded upon the door. When the frightened churls came running, he brushed them aside and went swiftly to Gytha, sitting by the fire.

Cerdic did not kneel to his lord's mother; if he should let his knees go, he might never be able to rise. He leaned against the board.

There was no need for words of his.

Gytha said quietly, *"He has come."*

"This morning," answered Cerdic. "This morning at Pevensey . . . a thousand great ships, my lady."

"There is no one to stop them now."

He did not answer, only looked at her. At length he asked, "And what of my lord? Is there news from the north?"

Gytha shook her head. Then she suddenly rose. "Forgive me! Meat, drink, for this bode. Quickly!" Servants ran with food, and she made him sit and eat.

"There is scarcely a decent horse left in the stables," she told him. "But I will find the best we have; you will have to get others as you go. But I mistrust that Harold in his march north has swept the country clean."

And so Cerdic was to find as he rode on that night alone. He had wished for one to ride with him, so that if he suffered mischance, his companion might get through. But there was no one, no one fit for such a task. All who could fight—and ride—were gone with Harold. So Cerdic rode alone, bearing his gilded banderole, which Gytha put into his hand again as he mounted at her gate.

Last night, which had been Thor's eve, before the Norman fleet had come he had scarce slept at all. And tonight, Freya's eve, September 28, he rode on and on, with a fresh horse and his way clear under the stars. Yet he wished that English roads were as well kept as he remembered the Norman roads to be. Sometimes he thought that nothing had been done to this north-leading way since the Romans had left Britain. Especially the bridges. They were all in disrepair, and before he was gone two hours beyond London, he was wet to the waist from the fords.

Still, the weather was not yet cold; he pressed on and on. Dawn came, and he was lucky enough to get a fresh horse at a farm and a little food for himself, bread and sausage to eat as he rode. How many leagues to York? Sixty, maybe more, almost two hundred English miles, he thought. And all the south of England open to the Norman host, and Harold and the carls far away.

Somewhere now they were meeting the fierce Norsemen with their giant king, Harald Hardrada, wasting England under his awful banner, the Raven. Cerdic pressed on, whipping his flagging horse. He hoped that the battle had not been joined. He would like to stand shoulder to shoulder with his brother carls, smashing the enemy shield-wall with a two-handed ax.

But when he really thought upon it, he hoped that the carls had made an utter end to the Norsemen, for now the fighting men of England must storm back down the long road.

As Freya's afternoon wore on, Cerdic's horse could no longer be urged to speed with whip and spur; slower and slower went the beast. There was no house in sight, the sun was low. And now a terrible lassitude overtook the bode, no doubt it had been close behind him for some time. His head spun round, his feet cried out in an agony of little pains. All the nerves in his body protested, calling out for rest and sleep.

Only for a moment will I alight and lay me down, he thought, seeing a lone hayrick beside the way. He let his horse loose with reins over head in the lush grass by the road. He planted his bode's banderole in the ditch, thought earnestly for a moment of his ride still to come, the carls, the king. . . .

The sun went to the horizon, the shadows lengthened. Cerdic lay on the hay as one dead.

Suddenly there came down from the north three riders coming fast, with lathered horses. They bore the banderoles of bodes. A last ray of sunlight glinted on Cerdic's ensign, and they saw it, saw him lying there and pulled up, shouting at him. He sat up, rubbing his head.

The oldest of the bodes was a man Cerdic knew—Breame the Anglo-Dane—who jumped from his horse and ran to him. As he saw him coming over the field, Cerdic cried, "You are from the king—what news?"

Almost at the same time Breame cried out, "You are from the coast—what news?"

Cerdic jumped to his feet. "Mine's Normans! A thousand ships, thirty thousand knights!"

"When?"

"Thor's morning. Was that . . . yesterday?"

"You have come fast, and this was your first sleep, that I can see." Breame looked as if he could sleep some himself. "Well, we have good news to take to London to offset yours. Great news indeed! The river Derwent runs red, the ravens and the wolves gather, for the slain of the Northmen lie there now in uncounted thousands."

"Praise God!" cried Cerdic, thinking of his grandam's banner, triumphant against the Land-Waster. And he had not been there to share this glory of his friends. Nay—the glory of all England!

"And the king?" he hastened to ask. "Is Harold well?"

"He is strong and hearty. On the march from London he was weak and ill, but a holy man saw a vision of Edward King with a healing message for Harold—and on the march our lord was healed."

Hastily then the bodes told Cerdic of the battle. How the Northmen had ravaged the coast, burning, taking spoil from the towns. How they had brought their ships into the mouth of the Humber, into the Ouse and up to Riccall, where they anchored, bottling up the English fleet. They told how Harald Hardrada with Tostig and allies from the isles, from Iceland and Scotland, had met the northern earls, those laggardly brothers Eadwine and Morcar, in battle at Fulford Gate, and how the Norsemen had been victorious there. This Norse king had been so sure that he would be king in Albion that he had melted all his treasure into one mammoth ingot of gold and taken it with him.

164

"This treasure is now Harold's!"

"This first battle was joined on Woden's day, September 20, you understand—before our king got there—while he and his carls, the Thingmen, the shire levies, were still on the road," said Breame. "So the next Sunday, Eadwine and Morcar—I will not say what I think of them!—they gave over the city of York to the invaders without another blow."

"No resistance—no siege?"

"Nothing! But mind you, Cerdic, at that very hour we were coming up into the valley where our fleet lay; we had already passed Tadcaster. Messengers began to reach us. Our own people were still ready to fight; it was the earls who gave up.

"The host of Hardrada had gone beyond York over into the valley of the Derwent, scarce more than three leagues. There at the earl's seat they waited to receive the hundred hostages they had demanded. So matters stood last Sunday afternoon.

"Well, Harold took us all into York; there was no Norse guard. We kept quiet and set our own guards about. And the great wonder is this: that in all that country that saw us passing twenty thousand strong, not even a thrall did run and warn our enemies. No word went to them of our coming. So the next day we took them quite by surprise. Coming suddenly into the valley of the Derwent, we caught them unprepared. Great slaughter we made there, forcing them back over a little bridge; then we shattered the shield-wall they made along the plain. Ah . . . you should have been there, lad!

"The Norse king was cut down, as was Tostig, that

traitor! You should have seen the carls, how they struck shields and helms, and red swung their axes!"

They were silent awhile. Cerdic was thinking of Gytha, sending him away on this ride. He knew she had gone to the chapel to pray, for him and for her sons in the north. But they had already met in battle and one, the ever-rebellious Tostig, was dead.

Now the bodes held consultation together. At the end Cerdic and Breame went north on the two best horses among them, and the others went on south to London.

Breame, having just gone over this road, was a most valuable traveling companion. He knew what mudholes were shallow and which ones were like bottomless bogs. He knew the best fords and where to find horses in a country swept almost bare. And four times a day he made Cerdic rest for a short space. It also rested the horses, and in the end they made better speed.

More than forty leagues they made on Saturday, the last day of September. Now they neared their goal. The next day, pressing on, they made Tadcaster in late afternoon and with fresh horses galloped on to York. The sun was down when they came to the gate; their ensigns passed them speedily by the guards, and they whipped up their horses to the doors of the great hall where Harold was holding feast with his men and certain thanes of the north.

Dropping from the saddle, they ran into the hall. Men made way for them to Harold's chair. Breame stood back; this was Cerdic's ride, he said, let Cerdic now give the word to the king.

Cerdic knelt to Harold. He could not speak but looked up at the Dragon banner swinging there behind his lord.

He thought of Adela stitching it at home . . . and he thought of the Pevensey shore.

Harold leaned down to him, then lifted him up, led him aside, half carrying him, for Cerdic's big frame was sagging; somehow his knees would not obey his command to straighten.

Cerdic thought, how weary the king looks!

Softly Harold spoke. "When did they come?"

"Eve of St. Michael's, my lord. About the third hour after sunrise."

"Thor's day! And this is Sunday! You have come quickly. How many of them? Did you see, could you tell?"

"They seemed countless; there must have been a thousand ships. Horses, knights, servants, as skilled bowmen as ever I saw."

Harold seemed very quiet, very weary. "So the south wind blew for them—and to Pevensey they sailed in." He asked many questions, and Cerdic answered.

Then Harold had food and drink brought for him and Breame and called Engelric to care for his son. So Cerdic, dropping into a bed of goose feathers, sank away into sleep for a night and a day. When he roused up at last, he found that Harold and his army were already on the road to London.

Harold had taken council with the northern lords, requiring them to help their countrymen in the south, even as the men from the south had come this long march and suffered these dangers to free them.

Breame, telling Cerdic of this as they ate a hasty meal, shook his head, looked about, and then leaned to him. "It is well to be careful what we say here. I fear that Harold is betrayed by these earls. Does this place look as if they were getting ready to follow Harold? Let me tell you—I saw them this morning, and they all act like folk out to save their own hides!"

So it proved to be, for though Cerdic and Breame were five days on the return road, having trouble to find horses and even food, there were no messengers from the northern earls. And no levies from Northumbria and Mercia ever came south to stand with Harold against the Normans.

London swarmed with men pouring in to defend the land against the Normans. There was wild excitement over the tales that came hourly with men and women flying from the south coast. There William was harrying the land, burning not only houses but fields of grain, barns of hay, and mills. And slaying all who resisted him.

For miles about Hastings, where the Normans now made camp, the country was more and more cleaned of animals and food. What they could not carry away, they destroyed. They made great areas of Sussex a wasteland, so that after, in the great survey taken twenty years later, much of this country was unrecovered for use and was written down as *wasta*.

Some remembered that crazed monk who had preached last summer of the scourge that was to come upon the land: *"Behold, his chariots shall be as a whirlwind, his horses swifter than eagles. Woe unto us, for we are spoiled!"*

And Cerdic, riding to the palace by the new West Minster, heard these tales along the road and thought upon Adela, alone at Farthingwold with a few churls and thralls.

ND with Turold too, Adela was constantly in thought.

Turold looked on at the progress of William's invasion as if in a dream. That first evening on the Pevensey shore, the duke sat down with his captains to a sumptuous feast around a great curved table under a crimson awning. Turold went to mass. He saw raiding parties going out, coming back with food taken from the farms and manors of Sussex. For almost all the space in William's fleet had been used for men, horses, and equipment. They had carried food for only two days; England was to supply all they needed. And England—or Sussex—did. But soon they were going farther and farther afield to find what was needed. And among these men the fat creature, Haimo, bloated and offensive, strutted and bullied.

Turold kept out of his way as much as he could. He no longer felt like laughing at jests concerning pretty Saxon widows. Indeed, he thought more and more about Adela. The south of England was almost drained of men. How fared his little grandam, keeping watch at Farthing-wold?

The duke noticed his moodiness, therefore when messengers came from the Normans near Canterbury—and they proved to be Rolph and Roger—then William sent

Turold home to his manor to see that all was well there.

En route to Dover in a small ship Turold eagerly plied Roger with questions. How did his grandam fare? But Roger was ashamed and wished that he had ridden over to Farthingwold to see that Adela was safe. He did not know what was going on at the Saxon manors in Scray. He did know that the district was stripped of men. Turold reassured him.

And how was it with Lucy? Roger said she was well, she hoped to see Turold. But she wearied of the Tower. No longer could she ride safely over moor and In Blean, for the wild men ran in packs. Only last week they had raided a manor near Bob-up-and-Down.

Turold felt very sober at this news; he was thankful that he had thought to wear a sword on this trip.

Of the invasion, of the battle that must come soon, neither of them cared to speak, but the thought of it lay heavily on them. Turold fell silent, looking to the shore, and there he saw something which made his heart sick. Westward scores of smokes rose lazily into the hazy air of month of Winter-Falls. And he heard again the words of the monk: *"And ye shall look to the plain—and lo! the smoke of it shall go up as the smoke of a furnace."*

They found horses at Dover and cantered out on the Canterbury Way. Six they rode: Roger and Rolph and two men-at-arms, and Turold and Eadnoth. The road was dry, for there had been a day or two of high winds, and so they made fast pace into Canterbury.

The sun was setting red as blood beyond Bob-up-and-Down hill. It was quite dark when Turold said "God be wi' ye!" to Roger and his father and reined in under Beech of the Rood. He sat his horse for a moment under the old tree and looked about him at the familiar place: the ford, the lane, the thicket where he had crouched, talking so carelessly with a stranger. And he bowed his head for a moment and thought of God and the saints. But what had God to do with all this?

He turned into the lane; wearily his horse climbed the rise out of the wood, and they came onto the open moor. And as Turold looked to see the manor roofs he heard a voice crying out—and someone stumbled out from the little sheep herd's hut by the track and ran almost under his horse's heels.

The horse reared in fright and almost stepped upon the man under his neck, yet the fellow paid no heed. Turold leaned from the saddle. It was an old man, his withered hands stretched out before his face, unflinching though the horse's hoofs crashed so close to him. Turold knew then that he was blind.

He spoke, that sightless one, "For the love of St. Mildred! If it be you, little master, speak to old Ulfnoth!"

Turold swung out of the saddle, took the old man's arm, looked at him closely. Beside him, Eadnoth said, "See master, they have put out his eyes!"

"Now praise God!" sobbed the old man. "All night," he said, "all night I have hidden here, hoping . . . be it you, Cerdic?"

"Nay, it is Turold. Who did this?"

"The Blean men have taken the manor. Engelric came —when was it—came and took away the big wain full of provisions for the lord Harold. Then after that at night came the wild men. Your father but lately hanged one of them for sheep stealing. They took a tree and broke down the gate—my gate! There was no strong man to stay them! Alric, the other old slaves who did not go with the master —God in heaven! they are all—"

"Where is Adela?"

"Blessed mistress! They could not touch her—safe in chapel. Even wolves that they be. The little maids with her—I saw them, safe inside, before, before . . ."

"I ken you held the gate well for her." Turold soothed him. He was silent then, hearing only his own heartbeats. When he lifted his head, it was to ask Ulfnoth to hide again in the hut for awhile and to assure him they would return. They led him in and shut the door. Then Turold and Eadnoth looked at one another, and there was little need for words between them. Only that Turold said, "How long is it, think you, since they came?"

Eadnoth shook his head.

Said Turold, "I grieve to leave this old man. He's been here overlong, that's sure."

"The other first, master," replied the man.

"There is an oak by the wall we can use. Cerdic and I used to come in that way—without leave of this very gateward!"

So they laughed shortly, though their eyes were wet.

Eadnoth asked, "Should we go to Roger for help?"

"Are not two carls the match for Blean men, any number? Do you cry succor?"

"Come on, come on!" The old carl's voice sounded happy—it was hard to see his face in the gloom.

They tied up their horses behind the hut and moved cautiously up the lane. Circling the wall, they found the oak tree and swung into it, and lay on a branch to watch the close. At the gate there was a barricade and men on watch. The horse barn was burned, and above the glowing ashes a few spires of smoke still rose. It was God's mercy that the great barn with the stored harvest had not burned too.

Dense smoke was rising from the hall louvers. Better than that, there was a tiny reflection of light from the chapel. Adela was still safe! Now they heard yells and turmoil from the hall. Blean troop held frolic in Engelric's hall and, it was devoutly hoped, were well soused with Engelric's sack and ale.

Turold loosed his sword in the scabbard, and Eadnoth picked from the woodpile a knotty root. Grinning in the dark, he whispered, "Let me fright them with a werewolf's howl. Do you dash out the torches—I'll show ye what'll clear 'em out, master!"

Turold agreed, but added, "Keep out of my way. And by St. Swithin! You don't need to show me; don't crash that thing down on my head!"

"Then master," said Eadnoth, "you'd best keep back, well back of the fire trench, and lay about you there. And I'll get them by the door as they break for the air."

Turold wanted to laugh as he swung the door and jumped through it. Here at last was something to hit at!

By the light of the smoky torches, he saw that shaggy bear man who had attacked the Norman under Beech of the Rood—so long ago it seemed. He was leaning drunkenly at the head of the board; others sprawled about him. It seemed unknightly to take them so, but Turold bethought him of Ulfnoth and Adela, and heartily he swung the

173

blade and heard screaming—men were they? He hardly knew, then or after, what he did. Was it thus that a man felt when the berserker rage possessed him?

Then the torches began to go out, and as the last one was dashed to the floor, there was a weird howling, and the outlaws of Blean began to scream in utmost terror.

Turold laid about him wherever he saw or heard anything move. That awful wailing came again and there was a rush for the door. Someone screamed, "Werewolf!" The crack of the club spoke again and again. So they fled, the howling mob, scrambling somehow over the wall and the broken gate, bearing the guards with them, and away up the lane and down into Blean.

After a little space the cool October stars, behind scudding clouds, looked down on silence and peace. Turold and Eadnoth leaned on their weapons outside the hall door and laughed. They wiped their streaming faces and laughed.

"They will never dare come near this place again as long as they live, nor their children after them!" cried Turold. "If there be minstrels in Blean dens, they will sing a great tale of this night's work. How a giant came upon them with a great sword while they sat at council—and of course sober as a duck. How a devil brought thick darkness and beat out their brains with a tree. And then a werewolf. This manor is safe from them now."

Eadnoth asked earnestly, "How will you hold this manor now? There be other dangers . . . soon."

Turold shook his head. They went then to the chapel and knocked on the door. There was no answer, only a heavy silence. Turold cried "Adela, Adela!" When there was still no answer, he beat frantically on the door shouting, "Grandam, for the love of Heaven—it is Turold!"

So the door opened a crack and then was flung suddenly back. Adela was pale but quite calm. "Good St. Mildred," she murmured, trying to smile, "you make more noise than Blean men! And look at your breeches. I must get you a whole pair." Thus she welcomed him back from overseas as if he had but come from hunting In Blean.

The frightened maids were sobbing and laughing in their sudden release, and now came Pig-Boy, swaggering through them, showing the rake he held as a weapon, poised as if still ready to have a crack at Blean men's heads. But his face was white under the grime, and Turold almost laughed at sight of him. Instead he said solemnly, "Pig-Boy, you really saved Adela," and so left him blushing and gaping, still holding to the rake.

Suddenly Adela was leaning against him, and he picked her up. How frail she was! Yet now she laughed up at him. The maids told him they had not broken bread nor had aught to drink since the outlaws swarmed upon them the night before. They carried Adela into her bower and at her feet made up a roaring fire. Then Turold found four churls lurking around, and with lusty shouting he got Kyndritha and some of the other women out from hiding places in the lofts. Together they set to and cleaned up the mess in the hall.

Then Kyndritha prepared meats and sweet broth and found bread she had hidden. The bake mistress did not scold now, but she leaned over the fire, and Turold saw the slow tears slipping down her cheeks. Ulfnoth sat on a bench, his eyes bandaged with one of Adela's best kerchiefs, and Turold fed him from a bowl.

In the morning Turold and Eadnoth repaired the gate and buried Alric and four others who had given their lives for their mistress. And then Turold must hold long reasoning with Adela, for she was determined to stay at the manor—and Turold was determined that she must go to a safer place.

As they sat at meat, still undecided what to do, Eadnoth took Turold aside and spoke earnestly to him. "Master, you be minstrel to the lord duke, and I do not question nor ask you how it can be so. But I am an old carl of Harold's and of his father, Godwine, before him." He looked at his cap, turning it awkwardly in his hands. "I would I might be with my lord Harold now! I must be with them, my old comrades. There will be a great fight soon."

"I have been selfish," Turold admitted sadly. "You must go to be with the carls. I will return to Hastings alone."

Turold now gave Adela her choice. She could go to refuge with Lucy at the Tower, or she could go to Edith Swanneshalls in Canterbury. Adela chose to go to Edith. They would go the next morning, using the sorry nags that Blean men had left in the byre.

That afternoon Turold set Eadnoth to guard the women and slipped away up the down. He wore no armor, was clad only in a light tunic and frieze breeches and he ran up the path, rejoicing in the freshness of the wind, seeing all the homely places as if they were wonderful, as if he had never seen them before. Aye, Kent was lovely. And worthy of invasion!

When he sighted the Tower, he wondered where

Lucy might be this day and what he could say to her. He did not have to ask admittance to the Tower. Long before he came to the moat, he heard the bugle blow, saw the bridge swinging down and Rolph's troop come riding out, headed by two riders who must be Roger and Lucy. He waited then on a slight rise of the down.

How bravely these Normans rode. Turold never wearied of seeing such horsemanship, though he had been many months in Normandy. Now they made a maneuver in coming up the slope to him, turning a complete circle, wheeling like seabirds in flight, orderly and graceful. Then Lucy was leaning from the saddle, eyes shining, saying nothing. Turold took her hand and when a horse was led up for him he leaped to the saddle and turned toward the Tower with them.

So Lucy, laughing softly, said, "We could not let you come afoot. And the country is bare of horses now." And Turold saw that though her lips smiled, her eyes were sad as if the tears lay close. He began to speak to her in feverish haste, but she hardly answered. He told her of his days with William, but she did not ask him if she had won her wager. When he spoke of what he had found at the manor on his return, both Lucy and Roger were very angry with themselves for not looking out for Adela.

Turold silenced them. "You could not send guards for every manor in Scray, could you? And Adela is proud . . ."

So they left it there.

When Turold had paid his respects to Rolph, Lucy took him up to the little tower window where she often sat and looked out over the wide countryside. In clear weather it was possible, she told him, to see far down in the Weald. But tonight, with the air so hazy, and the sun almost down, it was very murky in those far southern deeps. Turold did not tell her what he knew was true, that much of the haze came from the smoke of burning fields and houses and woods of the Sussex country.

Although he had scarce spoken a word to her alone, he now longed to get away. What could he say to her? Never could those cherished dreams come true. He was, it was true, far-famed for his songs and rich beyond the needs of a thane's son. And Rolph, it was plain, would never say nay to the minstrel beloved of the duke. Something more now came between them. He was, after all, a Saxon. And the folk of the Tower were Normans. And what of the future? When the coming event was resolved, who knew where anyone might be? Or who would be dead and who alive? But worst of all, he felt a stain upon his honor. He rendered service to two lords, two enemies. Therefore he was no true man.

So pride stiffened Turold. He threw up his head and suddenly told her, "I must go back now. I will not leave Adela alone there after dark."

She looked sadly at him, as if sensing his trouble. So she asked, "Will you bring her here? I will love and cherish her!"

He could hardly speak. He longed to touch her, to lean to the fragrance of her hair. Instead, he quickly led her down the winding stair, stiffly took his leave of them all, and ran back to the manor, refusing to ride.

When he was gone Lucy ran up to the little room

178

and flinging herself down on the bench burst into a storm of tears. And then, in spite of herself, she must look out the window slit to watch Turold as long as she could see him till he disappeared behind a dip in the moor.

The next morning Roger with Lucy and ten men-at-arms helped Turold escort Adela into Canterbury to the house of Edith.

Then Roger and Turold with two men-at-arms turned their faces westward into that smoky waste of the Weald, bearing with them food and water too. For it was said in Canterbury that even the wells were poisoned in that seared land. Back to Hastings they must go, Roger to fight with his people, and Turold, having divided duty, had no duty except to cheer the duke. And to be witness to this awful event, which in time to come would itself make a great song for some gleeman. And perchance, if Heaven should so favor him, he would find Harold before the battle and be loosed of his oath.

As Turold rode close to Lucy in parting, he touched her hand and she smiled at him through tears. So he knew, in spite of smoke and blood, they must still dream of one another.

FTER a night's rest, Cerdic bathed, trimmed his hair and short beard, and went into the hall to his lord. And there he heard a certain Frankish monk, one Hugh of Fécamp, deliver to Harold on his throne a message from the invader, Duke William.

It was a bold demand that Harold come down from the throne which, so Hugh said, he traitorously occupied, and acknowledge before his people that he himself was true man to William and as such must yield the kingdom to him. In the terrible silence that followed, the Norman shouted, "In God's name, do so! Else you and you alone will be guilty of all the blood that shall be shed in this quarrel."

The monk was standing at the very foot of the throne, and to Cerdic it seemed that he addressed the people in the hall, rather than the king, to whom he turned his back.

Harold rose up and stepping quickly down took him by the robe. It seemed that Harold would lay hands on him and choke him well. But Gyrth, who stood always close to his brother, spoke a word in the king's ear—and the moment passed. Harold turned wearily away and took his seat again.

"Hugh of Fécamp," said Harold, "go back to your

lord and tell him that the oath whereto he holds me was a forced oath as he knows. And tell him that the English crown cannot be given or passed by any man. The people have set it upon me of their own free will and them I must and will defend from your master." Then he stood up. *"And tell him that I will meet him in battle on Saturday next."*

A loud outcry rose up at Harold's challenge. On Saturday! There was not time!

Harold heeded not the display by his people but dismissed the monk, who then left the hall with great haughtiness.

Now Gyrth spoke boldly to Harold, "My lord, if you are going to stand to the issue so soon, let me set out with your carls and the levies which have already come in from the shires for London is thick with them. And they are eager to meet the Normans. Many indeed come from that south country William has ravaged.

"Let us go out to meet this insolent Norman. Your place is here, defending the city. If I fall in the first encounter—if the duke should worst us then—you will still be here to defend your city and rally the people. Time will bring more men to help you. The men from the west cannot get here for many days. We still hope for help from the north. And then, after I lead out the men who are now under arms, do you take raiders and lay waste all the land between here and the coast, between us and the enemy. Make it all barren! Burn everything, everything! It's certain that William could never hold his army together if you do that, for they would starve. They will go home, and we shall be free!"

Harold looked about him. Here in the hall of the palace stood some of his veterans of Stamford Bridge, here stood the carls who had broken the shield-wall of the Norsemen. He looked up at the Dragon banner, blazing on the wall behind him, and back again at his men, those vassals who had given the banner its bloody baptism only ten days since.

"Never," said Harold at last, "never will I send another man to face the perils that I should face. And never will I burn an English village, nor lay waste the lands of the men, my good vassals, whom I am sworn to protect."

It was kingly, Cerdic thought. Yet many said boldly that the king should take Gyrth's advice. He must not risk the kingdom on one battle.

Harold looked upon them with great earnestness. "Do you not understand," he asked, "that we cannot hold the army together much longer? It has served all summer. It has had a long march, a great battle, another long march. It is a simple matter, a question of food!"

Harold then called the thane, Mannig, and questioned him about his manor on the Hastings road. There was, Mannig told them, a ridge about two leagues out on the road where it branched off to go to Lewes. A few old apple trees stood there, but he used the hill to pasture cattle. "The ridge slopes sharply to the west, and drops steeply to the Hastings road as one faces the sea. And below this steepness the ground is wild and broken, with woods and swamps for at least a league southward."

"How far does this ridge extend?"

"A third of a league, maybe less. The steepest part is in the middle, right where the road climbs up to the fork. I had to build a log fence to keep the cattle in, lest they go down the slope and founder in the swamp and fall prey to wolves."

Harold said, "Mannig, we must take a stand near Hastings on some well-favored height where the heavy Norman horses will find it hard to climb to us. And where their heavily armed knights will find it hard to deliver blows against the shield-wall. This looks like a good place! The duke's horsemen will find the swamp difficult, even the bowmen would be hampered in the woods, and they will hardly be able to maneuver—and they love that.

"Though we English ride to battle, we fight on foot. If the log fence is still there we can throw up something of an earthwork against it. We must do it quickly! If we stand across William's path to London, he will have to attack us. But we will make our Saxon shield-wall as we have done since the times of old. As long as we stand, shoulder to shoulder, even the mounted knights can never break through."

Mannig kneeled to Harold and said humbly, "You know better than I do how my manor can serve you. Senlac, we call that ridge, because all the ledges there run red with something from the rocks. Senlac hill is yours to use, lord."

Harold answered, "Stand up, Mannig. I am only a man and now who can tell how long I shall be king?"

At the king's request Cerdic brought a piece of parchment, and Mannig traced the roadway from Hastings with the ridge of Senlac and the lay of the ground about it. Then Harold sent out his orders: "Day after tomorrow, twelfth day of Winter-Falls, let all men stand ready to march. For on that day, Thor's day, we will go down into Sussex, into the Weald. And on Saturday, October 14, this year of our Lord ten sixty-six, we stand to the battle."

The next night Harold went hastily down to Waltham Holy Cross, to his minster he had builded there, to ask help of the Holy Rood by which he swore. It was a rainy windy night.

A small troop went down with the king, among them Cerdic and Engelric. On the way Cerdic spoke with his father for the first time in many weeks. He found out that Engelric had been to Farthingwold the week before and brought back a great wain loaded with grain and dressed pork and mutton. And he heard with concern that Adela was there almost alone.

When they came into Waltham minster and knelt on the cold stone, it seemed to Cerdic he had never seen anyone so pitifully alone as Harold appeared to be. It was true that his brothers, Gyrth and Leofwine, stood always shoulder to shoulder with him. And Gytha his mother was ever tender and loyal. But Edith he had left with his own true sons in Canterbury. His new wife, sister to the northern earls, was not there. She was not, it seemed, going to share this travail with him.

The king prostrated himself before the Holy Rood. In the cold his men shivered as they waited for him. It was almost gray dawn when Harold rose and took horse back to London. Afterward, after the fight, Thurkill, the sexton of Waltham, told the story of how, at the end as Harold was turning away, the image of the Christ had bowed its head as if to say, "It is finished."

But Cerdic had not seen this miracle. He had been looking at the sad face of his king.

The levies were gathering, from all quarters, with all sorts of weapons. Men from Hertford and Essex, from Norfolk and Surrey, from Kent, Suffolk, Staffordshire, Bedfordshire, Huntingdonshire, Berkshire, Wiltshire, and from the districts of Gloucester, Worcester, Winton, and Bath. Many of these thanes and freemen had lances, swords, or two-handed axes and wore closefitting hauberks with joining helms. And with them they brought their sokemen and churls in frieze kirtles, armed only with farm tools.

Now Harold rallied his great force of house carls, and in shining array they rode over London Bridge and down the old Way. Cerdic rode close before his lord bearing in a socket the Dragon standard which floated over the kingly three, Harold and Gyrth and Leofwine.

All day they rode. Slowly they rode, for all the way men gathered to them, coming in haste, going down to fight under the Dragon.

They stopped at Sevenoaks for dinner and then went on. The far weald, the Andredes Leag, opened before them when they breasted the top of a hill. And there they waited, while Harold sat his horse at the head of the long column of thousands of men and looked down into the hazy distance where the invaders were camped. There were smokes rising, far in the distance. But the sky above was still blue.

Now they rode on again and Cerdic could hear the carls behind them singing the old tales. They sang of battles of old, of Brunanburgh, Maldon, and Ashingdon.

They sang of high-hearted heroes and their brave-hearted battle swords; of the men of Albion, standing with their comrades, shoulder to shoulder in the death-dealing struggle. Shoulder-companions, hearth-brothers, they rode down behind their king. And of him they sang too and of his great victory in the north. And they sang of the Dragon which had led them to victory, saluting the banner which rode before them down to battle again.

> *"Ever in Albion, land of the heroes,*
> *Leads us our king, Harold beloved.*
> *Under the Dragon, ancient of Wessex,*
> *Broke we the Northmen's strong-held shield-*
>   *wall!*
> *Fallen their king, parted from life-joys . . . ."*

And behind the carls came the long lines of the levies, thanes, sokemen, and bordars, men from London, men from the east coast, they too sang the old songs as they came.

As the sun set that evening they made camp along the way, among the fields and woods where they found themselves, where water ran for men and animals. The great wains swayed and creaked and stopped and were almost emptied of food to cook around the fires.

Cerdic saw Black Jarn having trouble with his father's wain brought from Farthingwold. The high rear wheels had got stuck in a mudhole, and Black Jarn was standing on the front, wielding the long whip over the four horses, cursing and yelling. It took two more teams hitched on before they could get it out.

So they gathered about their fires, eating, more quiet

186

now as night drew in. Little fires the king had them make, for he was coming down into the weald swiftly, as he had gone up to York, and he did not intend to have William's scouts see their fires this night.

The Saxon host lay and slept where it ate; they lay on the frosty ground sleeping on their arms. Only for a few hours did the stars wheel over them and the night wind sing. Then they were all astir. In the dark they saddled and mounted, and Cerdic lifted the banner again, to swing over his lord.

All in the dark they came, with shielded torches to keep them out of bogs, by narrow rutted ways, through swamps and deep forests where night animals still moved. And as day came, bursting into flower on their left hand, Mannig told the king that they neared the place they sought, the ridge of Senlac.

N the afternoon of Freya's day, the thirteenth of the month of Winter-Falls, Turold and Roger rode wearily into the camp at Hastings. Turold sagged in the saddle, and there was a strange dullness as of fever in his eyes.

For Turold had passed through the furnace of Sussex. He had seen by the wayside a broken shrine with the figure of Jesus lying in the dust. This desecration seemed more horrible than burnt manors. There was no telling who had done it. It could have been fear-crazed Saxons seeking the favor of Woden. Or William's men—some cared only for spoil. Turold took the broken rood, and when he found a stone shrine on a hill, he fastened it there and knelt a long time.

Now England too was crucified, and now there were burdens too great for human hearts to bear. He dared not go into battle with William, yet he could not stay away. He must go on and see the end. Above all he yearned to find Harold, whose ring he wore. How great a man he was, and what burdens he bore now! But who knew where Harold was, when he would meet the Norman host, and where. There had been wild rumors in Canterbury, but in this waste there was nothing, no men and no news.

188

Would all England be like this if William won? Did he want to be king over desolation?

When his little page, who took special charge of the French harp Matilda had given him, ran eagerly to meet him, babbling of a wonderful white horse, Turold could hardly answer.

"The duke sent it, master," the lad said. "He noted that the white horse you brought from England was gone. Did you leave it here last summer?"

Turold turned away.

The page returned leading a spirited barb, a creature of fire and beauty. But Turold could hardly look at it. The page began to sing softly Turold's own lines of the white horse which Charlemagne's bishop rode into the battle at Roncevalles:

> "That charger is swift and of a noble race;
> Fine are his hooves, his legs are smooth and
>   straight.
> Short are his thighs, broad cruppers he displays,
> Long are his ribs, aloft his spine is raised,
> White is his tail and yellow is his mane.
> Little his ears and tawny all his face;
> No beast is there can match him in a race."

The beautiful horse pranced. "See, master, you shall ride him into battle, spurring on as did that archbishop of old, by great vassalage to our lord, the most worthiest lord in all Christendom!"

Then did the page see that his master was ill, for without any word or stroking of the beast, he went into his tent and lay down on his pallet with closed eyes.

189

Roger came to him there. "The duke commands your presence!"

They found William sitting on his camp bed in the red tent, watching Taillefer. The old minstrel was striding up and down, pouring out words. Someone said, "He fell from his horse last night and lay in a stupor for hours. This morning he came here—you see how he is!"

Taillefer was speaking Saxon with a broad Kent turn to it. Turold whispered to William, "My lord, I think he has come to himself at last."

He took Taillefer by the arm and spoke in Saxon. "Turold, son of Wilfred, who was thane of Canute and lord of Farthingwold-under-Blean, speak to me. I am son to Engelric your brother. I too am called Turold, as you were before you left Scray to go to Normandy with William."

Taillefer looked at him calmly. "My head has been hurting me, but now I remember many things. You cannot be my brother's little boy! A hawk got his white dove by Beech of the Rood . . ."

"Aye, so it did. But that was long ago."

The minstrel cried, "Yes, yes! The duke threw a chain . . . it shone as it fell. But is this the duke? I cannot remember! He does not look as he did."

"For a long time you have been Taillefer, of William's court," said the nephew. "All of us are many years older than you remember since you left Adela, your mother, that day by the beech. You have been hurt, you have been ill, but now you do remember. It's been many years, Turold of Farthingwold!"

"What is this place? Why are we here?"

190

"Remember that you were a Saxon named Turold. And long you served the duke in Normandy."

"St. Mildred help me! And Adela my mother, how fares she?"

"Well and safe. Think, man! Try to remember."

"What is this great army?"

The duke said, "I have come into England to claim the crown that is rightfully mine."

"The crown of England? But where is King Edward?"

Turold explained, "He is dead, and Harold, son of Godwine, is raised to the kingdom."

Taillefer shook his head. "He is not an atheling of the old kingly line."

Now William broke in. "Speak our tongue, I must know what you two say."

"I tell him," Turold answered, "of your coming and of his mother. You saw her that day under the Beech."

Taillefer bowed to William, but spoke to Turold, this time in the French tongue. "Are the Saxons close by? Before the battle is joined, I want to see Engelric."

"Two leagues only, north of us!" cried the duke, pacing up and down. "Yesterday our scouts had not seen any of Harold's men, yet today he comes down like a flight of eagles. Two great marches has Harold made in three weeks—nay, three! This man is brave, and men love him. He has pulled with him a host of men who must be well weary of battle and marching. Yet . . . yet is he false." He put his hand on Turold's shoulder. "Turold, after this is over, you shall make a great song for me. Of the greatness of Harold. And of this great battle here."

Turold bent one knee to William and looked up at

191

him. "It pleases my lord to forget that if he wins I must sing the downfall of my countrymen. But if Harold wins, then perforce must I sing the downfall of my lord, who has never known downfall! How then shall I sing?"

William looked down at him. "It is a sadness either way. Pray then that the will of God be triumphant."

"The battle then is sure?"

"It is sure. They stand in our path. In the morning we go out to meet them."

As Turold rose, Taillefer took him by the arm. "Where is my brother? Where is Engelric?"

"With Harold—somewhere out there."

Then Taillefer knelt to the duke. "A boon, a boon!"

"You shall have it."

"Tomorrow, when the battle joins, I will die for you as I have lived for you these many years. But tonight let me go into the Saxon camp and seek my kin."

William protested, "You will be taken for a spy."

"I can get through," Turold told them. Perhaps, even now, it might not be too late to see Harold!

"Let me go with Taillefer. I speak Saxon, and I was up that road once."

The duke sighed. "Go then. You, my young falcon— maybe you can help this dear fool to return to me alive. I want him alive. I want you both alive, to sing, to make us happy. Go then. Fitz-Osbern shall fit you out with the clothing we use for our spies."

In their tent, changing into ragged garments, Turold remembered that he had failed to tell Adela of Taillefer. Yet, would it have made her less sorrowful? Perhaps it was better never to tell her. Tomorrow there would be a new world. It might be better, it might be worse. It would certainly be different.

After they were clear of the camp and well into the woods where the camp noises faded, then he set their course by stars he knew. They crept past a Norman outpost in the shadows. Sometimes they heard the Norman patrol on their heavy-footed horses and hid in the ditch till they had passed. Turold didn't want to show the duke's pass unless he had to.

After what seemed a long time, Turold saw ahead of them lights reflected in the sky and smelled wood smoke. Topping a rise, across an intervening valley lay another hill—a long ridge where countless watch fires glowed in the dark. A dull roar from the army encamped there made Turold's breath come faster. Below and to the left a big fire leaped beside a knoll, the dark shadows of men wavering about it.

The Saxon sentries must be close now, unless they had already cleared them.

But in a moment they heard a challenge. Crouching, they waited and heard a lance crash through the brush. Turold sprang to his feet then, cursing the sentry in broad Kent. The rabbit, he said, had been almost in his hands, why did he have to be such a lunkhead and scare him off? Then he tossed back the lance and asked, "Y' thought we was slinkin' Normans, eh?"

The sentry laughed. "Kent ye be, lad! As for the rabbit, me belly's fair achin'. But go down to that fire in the swamp, they got vittles there."

"Be they Kentish men?" asked Turold. "I look for my father, Engelric of Farthingwold-under-Blean."

"It might be. Men of Canterbury, I heard. It will be horrid lonesome on that post when the Normans ride down this hill."

The sentry moved on.

They went boldly down the hill and floundered in the swampy ground below. How bright the watch fires burned tonight along the Saxon battle line!

At the big fire, Turold challenged the first man he met and asked for his father. Engelric, the man said, was yonder cutting up roasted mutton. He stared when Turold suddenly came to him out of the shadows but said nothing, only leaned to hear his message. Turold made brief telling of the story of Taillefer, then led his father back to the minstrel and left them together.

Now Turold was free to seek Harold, and he hurried toward the dancing fires on the ridge. Harold's tent was pitched near the center of the rise close to an old apple tree. This was a very different kind of camp from the one at Hastings. Men were working in a frenzy of haste to bank earth and brush against the long fence which Mannig had made to keep his cows safe.

Within the fence lay the great host of men. Turold almost recoiled from the din of the roistering army. Some were asleep on the ground, but most of them were gathered about the fires cooking and eating, singing, shouting, drinking, looking to their arms. Too many were drinking deeply, Turold thought, but it was ever so with Saxons.

Above the tent of Harold had been planted the Dragon banner. It swung slowly in the dark, and the light of the up-shooting flames before the royal tent made the golden Dragon look like a living creature, writhing in the breeze.

194

All around the tent the house carls lay massed, holding more orderly rank than the county levies. Line upon line their shields lay beside their pointed lances. So their accoutrements showed where the companies of the king's thingmen, the fierce, far-renowned, ax-wielding carls, lay in their last bivouac.

Turold climbed over the fence near the banner. He was well muddied from the swamp, his face streaked, yet it was still the face of Turold—and the face of Cerdic.

Gyrth was standing guard before Harold's tent, and when he saw Turold he said, "Cerdic, for God's sake, go speak to the king! He prays—I would he might sleep. Another messenger has come from the Norman. I dare not go in, and I cannot make answer myself. He ever loved you. But he has borne more than he should."

Turold started to speak, but instead turned and parted the tent flaps. Harold was there, kneeling. He rose to his feet. "Lad, cannot Gyrth keep guard for me one hour?"

Turold kneeled to him then and spoke softly. "My lord Harold, I am here because Gyrth thought I was Cerdic. Has everyone forgotten that Cerdic has a brother? Even so, I have lived many months, falsely, in your service. Have you forgotten your falcon whom you sent overseas even before you were crowned?"

Harold's face was thinner than Turold remembered, and there was a look on it very different from William's ruddy energy. This was not the man who had sat his horse that day in the manor close and laughed at Rolph—and let William slip from his grasp. The king looked like an aged abbot whom Turold had seen at prayer with the evening light on his uplifted face. Where now was the conqueror

195

of Gruffyd the Wild, the knight whose exploits were already legend, even in France?

Gently Harold said, "I remember now when it is too late. It was a hard task I gave you, yet you sent the word I asked. . . . I now release you from all allegiance to me. I know William. Aye! Is this what you wish?"

Suddenly Turold rose and turned away. He should stay and give comfort to Harold in this hour. Stay and share with him the battle fortune of the morrow. He longed to cry out—for a moment he almost did—"I am your man! Let me die at your side!"

Then perhaps he could be good vassal and know honor and truth. But was that really truth?

His lips would not speak. In his heart he was William's man. Yet he longed for the gift of the single heart, that he might lose the terrible awareness of this man's troubles, the crisis of England. But felon he must not be!

He knelt to Harold again, kissed his hand, looked up at him a moment, then rose and passed quickly from the tent, running down to the swamp. He found Taillefer at the outpost rock, sitting quietly with Engelric, looking into the flames. They both looked tired—and something more.

He could find no words for his father, only raised his hand to him and with Taillefer at his side went off up the slope.

All the way he could see the Dragon banner, a thing of fire. And a kneeling king. And it seemed he could still hear the Saxons on Senlac: *"Drink home, boys, drink home! He who drinks goes ruthless to combat nor fears the stake of doom. Drink home and find courage, ye faintest of heart, to face the sword's edge or the point of the dart . . ."*

Afterward he wished he had thought more about Taillefer on that return trip to the Norman camp. Blindly they had walked together, blind in truth, for when he went into his tent later, he found Taillefer face down on his pallet, the torch smoking unheeded. The old harp that had once hung on the wall of Adela's bower was thrown down, the strings torn, the leopard's head broken.

UROLD could remember little of the rest of that night. Had he slept? Had he prayed? Had he talked with Taillefer as he longed to do? Had he thought of Lucy?

And what of the morning, the dawn of the fourteenth day of Winter-Falls?

He only knew that two great hosts were face to face under the bright morning sun. Yonder lay the Saxons on the ridge of Senlac—an incredible mass of men waiting on foot for their attackers. They had made the shield-wall, the bright strong barrier which of old had brought victory and glory to the Saxons and Danes in many battles. Many times Turold had sung of this shield-wall in songs of Brunanburgh, of Maldon and Ashingdon. So long as it held immovable, unbroken, the army of Harold was invincible.

On the slope facing Senlac ridge, almost on the very spot where he had fooled the sentry last night, Turold rode the white barb behind his lord with the oncoming Frankish host spread out behind him and on either side. The consecrated banner from Rome floated over them; Taillefer was beside him on a sorrel mount. Those who carried the armor for the knights had now finished the harnessing of their masters; the war horses were mounted, and away on either side, half seen through trees, the French hosts were drawn up in support.

198

On the slope below, where Turold had seen the fires of the Saxon outposts the night before, were ranked the Norman infantry, and ahead of them deep in the swamp he caught sight of the orderly bands of the bowmen. Below on the left was the outpost rock, and the Saxons still held it; it bristled with defenders.

Turold lifted his eyes to the ridge directly ahead. It was perhaps a thousand feet from where William waited on the slope, to the log barrier at the brow of Senlac hill. Beyond he could plainly see the standard of Harold, the flashing folds of the Dragon of Wessex. And there stood Harold with his brothers. Massed about them were the house carls and men of London and of Kent, who from ancient time kept always this honor, to hold their place by the king's standard. To the left and right were the county levies, and there was less glint of sun on mail and shield there. Many of these men, Turold knew, were armed only with their sharpened scythes, and with clubs. Indeed, many of his father's churls must be in those solid ranks with only an ax. There were so many of the English massed on the ridge that there was no space at all between their bodies. The outward ranks, standing thickly shield to shield, made a defense it would be all but impossible to break through.

Back on Telham Hill William had earlier exhorted his army. Now Turold wondered what Harold had said to his people that morning. William had commended the Normans to conquest, to noble deeds, for the glory of God and the saints, and their own honor and profit. What had Harold said to the Saxons, men who were fighting for the second time in defense of their own hearths?

Couriers were dashing up to the duke and away again;

from the right, which was held by the men of Picardy, and from the left, where men of Gaulish Bretagne faced their ancient enemy, the Saxon, these messengers came and went from the captains to the duke.

It was strange, Turold thought, as he held in his restless horse, how these two armies and their leaders both called on one God. It seemed to him better that if men must kill each other, they should have their own private gods like the warriors of old. Then let god strive against god, and the better win if there be any justice in the halls of Heaven.

For William had made a vow before all the army. He wore always about his neck his reliquary and some of the relics in it were the very ones over which Harold had made his oath concerning the English crown. Now William swore by these holy relics, these sacred bones, that if he won the battle this day he would rear a mighty minster to God on the very spot where the Saxon standard now waved.

When Odo cried out that it should be to the honor of St. Martin, the patron of Gaul, who would surely aid them that day, William agreed. A great abbey he would rear, with a minster, to the blessed St. Martin! And when he spoke this holy pledge the Frankish host bowed their heads and made the sign of the cross.

Aye, the gods of men were strange, or men's worship of them was strange. For William now swore to rear in time to come a minster for his own victory on that very spot where Turold had seen Harold kneeling in prayer to that same God the night before.

Now Turold no longer wondered at his own lack of

praying. He saw that the battle was a portentous contest between the old gods and the new. Aye, the very way of fighting was a test between the old and the new. The shield-wall, with the two-handed axes that took both a man's hands to swing—such could be no match for the armored knights, rushing upon them with all the force of the horses' charge behind their lance points. The archers, wonderful bowmen, were also strange to Saxon warfare. And the immovable shield-wall was the perfect symbol for Saxons: as long as they could stand firm they could hold. But when a moving force should come upon them, must not their stubborn holding to the old ways be trampled and scattered?

Now Taillefer pressed his horse close to the duke's side. His face shone in a wonderful way; never had Turold seen him look like this. He thought with anguish that he had not helped Taillefer in his sorrow.

"A boon, sire," he heard his father's brother beg the duke. "For service now I claim it from thee."

William bent his head.

"Grant me that I may have the honor to strike the first blow that is dealt in the fray."

So William raised his hand, and the ranks of the trumpets behind them spoke in the clear morning air. An echo came back from the hill and wild shouts from the army that faced them there. Watching, Turold knew that Taillefer saw the end of his road.

Taillefer rode forward a few paces in front of the line. He was singing of great vassalage. He tossed up his sword, he curvetted his horse, he made him rear all the while he sang. For Taillefer sang the Song of Rollant.

Then he uttered a piercing cry, "From every part they come to break the line!"

With sudden spurs he rowelled his horse and drove him down the slope and up to the Saxon shield-wall and there he made swift and terrible attack. With his lance he pierced an enemy, and in his turn was reached by one of the great Danish axes and turned.

Once more the Norman ranks heard Taillefer's voice, shouting almost as if he laughed, "Comrades, come, lay on, lay on! These Saxon dogs do bark!"

For now there was a great roar of rage and defiance from the Saxon ranks.

The Norman trumpets were blowing, the massed ranks of the knights were sweeping forward, their lances waving banners, the sun flashing on their brave array. Turold, who had meant to keep back, found himself swept savagely away in the attack. He saw as he rode that Taillefer at the barrier was swaying, his horse stumbling.

The Saxons were shouting, "Holy Cross!" and the Normans as they swept along, *"Dieu nous aide!"*

But Turold was not shouting. Confused fragments of his song rang in his mind, pounding out a rhythm to the thunder of the galloping ranks. So in a dream he saw Taillefer was fallen from his horse and that the knights had reached the shields and with fearful din were making general attack.

All that he knew now was that the first blow had been struck and the first knight fallen, he whom William had loved.

Thus the battle was joined.

Soon Turold was kneeling in the mud beside the body

of Taillefer. Somehow, while the knights crashed up the slope around him he got the minstrel's body onto his horse and bore him away down through the swamp and up the hill slope. There he eased him to the ground and saw that he had deserted his bone-house, was parted from life-joys.

Turold covered him with his cape and went back to his place by William on the hill, but the duke was spurring down to enter the fight.

The first attack was well under way, the din overwhelming, the very sky seemed beaten with the clamor. The archers and light-armed had fallen back from the shield-wall, but the knights continued their attack. The duke was urging them on. When Turold pressed to his side, he was looking anxiously to the left, for there the Bretons seemed to be falling back in disorder.

The steepness of the hill took the force from the charges of the knights, their blows failed in power, and when they turned their horses, then often the deadly ax did its work. It was a fearful weapon in the hands of the carls! None could escape its power, and more than one knight fell with his horse, both cloven through at one terrible blow.

And everywhere along the ridge the shield-wall was unbroken. The Saxons stood immovable on Senlac ridge.

As he saw how they stood, a feeling of savage triumph swept over Turold. His father . . . the house carls . . . . Cerdic . . . Harold—they held that wall. As long as the shields held they triumphed. Turold looked up at the blazing sky.

Suddenly there was a dreadful outcry from the Bretons at the left; they were falling back, and the Saxons who stood opposite them at the west end of the ridge, the light-armed, were pouring out from their places. The Saxon light-armed were pursuing the Breton light-armed!

Yet on Senlac ridge the shield-wall still held.

Turold saw men running from the little Saxon rock-fortress in the swamp, and then the press of the Breton fugitives was forcing the whole Norman line into confusion, pushing back the horses, making some to stumble and fall. There were cries of dismay in the Norman ranks, and before he could reach William there seemed to be a general rout in progress. Men cried out, "The duke, the duke, he is slain!"

Then in the front ranks between them and the enemy came William spurring along the line, plucking off his helm, shouting to them in a voice of thunder, "I live, I live . . . he lies who says I am slain. Madmen! Backward lies death—forward, victory!"

The host heard him, the host turned back from its flight. They rallied, they turned, they swept back in fresh attack.

But still the shield-wall stood immovable on Senlac ridge.

All sense of what was happening was lost on Turold. He was swept along in this new attack on the ridge and could not see far along the line; it was all he could do to guide his horse. As his mount breasted the slope, he saw William in front of him. Beside his two brothers, he was dealing death at the barricade with his great mace. A Saxon ax was lifted against him, but it was only his horse that fell. William was springing up, seizing a riderless horse, mounting again, attacking again.

206

Then Turold saw a mighty figure rise above the others behind the shields. An ax was lifted, and the duke faced it with his mace. Turold, unknowing what he did, shouted, "Gyrth! God against god now!"

And Gyrth fell, his helmet shattered. But William was unhurt.

Now William and Odo were again making mighty rain of blows on the shields and again a figure, mighty and valorous, rose ax in hand against them. Turold felt he must be mad, for this new defender was Leofwine. Again mace and ax crashed together with all the force of the war-trained men who wielded them. Again the duke's horse fell under him. But the body of Leofwine came hurtling down from the barricade and was trampled underfoot of the knights.

Both Harold's brothers were dead.

This time the duke was still on foot, in danger from the attacking charges of his own knights. Turold spurred to the duke's side, yielded the barb to him. Instantly William was in the saddle again.

And then he gave order for all his host to fall back into the valley and rest.

The sun was now high in the sky, and the Norman ranks must rest their sweated horses and themselves. William gathered his captains and barons and held council for an hour. Then couriers went out to all parts of the army. Turold did not know what it meant, for he was running back to the place where he had laid the body of Taillefer. In spite of the minstrel's high renown, the Norman camp followers had already stripped his body of arms and clothes. Sorrowfully Turold left him there, for now he heard the trumpets blowing a great blast. The ranks were forming again, and he ran back to find the duke. He saw William's face as he was lowering the helm, and there was a strange look of triumph on it. Later, he remembered it and saw that the trap had been cleverly laid. Aye, William was a lion, but he could also play the fox.

Now when the attack swept down the hill, Turold could not go with them, for he was without horse. On foot he made his way around the left flank, wishing to see if the Saxons still held the outpost rock in the swamp. It was no longer defended. There had been fierce fighting, and many of the dead and wounded of both armies were lying on the wet ground. But there were no folk he knew among them.

Again the attack was general all along the ridge. The Normans, the Picards, the Bretons, all hurled themselves fervently against the shields. Though the Saxons had not had respite since they made the line at dawn, shoulder to shoulder, yet still they stood.

Unbroken was the shield-wall on Senlac ridge. The new gods could not beat down the old. The Saxons stood immovable!

It was the song of the Old Time, thought Turold, alive here for the men of Wessex.

. . . when with their hammered blades the sons of Cerdic, the great sea-rangers, clove the serried bucklers and stood firm behind the shields of linden-wood. When spear met spear and man encountered man, and they yielded not. . . .

Then a lone trumpet sounded.

There was a pause. Knights left off their blows, archers left the arrow in the bow. Foot soldiers lowered swords. The Normans began to give way, to fall back down the slope. Then they turned, they ran, there was retreat. Was it rout? Was it truly retreat? This time William did not spur across his lines, shouting, turning them back.

A great cry arose from the ridge. Immovable had the Saxons stood under the sun all day. Hot, thirsty, aching, pressed man against man so solidly that they could not move a hair's breadth as long as they remained alive. The dead fell under their feet, and they pressed together again. They had borne attacks by mounted knights in mail, they had been harried by infantry and archers, blinded by the glare of the sun, their legs, arms, throats, heads, in torment.

Now they saw their foes in general retreat.

It was too much! They cried out, they broke the shield-wall, poured down the hill, and ran after their enemies. The stern wall of bucklers and men was dissolved.

No longer stood the Saxons immovable on Senlac hill.

Suddenly the Normans turned upon them, turned back upon them, caught them in the open and fell upon them with a terrible fury. The men of Wessex, without horses, could be no match for knights in single combat. Harold and his carls still stood fast under the Dragon, but to right and left the defense was broken.

Turold saw it, saw it and ran for shelter to the rock in the swamp. While the rout streamed by him, he pressed close to the rough wall, soon seeing with tightening throat the Normans turning back, falling fiercely upon the scattered Saxons. Then he heard a noise above him, looked up at a wild-haired fellow with upraised club. He leaped away, but a galloping knight knocked him over. He saw the horse that felled him, whirled, fell close to the rock and sank into unfeeling darkness.

Now the tide was pressing back, up, up to Senlac. The knights were urging their horses over the fence and were within the ranks of the defenders in some places. Back, back the knights pressed and hacked. All was personal prowess now in separate combats between the brave men on both sides.

Still the mounted knights attacked, and inch by inch the Saxons gave way. William and his brothers tried always to come at the Dragon standard waving still above king and house carls, who were now fighting desperately as the knights came upon them, dying each man in his place. The setting sun blazed upon the golden Dragon and its defenders, and it filled their last of earthly vision.

But still the ground was not wholly lost by Harold nor wholly won by William. To win the battle one leader and his men must camp that night on the place of battle and night was almost come. Then the duke sent orders to his archers. In the lengthening shadows showers of arrows swooped like birds of prey upon the heads of those close to the banner. Shot high into the air, they rained upon the heads of the carls and the men at the standard so that they raised their shields to keep off these torments from above. Thicker and faster sped the arrows, the air was dark with them. Or was it the light of day going so suddenly?

Then a lamentable cry went up from the ranks about the Dragon. An arrow had pierced the eye of the king.

All day Cerdic had been holding and guarding the

Dragon standard. While men fought at the barrier, while they left the safe shield-wall, while a thousand combats raged about him and knights pressed ever nearer, he had stood immovable in his place.

And now the sun was sinking and showers of arrows came down on their heads. They tore the stiff fabric of the banner, and they fell upon Cerdic's coat of mail, so like Turold's except for the bars. Harold was looking up as if in prayer—Cerdic cried out to his lord just as the arrow struck him. He wished to leave the heavy pole of the standard and longed to help his king. But he had sworn not to desert the standard, and he kept his post. Harold was sinking to the ground and those near him uttered a terrible cry of woe.

Now the Normans were close, hacking wildly. Not a house carl left his post, though they could no longer hear the voice of their lord cheering them. They fell every man where he stood. Every man of the house of Godwine and every carl fell where he stood.

Now all about the standard were slain! Only Cerdic was left. He saw knights hacking at Harold's body.

Harold was dead. The kingly three were dead, all the sons of Gytha, the high-hearted heroes, the shoulder-companions, were parted from life-joys, their soul-houses forsaken.

Cerdic looked up into the face of a Norman—he saw the horse rear over him. He touched not his sword, only clung to the standard.

Then he was felled with a great blow on his helm.

Slowly then the Dragon leaned and fell, spreading its folds over king and carl.

LL the day of battle Turold had moved in a vision of glory and terror. All through the night, while watch fires burned on Senlac ridge and the Norman host camped on the place of battle, Turold lay on the cold ground in the swamp with limbs inert and eyes closed.

But in a sort of dream he was riding the fabled Night Mare, and it was a white horse, not a black. It was his lost White Boy who cantered on and on with him through the smoking forests of Wessex, past blackened manors and ruined mills. Sometimes they were on the ground, sometimes sailing through the air looking down. He saw wrecks of the English ships along the coast and fallen crosses on the downs. He saw towns smoking, and he swooped up Canterbury Way and came to Brothercrosse and found that the old beech bore now no cross.

And as he was carried swiftly up the lane, suddenly a red flame blossomed before him and he knew it was the burning of Farthingwold. Looking up into the red glare reflected in the sky, he saw a monstrous eagle descending upon him, upon White Boy, and he tried to say his Pater Noster, and shut his eyes.

Then he opened them again, for the eagle did not strike. He looked up and found it was another day. He was lying on his back in the foul mud of the battlefield. Above him, circling in the dawn-lit sky, were myriads of death birds. Some of them lunged down in their flight, down, down to the earth and what lay upon it.

He turned over and saw that William's red tent now was pitched on the spot where the Dragon standard had stood. All along the ridge men moved about fires, and everywhere the camp followers had begun again their stripping of bodies of slain and wounded for their spoil. Even now some of them were coming this way.

Yet there was after all something strange with the world. Could it be that this was the encampment of the dead? Was William and his host defeated and this their ghostly rendezvous?

Aye, Turold knew now that he was dead, for he had awakened to a terrifying silence. The birds of prey wheeled but made no sound. No dogs barked, no birds sang, a wind blew through ghostlike trees. The brook was running as natural as life on the slope, yet there was no song in it. No song anywhere.

Now the sun, rising above the ridge, struck him full in the face. He sat up with a great sense of shock. It was warm, this sun, it warmed all the horrid dampness out of him. He struggled to his feet. He was alive, not dead—he was alive and warm! There was blood caked on the side of his head and over his blue tunic and the baldric broidered with Norman leopards. But he could lift his arms, move his feet.

He was alive in a silent world. He stood and stared at what was happening on the ridge. Men were striking the red tent. William was mounting the white barb, he was descending the road toward Hastings followed by the captains, the knights, the whole host falling in behind. Where were they going? Back to Hastings?

Turold stood quietly and watched them go. What had they to do with him? He remembered that he had loved William, that he had sung to those men, the conquering knights, long ago. But what had love and songs to do with him now—what place was there in the world for anything gentle?

Before they were all gone from sight, Turold began to walk. The wind was too warm for the month of Winter-Falls. It was warm on Turold's face, yet he felt cold.

There were names which lay heavy now in his breast, cold names, dead names. Yes, they must be dead, those names, or William could not have camped on Senlac last night. Harold and Gyrth, Leofwine and Eadnoth, carls who had been his brothers-in-arms, his neighbors and their own churls—Black Jarn, Roger, Engelric, Cerdic!

So Turold began walking. Steadily, quickly, he ranged up and down the wide scene of battle. He looked into the face of every man, and some of them he knew. Although almost all, conquering and conquered, had been stripped by camp followers, it was easy to tell a dead Saxon from a dead Norman. All the Saxons, save the boys, were bearded, all the Normans were clean shaven.

He stalked on, quartering the field like a hound ranging for rabbits. I made songs about these things, and what did I know of them? What is glory now to these dead men?

So Turold came to the place where the Saxon standard had been, and nearby he looked upon a great heap of slain carls. Many of the faces he knew.

As he passed along, one of the Norman spoilers cried to another, "Look! There is the duke's minstrel. He is mazed . . . he suffers the battle shock, see how he walks!"

His mate shook his head. "Not so! That is not the minstrel. I was here last night when they found him, wounded here by the Saxon standard, and the duke had him tenderly looked after by his own barber."

"His own barber! And men like us, who do the real work, get the wood, dig the ditches, dress meat, what do we get? We ought to warble like the little birdies in the trees. But wait—no, I think you are wrong. This is the very image of that singer!"

"I tell you, I saw him taken into the tent. And after, when the Saxon females began to flock about, taking away our rightful spoil, then came that Saxon woman they call Edith. The duke gave her Harold's body, hacked as it was. And the little old woman with her took away the wounded minstrel boy. I myself helped carry him to the cart they had up the road. They came here last night with food, not knowing when the battle would be fought—when it was all over."

But Turold heard nothing. He was walking along with steps of terrible precision as if to the sound of trumpets, through the great silence of the battle place.

Then he faced down into the swamp as he roamed and came again to the outpost rock. Behind it he could see a Saxon, with grizzled hair, roughly dressed, bending over a shallow grave he had been digging with a stick. Now he was scraping dirt and leaves over the place. When this man turned back, he stared, then cried out, "Turold!"

Turold tried to say, "Black Jarn, Black Jarn . . ." and

could not tell whether he had said it or not.

He saw that Black Jarn was wounded in the shoulder. And he looked down by the grave and saw his father's sword lying on the mud. Then Jarn came to him and put his arm tight about his shoulders.

As they stood so, looking down at the sword, Turold suddenly felt how thirst raged along all his bones. Without words they went to the trampled brook and drank, kneeling, splashing it into their mouths with their hands. Then he looked up at Jarn and tried to tell him that they must not forget to get the sheep down from the high moors— they must hurry and cap the ricks.

Suddenly he remembered the names, the poor cold names. He said to Jarn, "I must find them before they bury the names. Cerdic! They must not take him!"

Black Jarn took him strongly by the arm, picked up Engelric's sword and fastened the belt about Turold's waist. He pulled it up to the last notch and yet it hung but slackly, for the girth of Engelric had been greater than the girth of his sons.

But when Turold began again his walking, then Black Jarn held him strongly. When Turold struggled and cried out, with many confused words, that his songs were buried too, that all songs were now dead, that all the world was held in a black spell of silence, then Black Jarn slapped him hard across the face.

Turold staggered but did not hit back. "You do not see," he cried to Jarn, "you do not see what has died here. Not just these men, but manors, and women and fair cities and children yet unborn." Then he uttered a woeful cry. "I made brave songs, but I did not know! I thought . . .

216

I thought we would all come alive again afterward!"

Jarn answered gently, "They died with honor, as good vassals should, in defense of their lord and their lands."

"Aye," and now Turold's voice was so low that Jarn must lean to hear it, "good vassals!" But he had heard Jarn's words; his head was clear now.

"Ye think too much, master," said Jarn. "I'd rather see son o' mine a churl; minstrels think too much."

But Turold was thinking, "Nay, a singer feels too much. And I hate them all now—all who have done these bloody things. They were crazed!"

Then Black Jarn said, "Come away, lad, come away home. 'Tis sure they need us there."

Turold answered, "I'm going home. The ricks need capping. Home! Only an Englishman can go home, Jarn. A Frankish man has no word for it."

So Jarn led him away, walking slowly northward, leaving Senlac and its red ledges, going up into the dark reaches of the Andredes Leag.

T rained heavily that night. They found the deserted huts of some charcoal burners in the woods, but left them and went on when the sky cleared, for they needed food. They walked for two days, dizzy with hunger. The last afternoon Turold had to support Black Jarn, who was fevered from his wound.

Before the sun set that night, it rested on a line of hills seen clearly through the trees.

Jarn said, "On those hills is the Old Way, so old that no one knows much about it. It looks as if giant feet wore it in the chalk—beyond the memory of men. If we can get there, it leads home."

Turold shaded his eyes. "I see it! A line of trees marks it all along under the top of the hills. Why, I remember! It lies along our own hills at home."

"Aye," said Jarn. "It goes west from Canterbury, comes over there, and down to Winchester, and on to a place . . . a place where great stones lie on a plain, as they tell."

They did not travel east along the ancient Way that day nor for a week of days. For Black Jarn came very sick of the fever, and Turold at last found the hut of an anchorite in a glen below the track. And there they stopped, while the wound was tended and healing came to him.

And not only to Jarn did healing come, for Jarn needed healing of the body, and that the hermit tended with washings and simples and food. But Turold needed healing of the spirit and that the holy man saw too, and he quieted the tortured heart with the Word of Scripture.

Every night the hermit lighted a taper and read of eternal things. He read too of old wars—of battles so long ago that they were beyond memory. The troubles of the children of Israel.

The children of Israel, the old man said, were God's people, and yet they had their troubles too. But the Lord of Heaven was above all these things. Men made their own troubles, but they must find healing in the secret place of the Most High.

But Turold, rebelling, thinking that the old man could not understand, for he had not been at Senlac, cried out bitterly, "Where is God? I do not believe in Him. I hate all of them; they are but wolves, not men!"

Gently the hermit replied, "I was a soldier under Canute, and I have seen, I have seen! But you, my son— are you a wolf? Hate the evil, but not the people. Hate is a rust that eats away at the heart." And he prayed silently, kneeling beside the young minstrel. When he rose, Turold suddenly began to sob and went out and lay on the ground in the dark. But when he went in again, there was a different look in his eyes.

On their last night with the anchorite, Turold won to a great peace. The gentle voice read burning words: ". . . for your ways are not my ways. As the heavens are higher than the earth, so are my thoughts than your thoughts. . . . But the Lord will save, He will rejoice over thee with joy. . . . and my kingdom is not of this world."

Turold seized upon that thought. Kings and lords got them all into trouble with trifles. Trifles like crowns. The important thing was the care of the land. The harvest . . . the safety of Adela, of Lucy . . . of the children at Farthingwold.

Safety—where, in a world in ashes, was safety?

And as if feeling his thought the hermit read, "Look upon Zion, a quiet habitation, a tabernacle that shall not be taken down. But there the glorious Lord will be unto us a place of broad rivers and streams wherein shall go no galley with oars. For the Lord is our law-giver, the Lord is our judge, the Lord is our King, He will save us . . . and His banner over me is love."

This is a wonderful old man, thought Turold. I have not said to him: The king is fallen, the great banner, the glory of Albion, is fallen! Yet he understands. But this new banner. Can it be that men can live under love?

The next morning, before they set out eastward along the ancient way, Turold took off the ring carved like a dragon and put it in the hermit's hand.

The old man looked at the carving, then at Turold.

"This is very precious," he said.

"Except that we must always remember who gave it," answered Turold, "it is but a bauble, compared with what you have given us. Use it for the poor, if you care not to keep it. It really is not enough even to pay for my fresh clothes." He fingered the rough warm texture of the jerkin the hermit had given him. It was good to leave off the muddied ducal surcoat.

So they went away, leaving the old man in the door

of his hut looking after them.

Now the winds stripped the trees, the leaves whirled about them, the Old Way was lonely and mournful, and at night they lay on the frosty ground. Once they saw some frightened women, carrying bundles on their backs and little ones clinging to their skirts, scutter out from the lower slopes, cross the way like frightened rabbits, and toiling up, disappear into the mouth of a cave. Often during the day, they saw small smokes rising here and there to the south.

Black Jarn said once, "Saxon folk be like the wild things now and must hide in holes from the scourge of Israel. These hills will soon be full of folk."

He never spoke so again. They had some talk as they went, but it was of home things.

Sometimes Jarn talked of the cattle, the things they must do when they got back. "The sheep must still be in the high pasture—if Blean men have left any. As soon as we first get sight of smoke o' home-stall rising . . ."

Smoke of home-stall! It was, Turold knew, the most loveliest sight upon earth. The smoke rising from the fire where loved ones gathered, where Adela would be sitting, her feet tucked into her blue gown, where Kyndritha would be bent over a roast sheep, fork in hand. Lucy was in the picture too.

One day they saw, as they crossed a brook, a great manor house in flames, and when they got close to it, six Norman knights rode away eastward. They ran down a rutted lane, and near the gate, they found the bodies of a Saxon thane, an old serving man, two maidens richly dressed, and a little boy. They turned away after scraping up from a bin a few grains of barley.

Now at last, after some days on the Way, with belts pulled tight, they came to the ridge that separated them from sight of Farthingwold. They could see the Blean beyond, spreading darkly to the north. There was a sheep track here, which led down to their own folds. Turold wondered how soon they would sight a sheep with his father's mark, how soon they would breast the rise and see the smoke rising from the louvers of his father's hall. No . . . his father lay far away . . . by an outpost rock.

It was his hall, his and Cerdic's. Perhaps Cerdic was already home. In all that place of slaughter, he had not found Cerdic.

And beyond he would see the Broken Tower. Soon now he would meet with Roger and Lucy. No, not Roger. Roger would return no more.

As they slowly climbed this last rise, Turold held back. He stood a moment looking into the west whence they had come. Against the setting sun, the moors shone like gold. In the south many smokes were still rising. And by the sea rolled one dark smoke, like a sullen smudge.

"That would be where the town of Romney lies," said Jarn.

"Aye, Romney," said Turold.

Farther east was another smoke like it.

"That is sure to be Dover," said Jarn.

"Aye, Dover," answered Turold.

"The Normans have been all along the coast."

But Canterbury lay behind her walls, magnificent and untouched.

"Look at the road beyond Canterbury," said Black

Jarn. There a long column of dust streaked the country-side.

"He is coming then, almost to Canterbury," said Turold.

"It was a sightly city," said Jarn.

They looked steadfastly at the dusty line, where it was sure the conqueror came. What was that saying of Adela's Turold had been trying to remember? Now it came.

To a great night a great lanthorn.

But where could there be light in these ravagings? He had heard William say he wished no bloody conquest by fire and sword, but wished to be accepted as rightful sovereign over the nation. Why was he making it into a wilderness?

As Turold turned away to climb again, he knew that in the next minute or so he would see at last the homeplace lying below. Then a sharp pain, a kind of sickness almost overwhelmed him. Would the smoke he would see be the smoke of the ravagers?

No, no! He bowed himself together, then straightened. He must hold fast to the true picture of home. Then he knew a strange comfort, an easing of the tightness in his breast, and the fear passed.

He looked up. Birds were soaring above him, clean white birds from the sea, chirming and tossing on the wind with thin, lonely cries. So he had often seen them on the down.

Aye, he felt fear no longer, for strong and clear now he had a song, after all the way without a song.

It was the home song.

IG-BOY, with head up and hands behind his back, stood on a bare hilltop and looked southward. He felt almost freeborn. Every day for a fortnight he had run down the Way, sometimes even beyond Canterbury. The few pigs that hadn't gone to feed king's men were being kept In Blean by two smaller boys. And Adela had given him some old pants of Cerdic's.

Aye, Pig-Boy was king now In Blean and on moor track. Adela was counting on him to bring news of what was happening. And hoping for word of their lost ones.

Adela had brought Cerdic home in a cart from the battle, and his head was mending now, but they still looked for Engelric, Black Jarn, and a score of others. And Turold, where was he? A minstrel who kicked pig-boys, and a spy in Normandy he had been, yet Pig-Boy looked hopefully for him too.

Nearer and nearer the Normans were coming. Savage revenge they had taken at Romney, kindness they had given other towns where the people received them well. William had been at Dover several days now; part of the town was burned but that was an accident. Travelers, folk fleeing, had many tales to tell of what was happening along William's path. One said that he had repaid the men of Dover for the burnt houses.

Pig-Boy hitched up his sagging breeches, looked again to the Way beyond Canterbury, then scampered gaily along a path. Two leagues to Farthingwold gate; he could make it before the sun was an hour lower.

Kyndritha stood in the bakehouse, her floury arms akimbo before the vast trough heaped with dark meal. She sniffed again at the little stone crock on the table and said, "Faugh! Mischief comes by the pound and goes away by the ounce. The yeast—the barm—be all mold!"

Two of the women tending to the oven fire turned with looks of wistful pleasure when they heard her voice. When she broke off, they sighed and moved to the salt box.

"Aye," the first churl woman rocked her body to and fro. "Your man has not come back, and mine lies hurted in the hall. And of the forty-seven men who went out with the master, who has come back?"

"Twelve, Mary."

"Twelve. And five of them lie in hall with mistress tending on them. Master and Black Jarn missing too. Listen to Kyndritha . . . her man not seen after the bloody day. I cannot abide it!"

The other shook her head. "He was a good man, Black Jarn!"

Crooning under her breath, Kyndritha was taking a handful of barm to throw into the meal when Mary screamed, "The blessing, the blessing! It won't rise—and it's bad luck!"

Kyndritha stopped all motion, her hand poised over the trough. The churl women shook their heads. The unwearied scold of better days had strange lapses now. Then the habits of the good cook prevailed. Kyndritha said weakly, "God's good, God's good," and dropped in the barm, calling for one of the little lads to get water.

He was back in a minute. " 'Drithy," he asked, "are you doing a great baking? Will we have roast ox and blood pudding like we did when the lord Harold came, and Turold and Cerdic rode off with him?"

Kyndritha looked away, her lips trembled. She made a deep hole in the meal and poured in water from the noggin.

Mary sprang to her side, crying, "Now look! You've put the miller's eye out. You'll have to mix in more flour."

"But then the trough will not hold the dough when it rises." Kyndritha stared at it. Mary shook her head, reached for a small bowl and began to scrape some of the wet dough into it.

She was licking off her fingers when a little girl came running, "Mistress says, come quick! Pig-Boy has news!"

The women were all aflutter. They hurried to the hall. Pig-Boy stood with back to the fire, his skinny arms akimbo, his black eyes shining as he looked about at the circle of folk crowding to hear his news. He was almost as good as churl now!

"This very day," he told them with a flourish, "the duke rides up to Canterbury from Dover. His fierce knights will sack the city, and there'll be never a stone left to tell folk that any dwelt there."

Adela cried, "Hush, boy, hush! No need to fright them so. I wanted you all to know this, that William is coming close to us now with his army, and we must keep close watch. There are many with him who look on us all as conquered folk, yet William is no barbarian. He fought our men under arms, but I do not think he will harm women and children, neither does he violate sanctuary."

An old woman held out her arms. "Three sons I had —now they lie on that bloody hill. Mistress, we are not safe. We must take refuge In Blean!"

Others then took up the cry.

Adela said quietly, "Go, then. But I shall stay here."

Cerdic, pale but straightly standing, came to Adela's side. "As long as there is one churl left to us, one sheep to care for . . . as long as there is the sky over our heads and earth to stand on, I will not leave Farthingwold."

Some of the people looked at him sadly, murmuring, "Earth, earth to lie under." Some grumbled openly and loudly, but some were silent. Pig-Boy and Kyndritha were of these.

Then an old man cried, "Let us make refuge In Blean, as hunted folk have always done." Others took up the cry, "To Blean, mistress, to Blean!"

Adela looked at them. They could not meet her eyes. "You are children," she said. "Children all. But you need not be fools. Do you remember last year, when Rolph tried to take Turold for the high justice, do you remember a black knight who said strange words to our earl, gave a knife to Turold and then rode away, singing?

"That man," she told them slowly, "that man was William, duke of Normandy."

Some of them gasped, some crossed themselves, as if she had named the Evil One.

She went to a little chest and pulled out a gold chain, held it up for all to see. "William left this for me, that if this day ever came, it could be used to protect us." She dangled the medallion before them. "That is William's seal,

227

the ducal arms of Normandy. Even his fiercest knight must respect this!"

The hall echoed with glad cries. A few still looked doubtful.

Adela laughed. "Come, we'll all go down to the gate and fasten it there."

They all trooped after her; someone brought a ladder. Pig-Boy took a piece of bent iron which was handed him. Standing tip-toe on the top of the ladder he fastened the chain securely so that the medallion with leopards rampant was plain for all to see.

Adela bowed her head. "Let us ask God's blessing." They all bowed their heads.

She called to Pig-Boy, "Come, big ears and swift feet, go now on the down path and coax home that old ewe you saw up there. And the rest of you! To your tasks. You will want to taste the broth as soon as the meat is in!"

Off they all went, some even merry, and off clipped Pig-Boy. Scorning the gate, he was over the wall like a squirrel and away up the path with a flash of his skinny legs.

But suddenly they all heard his cries. They ran and looked up the slope with frightened eyes. Pig-Boy dropped off the wall into the close, shouting, "Coming! Oh, saints be praised! Coming, coming! Turold, Black Jarn . . . wounded . . . coming slow!" Men, women, children, dogs—they all ran out of the gate and around the wall and up the path. As Farthingwold folk came running madly to them, Turold and Jarn stood still; then they were engulfed in friendly arms. Turold hugged Adela; Cerdic, wordless, looked at Turold.

Then Kyndritha, who had been sobbing, "Hurted ye be!" drew back, and clutched Black Jarn's arm. He raised his hand and bellowed, "Come, lads. Get the sheep down before it snows!"

Springing back, Kyndritha laid back her head and shrieked, "By St. Dunstan! He's sound as a sow, and we mournin' him these three weeks—and scarce a man to the place. I'll wager ye and the lad been taking holiday, snarin' conies on the hills, for the fun of it!"

The manor folk shouted with glee like children at harvest time. The bakehouse women cried, "The old woman's back, praise be!" Then Adela drew her grandsons apart and pointed to the road from Dover, still heavy with dust as if a great company passed there.

"He comes," Turold told her. "And it looks as if some folk ride out to meet them from the town."

"That is good. I was hoping they would use some sense," answered Adela. "William's policy was ever to treat with kindness those who yielded—and to punish those who resisted him."

Cerdic's mouth set in a hard line. "Little grandam, we are Saxons and true men. At least . . . I was true man to Harold! You saved me when I lay wounded in William's tent. They all thought I was Turold, lying there naked after the battle. But had I known, had I been able to speak, I would have defied them and died at the standard with the others, as was my right."

Adela's eyes were cold blue like the sea in winter. "Don't be a fool! I told the duke who you were—did you think I wanted them to fail to keep watch for Turold also?"

Cerdic's face was red. "So I owe my life to the duke!"

"Rather than to your grandam's unblushing deceit?" Adela's voice was sharp. "Well, it is done!" Then she put her hand to her heart. "Two sons of my body died at Senlac. Engelric, and Turold, who was Taillefer. Do not stare so, Turold. I know the whole story now. Every man who got back had heard it. But now we must rebuild our world. We need you, Cerdic and Turold. These people need you. You can hold the manor at the hand of William."

Cerdic's eyes were blazing. "That I will never do!"

"Nor I," responded Turold, touching his brother's shoulder.

Adela stared at them.

Then a woman widowed at Senlac began to cry out against Turold. "He was with the Normans; he comes home untouched. Felon! Felon!"

But Black Jarn shouted her down. "Be still, you foolish female! Turold was only a minstrel; he bore no weapon in the battle, yet see his head. And he is my master's son—and now he is my master, master to all of us!"

Many cried, "It is so, master, master!" and Turold lifted his hand to them and then turned away lest they see tears on his face.

Then Adela told him how Lucy had come every day with a troop of her men to see that all was well at Farthingwold. "Every day we looked for you, Lucy and I. Every day, hoping! She would ride along the crest of the hills. This afternoon you must go to her. These times do not wait upon coyness. I know there is true love between you. If you wed her now, at once, then we can send our people to the Tower in case there is trouble."

230

Turold flushed. "I could not use her so."

Adela lifted her eyebrows. "But you love her—and you love our people. It is now your duty to protect them. And while I am on this matter, I wish Cerdic to be choosing of a wife. I think he's already chosen. Two maids at least will have protectors—and be a strength to you."

Now it was Cerdic who seemed amazed. He and Turold looked at each other in wonder. Who would have thought that Adela could be so strong-mooded?

"I tell you, it's true," insisted Adela. "You think because Lucy has a Tower and a knightly father with a troop of men that she is safe. It's not so. Twice since the battle have Normans from the Tower been ambushed by Saxons. Aye—Rolph is well hated, and his men are a wild lot. If anything happened to Rolph, Lucy wouldn't be safe a day. She needs a good husband. And who so safe a man for her as that minstrel whom William loves?"

Adela looked about her. "But you are weary and hungry. What are we doing here, talking!"

They all laughed and turned around. Turold looked down again to the haven that had drawn him all the way from Senlac. Dinner was cooking down there, and he and Jarn had their belts drawn tight. Smoke was rising near the bakehouse—and he thought he could smell a roasting pig.

And then they saw them, all the manor-folk saw them.

The troop of Norman riders all in mail came gaily out of Blean track, shouting and waving their bannered lances. They rode down through the battered gate and into the close, while Farthingwold folk stood on the slope above their walls and watched their enemies ride in.

Turold watched with tightening throat, his hand closing on Cerdic's shoulder. In the midst of the troop was a great bloated figure riding in a decorated cart. It rattled through the gate and drew up by the fire pit. Haimo, sutler to the duke, was inside Farthingwold walled place. They saw him lift the pig from the fire, they saw him lift it up on the spit and wave the smoking pig like a banner.

Turold's right hand closed tight about Engelric's sword.

T was strange, Turold thought, as he beheld this incredible thing happening below them, that he still heard the home song, clear and calm. He had seen what had happened at other manors; he had known it might happen to them. Now Normans were in the home close, but it did not seem real. It could not be true. In a moment he would look again; the close would be empty, the figure of Haimo waving the pig would vanish. And they would go laughing down into hall and eat and drink. . . .

But now the women and children came close, clinging to Adela's skirts, kneeling to her, hugging the knees of Turold and Cerdic and Black Jarn.

It was true and no dream. Turold put his hand on his father's sword—and took it away.

Then Adela said in a strong clear voice, "I am going down. It is my manor and my home. They shall not eat my food and muddy my bedcovers—the pigs!"

Turold answered her, "I will go too. Maybe we can cozen him. That is the duke's high sutler, the monstrous Haimo. But he will not forget that I was the duke's minstrel."

As he took Adela's arm, they heard a noise behind them. A throng of folk were running down the moor

233

toward them. Most of them were women with children. A few were big boys, some of them graybeards, some strong men with bloody rags over half-healed wounds. Most of them bore packs of their goods and tools rudely tied up; kettles, spades, bows and arrows sticking from wads of bedcovers.

Farthingwold folk greeted them, and the strangers told them who they were, though it was plain enough before they spoke. Out came the bleak story of ravage and burning, of manors taken, and Normans in force.

"I am Godric of Wormhill," said one, a cross-eyed little man with his arm in a sling. "Last night they came upon us."

"And I am Sbern of Suchborough-nether," said another, a sinewy old fellow who in spite of white hair bore a great pack upon his back. "We thought to take refuge here. I mind my father telling how he helped Wilfred build the wall when the Danes came."

"You are welcome. If you had come an hour earlier, and if only Black Jarn and I had come an hour earlier, we would not be here, watching the Normans do as they will in our close."

Sbern eased his pack to the ground. They all looked down into the close. The Normans were eating the pig, tossing half-baked bread from the oven. Two of them chased some hens about. Then horses were hitched to a big wain, the barn door swung, and men carried out sacks of grain.

Black Jarn said quietly, "It's the wood for us then."

But Adela said just as quietly, "You can go into Blean, but I am going down. They will not harm me."

"Lambs they are, no doubt," commented Cerdic. "Of course, grandam, we will let you go down alone while we run off into the wood."

But, as they started out, Turold turned to the Saxons who stood there, homeless. "Do you know that place In Blean," he asked Sbern, "where the deer trail goes down toward the glen where the great herd lies and then turns away east for a bit and winds up over the ledges of Elney-Lovet?"

"I know the place," answered Sbern.

"If you turn to the left just as you come to the steep part of the path and go under the branches of a tall pine and then around a thicket of hemlocks, you will find an entrance to a sort of cave. The place is dirty, filled with leaves, but you can clean it out. I think it was above ground once, a house made by men, but the wood has grown up over it. Anyway, there are big rooms with strong roof vaults. Take your people there."

"I never knew of it," answered Sbern.

"Nor I," added Godric of Wormhill. "But any shelter will be a help. We will get it ready for you too."

Turold nodded. "In case Adela's plan fails."

They watched the homeless ones make a circle to bring them down into Blean beyond the demesne. Then they went down. Cerdic and Turold and Black Jarn walked firmly down to the gate with Adela, and their people, as if unable to hang back, trailed after them.

Adela pointed to the top beam of the gate. They looked up. The magic medallion which Pig-Boy had fastened there less than an hour since, to keep out marauding Normans, was gone.

Adela said nothing at all. With her people close behind her, she advanced straitly into her close, on past staring Normans, up the steps and into her hall. And there the gross man Haimo was sitting on two benches placed one before the other, for his great bulk could not be crowded into the backed chair. But he had the chair for his table and was eating from it, slopping the food about. Around his fat neck lay the gold chain.

Adela went straight to a chest, took out a fine napkin of whitest linen, and offered it to the sutler. " I am sorry," she told him, "that you are not better served. We were all up on the moor. Will you wish some sack drawn and heated?"

Haimo looked at her sideways under his puffy lids and laughed silently. Norman men-at-arms, three of them, crowded close to Cerdic and Turold and Black Jarn, letting the weight of their pikes fall as by accident on the Saxons' toes. They did it together, and they laughed tauntingly. Turold put his hand on his sword—and again took it away.

Adela casually took a seat on a bench near the sutler. "I see you found my chain," she said smiling. "That was a gift to me from William. You could not know that, of course. The duke asked us to fasten it over our gate when he came this way—lest some of his people disturb us. He would be displeased to see you wearing it. You may return it to me now."

The fat man's eyelids did not even flicker. His bloated fingers caressed the leopards. "Gold," he whispered, "that is the most beautiful thing in the world. I could not give this back to you. I feed William's army, and he yields

236

to me all I wish. This manor . . . I had expected something grander. And I hoped for a wealthier widow." He shrugged his vast shoulders. "Well, no matter. I would rather marry you than take by force this freehold from your sons." He looked Cerdic and Turold up and down. "You, however, are beautiful, if a little wrinkled. We will celebrate the wedding in the morning. I am expecting a monk then."

"You are most flattering. I am not the mother of these young men but their grandmother. The thought of marriage wearies me."

"That is too bad. You must become reconciled to it," whispered the vast man. "I like my widows old, then so much the sooner am I a bereaved widower, and little gossip about it. Especially I like them old when they are rich." Haimo looked at the gold arm rings Adela wore. "In the meantime," he said, "we thank you for your good cheer to weary travelers. The food, of course, is not as delicate as that I once had ready at my place, ready each day and night for three weeks for certain messengers who were expected. But it will do. Yes—very thoughtful." He lifted Engelric's great cup and drank noisily.

Now Adela passed close to Turold and said softly, "Watch out . . . these men only wait for one bold move to kill you. Swallow your pride. I must not lose you too!" She fussed over some linen in the chest. "Have our people serve these men now, then meet together in the great loft as soon as it comes dark."

Turold, pretending to be absorbed in tending the fire, was watching the sutler. When Adela held a cup on the hearth to heat, he said, "We can't leave you here with him."

"Silly! I can handle him. Get them all to the barn!"

Turold rose to his feet and bowed to Haimo as he said, "We will make good cheer for you for a day or two. I am expecting the duke soon, and we must get ready for him. It will be all right if you seek other quarters in the morning."

Haimo's eyes gleamed as he patted his stomach. "You—you are expecting the duke?" he whispered. "Wait till he sees you. It was given out by the herald to look out for the young minstrel. You deserted, eh? The duke is going to the Tower of Rolph in the morning. He needs rest; he's been fevered. I am bidden to send great provision there. No . . . I like it here. It will be handy for me after the duke comes to the Tower. Even later I shall keep this place for my own. Now send your men to give help in loading the grain!"

Turold bowed. He went out slowly and saw a Norman squire reaching out for Brunhilda's dress as she brought a platter of bread to the hall. Turold knocked the man down with a sudden blow, watched her safely to the door, and went on to the barn, giving no heed to the laughter of a group of lounging Normans.

Turold found Cerdic, who agreed to stay close to Adela.

In the barn, Black Jarn was directing the loading of the wain. As soon as it was done, Turold had the high arched doors shut and drew Jarn aside. They were alone, yet they whispered.

"We've got to get away, that is plain," Turold said. "If I have to stand again before that great pig, I shall slit him. And that chain—the chain William gave us to protect us—on that great greasy neck!"

"Aye," answered Jarn. "But you can have the chain. Just give me his neck!"

"Take care! If we are killed, the women will be easy prey to them. Did you see him looking at Adela's arm rings?"

"Aye. And at our little maids. And some of our new widows are far too comely. These Norman dogs would scarce give them decent time to mourn the husband they themselves gave leave of their life-joys."

"Jarn, listen! Get them in here, one by one. Wait—I know just what we can do! You go out and stir up a great fuss about making these fellows comfortable for the night, but see that none of them come out here to sleep. Tell them the rats are too big! And act as wilted to them as last year's floor rushes, so they'll think you're just one of those lazy Saxon churls. Tell our folk to be wary, start no trouble. Pass the word to Kyndritha that she is to get the girls and women to come here secretly as soon as it is dark, all of them, mothers, babes, all. Oh—and the dogs too! Not one must be seen, not a sound heard by the watch they will set. We must get what bedcovers we can and some kettles. It will be cold lying out In Blean now. The women will know what to bring. But not enough to call attention!

"Now first of all, send Pig-Boy to me. I think he can help us to take the attention of the watch from this end of the close."

When the thick darkness of a cloudy night of Winter-Falls shrouded the paths and buildings, the Normans became much distracted by a wolf which somehow had gotten into the close, now yelping here, now there, causing uproar among their horses. Once they all ran clear down into the rickyard but found nothing. They came back cursing the night, the place, the Saxons, the wind. And one of them cursed loudly at a wild-haired boy he stumbled over in the rickyard. The boy only laughed at him and melted away into the shadows.

Exhausted, the Normans retired to their bed-places and dropped into troubled slumber.

By early dark all of Farthingwold folk were gathered in the great barn. They came in the dark, creeping up the ladders, up secret passages alongside the eave beams in lofts thick with hay, feeling their way to the place appointed. The word they gave each other was "In Blean" and when Cerdic at last counted them over they were all there but one—and that was Pig-Boy.

"Don't worry about him," chuckled Turold. "He's busy in his own way. Now we must go down, around the barn and over the wall. We are all to meet at the ambush thicket below Brothercrosse, and there we will count noses again. Black Jarn and I have set against the wall some siege steps. Jarn will go over first and help you on the outside; Cerdic will help the mothers with little ones. I'll stay this side with three of the men, as rear guard."

Kyndritha said, "Turold, our hurted men gave their beds by the fire to the Normans—and they thought it was only their due of course, being Normans. But we forgot to get the herbs and simples we need for our sick ones. You'll have get them for us somehow."

"Where are they?"

"By bad luck, on a shelf in the hall."

"We'll find some way," Turold told her. "But later."

They heard the howlings of Pig-Boy as they moved in a broken line, laden with goods, down to the ford. The first-comers greeted the others softly, almost gaily as they came in with the hounds stalking silently beside them. At last came Turold and asked how the wounded men bore the walking. They answered that they did well, and would liefer die in the open wood than rot with the Normans.

Now came the last one. Pig-Boy it was, coming merrily and openly, driving before him an old sow with five piglings.

"I got them out through a broken place at the back of the sty—it was easy," he boasted.

Adela's voice came to them as if she were laughing, "Did I not say that Pig-Boy is a very pixy? A merry and useful wight! Pigs can live forever at pannage, and Blean wood is their home."

It was scarce two leagues to Elney-Lovet as they went, yet because of the dark, the roughness of the path, or no path most of the way, it was a long time before they saw a light flickering through the trees and came at last to the campfire that Godric and his people had made.

Soon the women made up the beds in the cave place and hushed their little ones to rest.

Most of the men, too stirred up to sleep, sat about the fire making plans, after putting out guards.

But Turold took Pig-Boy and went off through the wood. It was almost to morning, yet he could not wait longer for news of Lucy.

N the castle of Rolph nothing could be seen, nothing moved as Turold and Pig-Boy ran up to the drawbridge.

Day was near, there should be people stirring, but the Tower was dark and silent. Turold shouted, and Pig-Boy chucked rocks at the gatehouse. There was no response.

Turold pulled up his belt. "I'm fair famished. Jarn and I didn't find much to eat coming home. I'm going back to camp."

"I can stay here and watch."

"No, you need to eat too. We'll come back—with help. Even though it's early, there should be a watch, someone should have answered us. There's something wrong, terribly wrong."

As they went back to Elney-Lovet, Pig-Boy suddenly stopped Turold. He acted most strangely, making grimaces, beating his head with his hands, crying out, "Oh, dolt that I be! Oh, niddering! I should have remembered to tell you . . . it was the getting away from those knaves . . . oh, master, master!"

Turold shook him. "Speak sense!"

He gasped, "One of Rolph's men! I was hanging around the hall door at early candlelight. This fellow came—I'd know him anywhere, master, he kicked me one day at the ford—this fellow spoke of Lucy! To that fat man!"

"What did he say?"

"He's going to bring her to him. They gave him something in a little bag. Think you it was gold?"

Turold felt as if the world had turned over. He choked, said only, "Her father . . . is selling her?"

"No, no—Rolph is missing; at least that is what that knave said. He went hunting several days ago and never came back."

"Maybe his own men murdered him!" And Turold shivered in spite of the heat. There was that French captain, knave, poltroon that he was—would he do this? If her father was gone, she was in gravest danger regardless of Haimo. If only William would come! But he might stay in Canterbury for days. It might be too late by the time he could reach William.

Pig-Boy was babbling, "He means to marry her. Tomorrow, master, before nooning."

Turold groaned. He remembered that once he had thrown Pig-Boy in the brook for snooping, and now snooping was of more worth than anything else.

But it was not yet come, the day in which Haimo would try to do this thing. Nay, it was come! For the sky above the bare trees was lightening with a brassy glow, and far in some distant croft a cock was crowing.

They listened to it for a moment as if they had forgotten to breathe.

"We must get help!" The next moment they were running as fast as they could toward Elney-Lovet.

There the women were up, stirring up the fires,

feeding men who decided to hunt. The men had action to help them in this crisis but with the women it was different. Some were noisy, laughing too loudly as if to build up a wall for safety. Others were too quiet and kept their children close as if to shield them from the vast wood which had swallowed them. Yet there was too a feeling of relief seen in their faces, a kind of awe to find that they still held the incredible gift of life itself. Aye, it was good to be alive with the sun rising through the wood, yellow leaves drifting down, fires blazing, food smoking, children laughing.

Adela was feeding broth to Elfgyva, one of the old women, when Cerdic came back with the hunters, scarce gone an hour. They carried a burden in a rude litter. It was the body of Rolph of the Tower, Cerdic told Adela. There was a Saxon arrow in his breast.

Cerdic asked, "Where's Turold?"

"He's not got back from the Tower."

Cerdic whistled. "If he reached Lucy, he should be back by now. I'll have to go see what's kept him."

As he turned away there was a noise, someone running with little caution, and as they looked up startled, Turold and Pig-Boy burst upon them.

Turold went at once to the litter, looked at Rolph's body. "A Saxon arrow! I just heard he'd been missing four days." And he unfolded to them Pig-Boy's story.

They wondered how such a thing could be, but Turold cut them short. "We must act, not talk." He put his hand to his stomach. "I wish I could learn how to do without food!"

Someone handed him a knuckle of pig, another, a

244

hunk of bread. "Thank you, gentle ones!" He ate standing, and begged between mouthfuls, "Get the men together! Hurry!"

More hunters were coming in with their dogs, and Turold shouted at them, "Saxons! We've got work to do today. We can waylay some Normans." They came running, growling like their dogs. So Turold spoke to them of Lucy, the danger she was in, and that he needed their help to save her.

He was amazed when an angry murmur rose and swelled among them. A man shouted, "We'll not raise finger for the Norman wench. Let the fat pig take her. They're both Normans!"

Turold threw down his meat, put his hand over his eyes for a moment, then looked at Cerdic, looked at Adela. He had never reckoned that they would turn against him. Old Sbern shouted, "This fellow Turold—don't you know? He served William. Shall we now follow him? To help a Norman woman? Put him out of camp. Let him go to the Normans. Put him out!"

There was a long pause. Turold turned away. There was a numbness in him, he neither saw nor heard anything.

Then Cerdic mounted a log, and they turned to hear him.

Someone said, "You are Cerdic, son of Engelric, and you were one of Harold's house carls."

"Will you believe me if I tell you what Turold was doing with William?"

There were murmurings, but William the Hauker shouted them down. "Shame! Can you doubt the carl who held the king's standard in the battle? I myself saw him holding to the Dragon when all about him were down."

They were quiet then, so that Cerdic spoke gently to them, and they listened. He told them of that night of King Edward's dying, of how Harold had sent Turold into Normandy to serve him there. How he had been in danger, had done Harold's bidding as true vassal. He told them of his own voyaging into Normandy, how Turold gave him the news for Harold. He told them how Tostig the traitor had attacked him, how Turold had hidden him for six days, while Tostig searched to kill him.

When he was done, there was a deep hush.

Then Adela said, "Let me speak to them while their hearts are softened."

She spoke of coming from Normandy, of wedding a Saxon thane, of Taillefer and his death and of Engelric buried on the field of battle by Black Jarn. She began pointing at the different men and women, naming their house and lineage. "You, Sbern—was not your father of Danish blood? And you—Gerelin of Shansford, your mother was of the north kingdom. And, Ascored, you too were Dane. And, William, whom they call the Hauker—have you too not Norman blood?

"And as for those of you who boast a clear descent from the old kingly house of Cerdic and Cynric—were they not too raiders from overseas? The only one I can lay eyes on now who is probably of those who belonged to Albion land is the boy who kept our pigs at pannage. Doubtless his folk were some noble ones; when the raiders of long ago took their lands, they fled into the forest. But, to stay their hungers, they came at last home to the places they had been born in, and there they were slaves and their children after them."

She made a long pause, then spoke sharply, "We are now in the same position, the very same! If we are to escape such an end for us and for our children, we must use great wisdom now."

Godric replied with great earnestness. "You speak well, mistress. Yet what would you have us do? Will the duke return our lands to us? Even if he does, how could we work them with so few men left after this great slaughter?"

Turold spoke for her. "I don't think it possible that William can return the lands his men have taken. Always in war the conquerors must have their reward."

"What then," asked Godric, and he spoke for Sbern and the others, "what then shall we do?"

And William the Hauker, looking about on the throng of women and children and the few men, said to them, "We should see clearly that even if we could bide safely here and get our food, much would ever be lost to us. We will be masterless men, the prey of all stronger than we. And worse. We should lose Holy Church and all her comforts to us."

Godric cried, "Aye—we will lose the very ways that lift us above the animals."

"It will be so," answered Ascored. "In thirty winters when we older ones are dead, then our children will be the wild people in Blean wood!"

Then they all cried out in sorrow, "No, no!"

And while they made outcries, "God help us! . . . May the saints look down on us!" Turold too looked up and remembered the words of the hermit, that good man who had never seen them before, but had taken them in and saved Black Jarn's life. Jarn, who had served Farthingwold all his life. So tears fell on Turold's cheeks, and he said, "Father, I see now what I must do."

Thy banner over me is love.

There were tears too on Adela's cheeks as she said, "Let us ask God's help," and slipping from the log she knelt in the trampled dirt beside the fire. Slowly, one by one, they came to their knees beside her. Turold saw, as he knelt by Cerdic, that Kyndritha threw a small charm into the fire.

The soft voice of Adela hung over them like warmth in winter. "Bread of heaven we ask, first. We can fill our bellies, do you, Lord, fill our hearts, give us strength and courage. Give us the boon of helping our people. Teach us to love those who are our enemies. And if we may not escape them, if they will take the whole land, then show us how to bear it. . . . Lead us in this wilderness, for we are far from home place. Give us light to show us the way out of this so great a darkness. Give us a great lanthorn!"

They rose to their feet. The morning sun was dazzling.

Turold knew what that great lanthorn was. It was strange to think that but a few hours since he had been so prideful and stubborn.

His banner over me is love.

Now Turold mounted a log and spoke to them. "In my pride I had said I would never hold land of William. I was Harold's man, yet in Normandy I loved William well, for he is a great lord and one that men love. Yet when he asked my devoir, I would not put my hand in his. Only on the battle night did I find Harold, and he

248

freed me. Therefore it will now be no dishonor for me to hold land of William. Cerdic can do the same. Harold is dead! The merchants of London will not fight. The northern earls will not come down. Moreover, if I wed Lucy of the Tower I can hold her lands—wide lands as you know. If we do this, hold these lands, will you come and be sokemen there?"

They all looked at him.

"I must be able to tell William that I have men to work the land. Many of my father's men fell in the battle. We can take all these widows, these poor children, and care for them as our own. All the men shall share alike and we will share with our helpless ones.

"We can do this. Or we can stay In Blean. But if you want to stand by me, we will have to save Lucy, or I would have no claim on her lands. She is a virtuous maid and loves Saxons. Choose! I have spoken!"

Godric answered, "Out of your word-store, you have given us wisdom and shown us duty. But are you sure you can get from William the holding of these lands?"

"I am Turold the minstrel! And though bearing no arms in the battle, I was wounded and struck down because I gave my horse to the duke when his fell under him."

There was excited talk then. "He gave the duke his horse!" "Aye, lords give great guerdon for such service!"

Suddenly William the Hauker stepped forward and faced them. "Let us agree to what Turold has said. He is young, but he knows the ways of the Normans. He is of our ancient blood, and we knew his father. Let us now show our good faith and be no more masterless men before the world. And some day, with God's blessing, we may be no more landless men. We can help him to get this Norman maid to wife. Come! We'll swear now to Turold to be his men, to follow either here, or to his lands, as it may fall out. I will be the first one!"

But Sbern shouted, "Will you then be William's men? No! My boy died in the battle. William's hands are red with our blood. Will he then give us good law?"

Godric answered, "He will give us good law if we yield to him. I saw how we Saxons used a Norman messenger, come under flag! We beat him, we robbed him, we sent him horseless and naked back to his master. And I saw how our messengers—aye, even our captured spies— were sent back to us by William. He gave them fine horses, cloaks, and food for their journey."

Cerdic laughed. "It is so! I know, for it was thus he served my father and me. Harold sent us to the Norman camp on the Dives last summer. William treated us generously when we were caught, like welcome envoys."

Cried an old man, "William is a great lord and knows how to deal with lesser folk."

Godric pressed the point. "Who now will swear to Turold?"

Joyfully then they all cried assent. All but Sbern who shouted, "No Norman lords for me!" and gathered his family and left the circle.

Turold was pale but did not falter.

"I am in truth young in years. Yet with God's help I will succeed." He took from its sheath Engelric's old two-edged sword and held the hilt before him as it were a cross, and kissed it.

"I swear by this cross and by our St. Mildred, before all these witnesses . . . I swear to protect and cherish you at all times, and to share with you all my good fortune in times to come, as you may have to share my ill fortune."

Then Godric and William the Hauker spread a cloak upon a log and made Turold sit down before them all. So they came, one by one, beginning with William the Hauker and ending with Pig-Boy. They laid their heads upon Turold's knee, they put their hands in his and swore to be his men and to follow him where he should lead them, in life or in death, and to be faithful vassals to God and to him.

Of them all, Pig-Boy was the proudest.

When they were done, they did not shout as they would have done in walled house after this ceremony. They looked about at the beech trees with the yellow cloud of leaves drifting down, at the evergreens turned to gold by the morning sun. They looked at the faces of the women and children about them. And they looked up at the sky as if they saw a new banner, invisible, glorious, floating over them.

UD-STREAKED from a slough he had fallen into, sweaty and panting, Pig-Boy burst from the edge of Blean wood onto the down. He was running lightly, hardly feeling touch of earth, for Pig-Boy was freeman now. He felt as tall as the trees. It would be easy to reach up and touch a cloud. Now he would not fear the fiercest knight in Kent, for cradled against his body he held young master's great sword and in his own belt swung a weapon so awe-inspiring that Turold, coming after him, marvelled how he ran at all without cutting off his legs. It was an old Danish battle ax that Pig-Boy had found in a ditch, and the blade, recently sharpened, had made the women shudder to look at.

Now Turold came up, held out his hand for the sword. But Pig-Boy waved him away and bent to strap it to his master's belt. Turold was grinning at him, but he didn't care. It was his duty—his right—to play squire to his knight.

Turold's sokemen were coming out of the wood now, six in the rear staggering under a swaying litter that held Rolph's body. They swarmed out onto the grassy sward, and laid down their burden. Pressing close, Pig-Boy listened to Turold and his men planning. They would take the body to the Tower and try to get in and get word of Lucy. There was no word of dissent, so they

252

tightened their belts, picked up the litter, and ran out across the down.

They laid Rolph's body down at the edge of the moat, in front of the upraised bridge, and shouted again and again, so that their cries echoed against the dark stones. They let the echoes die and heard the silence fall, waiting for the Tower to answer them.

Suddenly a shower of arrows spurted from the walls but fell short, hissing into the muddy water of the moat. Then the Saxons took the litter with the body and raising it over their heads shouted, "Rolph! Rolph!" At last they heard a sound, a cry of woe, thin and high and suddenly shut off. Looking up, Turold saw something white which fluttered a moment in a high opening and then was gone.

Now there was another sound—a clamor and shouting in the Tower, then the creak of chains. Slowly the bridge swung down to them. As the angle opened they could see men swarming upon it, then suddenly it was down, and knights in light armor were running out.

Turold stood at the head of his men before the litter and shouted to the Normans not to come too close. Before he would give up the body of Rolph, he must see Lucy, have proof that she was safe.

The captain of the Normans, that French knight, pushed up the facepiece of his helmet and slowly walked to Turold and boldly looked him in the eye.

Turold said calmly, "We must know the maid is well. Bring her to the parapet that we may speak with her."

Though Pig-Boy sensed what they would do, he could hardly raise his ax before the knights made a swift maneuver, pressing the Saxons back; the lesser men took up the body of Rolph and ran to the gate with it. There was a sound to make spines crawl, a creaking somewhere, the sharp screech of iron on iron . . . the portcullis it was. The Saxons knew what those iron teeth would do if it fell on them as they tried to enter the court.

Only for a second they hesitated. Pig-Boy's screeching brought them into wild attack upon the retreating Normans, surging onto the bridge after them. Some of the Normans yelled, "Saxon wolves!" and tried to turn again upon them, but the creatures swarmed all over them. Pig-Boy was thinking, this is very comical . . . I, who was once a herder of swine, I have struck off the arm of a man in light mail!

He peered over the edge of the bridge where the fellow had rolled off. The muddy water showed dark streaks. Now he could feel the sudden lift of the bridge under his feet; it went up by jerks and starts, and all the Saxons began to howl afresh and lay on more desperately. Pig-Boy lifted his great ax and leaped at a man near him. They mustn't lose their chance to get into the Tower! He shook his head to clear it and suddenly as he faced the Norman he knew who it was—that knave who had taken gold in his hand to deliver Lucy to Haimo. He grabbed him by the arm, shouting for Turold. The bridge gave a quick jerk, and the Saxons jumped for their lives. Pig-Boy slung his ax out behind him blindly, hoping it wouldn't hit one of his own people. Then he put both arms around his opponent and rolled off into the moat. He sputtered, came up, and thought how oily the slimy moat water tasted. There were jeers from above, but he had no time to look, for the Norman reached over and tried to choke him. Pig-Boy got

254

him by the hair, and through sheer rage got him under water till he was manageable. Now friendly hands were reached out, and a spear to hang onto, and so he got up somehow, dragging the Norman after him.

Pig-Boy gasped, "This is that son of the devil I saw take gold to deliver the lady Lucy, master!"

They bound the Norman with cords and led him away down into Blean wood and up onto a little hill where they could look down through the naked trees and see any who might pass along to or from the Tower. Fog was drifting in now, across down and wood with the sun a dull ball above them. Safe here, they went to work on their prisoner for information, without result.

"Let be! I'll make him talk," Turold told them. What he said was so low that it didn't reach beyond the Norman. But suddenly this man cried him mercy and began to talk of Lucy.

She was well, but there were two factions among her men. They had known that her father must be dead. They were aggrieved because they hadn't been at the battle to share the spoil, and Lucy was one kind of booty. So one faction was in favor of selling her to the highest bidder among their invading friends; at present it was Haimo. But another faction was minded to force her to wed with their French captain. They were the strongest and were planning to ride out that very day and take her westward to Rochester to find a priest. Most of the men expected better fortune by serving the master of a castle than to try and get gold for her. That very day it would be.

"How many men will go with her?"

The Norman hesitated. "About twenty, I think."

255

William the Hauker came up to him, fingering a belt knife. The Norman faltered, "Perhaps only fifteen." The Hauker came closer. The Norman turned quite pale and cried, "That is a mistake—yes—it's no more than eight. Only eight will go."

A cry of triumph went up. Voices cried, "Ambush, ambush!"

They bound their prisoner more securely, took him into a hollow and set a guard over him. Turold sent a man to watch at the edge of the down and another to climb a high tree on the ridge. Then he called Pig-Boy to him, and as Pig-Boy listened his dark eyes widened. He was to be a roving scout, to run up and down, around and about, using his eyes and ears. Aye—this whole business of saving Lucy just about lay on him, it seemed! So he straightened his shoulders and shifted his ax and was off, noiselessly.

Suddenly he was back before Turold, "Something's coming up from Canterbury, master. A herd of horses. Listen!"

In the silence, with fog dripping off the trees, they heard first a sound like a wind rising somewhere, then a rumbling.

Turold took Pig-Boy and two others and ran east toward the Way, then hid among the trees near the beginning of Tower lane. Now the rumbling swelled to a mighty sound that filled the wood; the very ground shook. Then they saw, ghostly in the drifting mist, the first of the horses with riders to guide them. More and more swept along, rushing past, turning up the Tower lane.

Turold said, "The duke's horses! Let's turn a few—we could use them."

There had been herders up front, probably more in the rear, but they saw none now. They jumped in among them and turned a few, waving them into the woods. Two of them turned back again, but they still had three, and the mist covered them as they drove them cautiously back to their post below the ridge, and secured them by their rope halters. Turold stood stroking one of them, the white barb he had ridden into battle.

Pig-Boy's eyes were popping. "What a head, what feet, what a tail!"

"Aye, this was my horse. I rode him—that day."

They talked about what use they could make of the animals.

"Let me take them back to the Tower," Pig-Boy cried. "I'll say I found them lost in the woods. They would have to give me something. I'll get into the Tower. I'll get to Lucy, warn her, help her. And when you waylay them, I can be there to lead her away into the woods, go round about, put them off the scent, while you smash them Normans right down into a pulp!" His feelings seemed to peter out, for he suddenly lifted the ax and stroked the edge with his thumb, then looked at the ground.

Turold laid a hand on his shoulder. "It is a noble part, and one that you alone could carry through. But you must take care! And let's disguise you a little. They must have seen you fighting on the bridge!"

They stripped him, washed him in a nearby rivulet, cut his wispy locks about his ears. "Now, who's the smallest man here?" and Turold caught hold of a little fellow, who protested loudly when they dressed up Pig-Boy in his jerkin, breeches, and cap.

257

Then Turold handed him his knife—the leopard knife. "Hide it under your shirt." Pig-Boy swallowed a big lump in his throat and secured the knife.

"Try to fix it so that Lucy rides the white barb out. He's tireless, and you can run by the stirrups. Take this gray horse too. I'll keep only the brown one."

They looked after Pig-Boy as he rode through the woods, with the barb between his knees and leading the other by the rope halter.

Turold ran to the edge of the wood to see how it fared with his freeman. There was a clear view to the Tower, for the wind was rising in gusts, and the fog was blowing away. Pig-Boy was catching up to the last of the herd, and riders were rounding up some stragglers. He rode up to one of these, talked a minute, then rode on with him over the bridge. The draw was lifted.

It was done! Pig-Boy was inside the Tower and would surely get to see Lucy.

Turold ran back to his men and told them of Pig-Boy's safe entry into the Tower.

"The saints be praised," said Godric. "Now, young master, let us plan the ambush."

Black Jarn said, "We'd best fell a tree to stop their horses." The rest agreed, and they found a place where the track from the Tower narrowed between high banks.

They found a young pine in just the right spot and soon had it down so that it fell into place with a rustle of thick branches. It lay just right, too high for horses to jump over, too low to go under.

Then Turold set the watch: William the Hauker to take his stand at the slope of the down half a mile away,

258

Ascored to watch eastward on the main road, the rest of the men hidden near the fallen tree. Behind tree trunks, lying under bushes or prone on the ground, they could not be seen by horsemen coming from the Tower.

Now came the hard part, to wait.

The sun broke through low clouds, and Turold wiped his face and leaned against a tree. Plague take the French knight, anyway! He must be a laggardly lover, in no haste to take his bride to a priest. Turold grinned to think that Lucy herself was probably the cause of the delay. Maybe she had locked herself into the little room at the top of the keep. But if there was a locked door like that anywhere, Pig-Boy would find it, would whisper through the keyhole. Then she would suffer a change of heart, would agree to go.

Turold ran his finger along the edge of his sword. He was remembering that day in London when that Frenchman had ordered Lucy to remove his muddy boots. Aye, there was one proper end to make of such a fellow, and now Turold and his vassals were on their own ground.

The signal, a long whistle, came so suddenly he was almost caught off guard, but only for a moment. The Normans were coming, and Saxons must crouch, every muscle tensed, ready to spring with weapons under hand.

Turold swung down from the look-out tree and went to meet William the Hauker, who was running back to them through the wood. A party had just ridden out from the castle, he said; the French captain, Lucy with Pig-Boy running at her stirrup, and eight men. They'd soon be off the moor and into the wood.

Turold whistled, his men all jumped up from their

hiding places, and he waved his arms and pointed uphill.
They waved back, then sank out of sight without a sound.
Turold mounted the brown horse and rode him among the
crouching men, stopping behind the wide bole of a beech.
He must get the man down at the first blow. Turold had
no intention of giving the French knight a fair chance at
all. The knight had mail; he did not. And too many people
would come to harm, maybe to hunger and death, if Turold and his men could not win this affray at the outset.

The horse quivered as a rabbit ran under his legs.
Turold shifted on his bare back and loosed his sword.
They were coming now, there were faint sounds, then all
at once they were loud. The Normans were riding into the
trap.

Somehow he was moving, was flying through the air,
the horse's flanks between his knees, then he was down
among the riders with his great sword raised. He heard his
men dropping, savage and quiet upon the Normans, like
wolves falling on sheep. And Normans were screaming. As
for that French knight, the two-handed sword did its part,
he was cloven through at one terrible blow. Aye—the old
sword knew the way of battle, for Turold had scarce
known battle himself. St. Mildred be praised! The French
knight was dead.

He turned hacking at another Norman. Hack and
crash! the scream of a horse, blood and outcries. Now the
Normans were trying to turn their horses in the narrow
space. Turold saw Lucy riding away at the upper end and
tried to get to her, but it was too far. He shouted for Black
Jarn, slashed about him, got through somehow, and trotted
into the wood a little way. At first he saw no sign of her,

then far between the trees it seemed that the white horse passed, something dark beside it. Pig-Boy was keeping his promise! But as he looked there was something else in that part of the wood, another rider trotting after them, dimly seen.

He was aware now that the din had ceased, the wood was silent, even the crows quiet. What was his duty now? He must ride after Lucy—but he could not leave his men yet! There must be no trail between here and Elney-Lovet when they left this place.

A cry rose behind him, someone shouting, "Turold, Turold!" He turned the horse and rode back to the place of ambush. Dead Normans lay about, and one Saxon was on the ground, men bending over him. Black Jarn stood up. "It's Godric. There's no wound, and his heart beats. He'll come round. But we've got to get out of here! Two Normans got away—they'll be back at the Tower soon, and there'll be more knights down on us. We must go!"

Turold said, "There were eight and the captain. You saw two ride away." They looked around. Six Normans lay dead, the captain and five men.

"That is only seven. The eighth man—he rode after Lucy and Pig-Boy. I was afraid of this. What shall we do?"

Jarn said quickly, "We couldn't find them now. Leave it to Pig-Boy. Now we have to think of the folk back at camp."

Turold was forced to agree. Heaven now would care for Lucy. These men had done all they could—they had got her away from a troop of armed Normans. And Pig-Boy was a woodsy wight.

Quickly they raised Godric to the brown horse with

261

a man to hold him, quickly they smoothed out their foot-
prints and left the place of ambush, going up over a ledge
of rock with Turold as rear guard to see that nothing was
dropped, no marks left. They took a roundabout way to
camp, and when they were near it, Turold ran ahead and
went in and told the women that they had met success and
no one hurt save Godric, and he was coming to himself.
He went to Adela and asked a wordless question, but she
shook her head.

"Pig-Boy is bringing her," he said. "You'll care for
her when they come. But now I must go back and be sure
we are not followed."

He was soon gone among the trees. Below the ridge
where they had waited, he heard men talking. The Normans were taking off their dead. He circled them, getting
quite close in a thicket, but heard no talk of pursuit.
Rather, they looked over their shoulders and seemed like
men in a hurry.

He went off into the part of the wood where he had
seen Lucy going into the shadows on the barb, but search
as he would there was no trace, none at all.

It was coming on to dusk now, and he himself was
lost.

He went to the top of a hill, and climbing a tree, got
his bearings by a far sight of the walls of the Tower. Now
he knew how to go, and he climbed down and headed east
through the wood. Soon he saw the bluff that rose above
the camp, and he slowed down. He was hungry, thirsty,
weary. The air was heavy—breathless and strange.

He came into camp and went straight to Adela, but
she could only shake her head.

Supper was cooking, the men lounging about, Godric getting wood for his women. All his vassals were safe returned, all who had gone out with him were safe returned. All except Pig-Boy.

Pig-Boy and Lucy had not come in.

DELA came with a cloak and put it over Turold where he lay asleep. It was, she thought, horrible to be young. You couldn't look ahead with any security, because you couldn't look back, couldn't see how trouble usually passed. The weight of present grief could be too heavy.

Turold lay where he had flung himself, his half-eaten meat fallen from his hand. She lifted his hanging arm, tucked the cloak around him. He had been under strain for so long.

He should sleep for a week, yet there was still much he must do, for he was the lord of all these people now. They had food enough for the present. But they must make defenses here, must set pitfalls to trap the Norman horses, should they ever come this way.

And there were three things they must get from the manor close: the bag of herbs for the sick and wounded, the holy vessel of the sacrament, and the big candlestick which always lighted the last hours of their people. Old Elfgyva was dying.

Turold woke after the briefest snatch of sleep. Adela spoke of the things needed from Farthingwold. His response was instant. "We'll go. I'll call the men."

Black Jarn and some of the others would go with him,

Turold decided. It would not be too difficult to raid their own manor. He looked for Cerdic and saw him coming from the shadows, hand in hand with Brunhilda. To his brother Turold said, "You'd best bide here and look out for the folk. Tell the men I'll be ready in a minute."

He walked quickly away from the fire into the darkness beyond. The wind had risen; it whirled the dry leaves about, so that they clung to hands and face. The wood was in a tumult; there was not a star overhead. Turold leaned against the smooth trunk of a beech, looking out into the darkness.

He tried not to think of Lucy. Lucy was his love, his true love. But Pig-Boy the little thrall, freeman now, was special. They had been through so much together. He lifted his sword and kissed the cross of the hilt, remembering duty.

Then he saw to his amazement that there was a whiteness in the wood. It moved, it walked. It was the barb! The silver horse moved through the dim aisles of the wood like some unearthly creature. He bore Lucy, and Pig-Boy, still holding to the stirrup, was running beside her.

Turold could not take a step, but watched their coming. How fair she was! Her hair shone red where it fell from under her hood. The firelight made leaping red shadows too over her cloak.

He walked out from the shadows and looked up at her without a word. Then he lifted her from the saddle and held her close.

"Dear God!" His voice was hoarse. "That Norman who went after you!"

"He will not trouble us any more." And he felt how

she shivered in the circle of his arms.

"Pig-Boy!" he said. And when Pig-Boy stood before him, "That Norman—you know that I tried to find you, not leave you alone to face him!"

Pig-Boy said simply, "It was all right, master. I took care of him." He held out to Turold the leopard knife, and Turold took it and looked at the blade a moment. He put it into his belt. "Your ax," he said. "Ascored will have it for you. It is well fleshed now."

Pig-Boy grinned and went off leading the barb.

Lucy leaned against Turold now as if she had come home at last. He was not ashamed to let the salt tears fall on his cheeks. Now there was a great song for him. Nothing could rob him of it. Not battle, not outlawry, not death itself. So they clung to each other and needed no words.

Then they were by the fire, and all the folk came running to meet them. Adela put her arms about the girl, and Lucy kissed her shyly.

The men who had taken part in the ambush then came and spoke gently to her, and she thanked them for their great risks in freeing her. Cerdic came and saluted her, kissing her on both cheeks. They stood together for a moment, Cerdic, Brunhilda, Lucy and Turold, Adela, Black Jarn, and Pig-Boy. Then Turold, uneasy to get their new escapade over with, spoke of it, but Adela shook her head. She turned to Lucy.

"You have come to Turold to share his life. For better or worse?"

Lucy lifted her head. "I have come to share my life— with Turold, of course. But to share it with all of you!"

"Then," smiled Adela, "let us have a wedding. Nay,

let us have two weddings! At once, lest we seem to spurn God's good gifts."

Lucy put her hand in Turold's. "I am ready. Where is the other bride?"

Brunhilda took Cerdic's hand, but Turold made earnest protest. "Grandam! We have here no monk to give us the blessing of church. How then shall we have a wedding?"

But Lucy spoke gently, "In such a case as this, God and these witnesses will hear our vows, and later you can take me to churching. What do you say, Brunhilda?"

"I too shall be proud to be wife after the ancient custom."

Turold looked amazed. "But that is the Dane-way," he burst out, "and I will never ask you to wed me in such fashion. You yourself once said of Harold and Edith Swanneshalls . . ."

Lucy's eyes were laughing. She put her finger on his lips. "You didn't ask me! I asked you! Times change."

While the people made a circle near the fire, Pig-Boy ran and got a cloak and laid it down so that the two couples could kneel upon it. The fire blazed up with fresh faggots, the wood was black beyond the flames. There was a deep hush as these four made their vows to each other before God and the witnesses.

How soon it was done!

Turold lifted Lucy up; tenderly he reminded her of his present duty, and she answered, "Go now. I will be here when you get back."

Quickly Turold gathered his men, quickly they girded themselves. Turold said, "God be wi' ye!" to Cerdic. Now they were ready for the raid on Farthingwold; there was nothing more to stay for.

But Turold looked back as long as he could see them, Adela and Lucy, standing by the light of the fire.

As long as they could still feel that the men were near at hand, the women stood looking into the darkness after them. Then Adela, looking for something to keep them busy till their menfolk should come again, told Lucy they must take some food to the prisoner, one of her men.

"Even a knave has to eat," said Adela. But when they went to the place where he had been tied to a tree he was gone. Something else was gone too, as they soon found. There had been two horses near the cave—and one of them was gone.

Trembling a little, as the meaning of this escape came upon them, the two women got a torch and hunted through the woods till they found horse's tracks leading away through soft ground. From the stride, the way the mud was thrown off the hoofs, the escaped varlet had been in a vast hurry.

Lucy said, "Adela—he has gone to betray us. He will bring my men here. Or that fat man."

But Adela was quite calm. "William is at Canterbury now," she said.

"Aye, aye! But how . . ."

"And we still have two horses, the barb and that other nag."

The two women looked at each other. Adela chuckled. "Be quiet now. The other men must not know what we are going to do. They'd want to go themselves and get run through by the Norman sentries for their pains. But we can get through, lass, we can get to William!"

It was Pig-Boy who saw them as they rode away. Turold had stopped a furlong from camp to hold council. He felt their best chance to get what they wanted at the manor was to fire a rick and pray it would not spread. It was too bad to take a chance with the Great Barn; there was still good store of food there for man and beast. Yet it might never be theirs again to use, and right now they needed those other things. So he sent Pig-Boy back to get some live coals in a mug.

Warned not to let the women see him taking the coals, Pig-Boy sneaked into the cave for the mug, then to the fire for the coals. His black eyes searched everywhere as he crouched in the shadows, and he saw two riders going off among the trees. Someone was taking their horses! He ran after them, got near enough to see that it was Lucy and Adela. He kept on running, then suddenly stopped in his tracks. Adela must know what she was doing! And Turold was waiting for the coals.

It was, after all, easy to raid their own manor. There was a watch set, all in good order as if they had been guarding a castle. But the Saxons knew every inch of their manor close. Not a dog barked as they climbed into the oak behind the hall and lay along the wall, watching at the same place where Turold and Eadnoth had lain a month before when Blean men howled below. Turold thought, laughing to himself, I am Blean man myself now.

When they saw how the watch were placed and knew that the others were probably asleep, they put their heads together a moment to see that each man knew his part.

They did it so quickly that they were over the wall

again and halfway to Beech of the Rood before the Normans knew what had really happened. Turold crept to the
chapel, tried the door, and found it open. He waited till
he thought the others had reached their places; one by the
hall ready to snatch Kyndritha's bag of herbs, another near
the bakehouse ready to get the big kettle the women said
they wanted, and three men on guard, ready to help, and
last, and most important, Pig-Boy in the farthest corner
where the ricks stood.

Turold waited for what seemed a long time. He saw
a sentinel pass near and waited till he had gone by. Then
he crowed softly, like a sleepy young cock making a mistake about dawn. Instantly he wished he hadn't given the
signal, for the wind was on the rise, and there came a
sharp gust. A gale, maybe a tempest, was about to burst
upon them. A fire was dangerous, but it was already too
late, for a flame blossomed in the dark. It wavered, licked
like a tongue at the rick, then burst into a blaze.

At once the watch saw the fire and shouted the alarm.
And while they were waking their fellows, while men
poured out of the hall bringing buckets, making a line to
the well, then Black Jarn had the herbs, someone else took
up the kettle, and Turold was putting his hands on the
candlestick on Adela's little altar.

Over the wall they were then, while the first buckets
of water were being passed by the Normans. All were
safely up and over and away—all, that is, except Turold.

A sudden flash of lightning tore the sky as he stepped
from the chapel door. He ran straight into the bulk, the
feather-bed stomach of Haimo. He fought blindly, thrust
the candlestick into Haimo's face, whirled against the men

who pressed against him. He tried to reach his sword, but they pinned his arms and took it from him. He was helpless.

They put a rope around his neck, and while he was wondering if they meant to hang him out of hand, someone came with heavy shackles and closed them about his wrists. They were too small for his big bones and cut into his flesh. The chains fastened to them were heavy also, and made it worse. He protested loudly.

Haimo's big belly shook with mirth. "The fair maid will come when she hears of this. But I will have you safe."

They led him down the lane and pricked him with their lances when he stumbled in the ruts. Two torches, guttering in the wind, lighted the way. There was indeed a storm, a great wind tearing through the wood, pressing their clothes flat to their bodies. It was so strong you could lean against it, but Turold hardly noticed. As they went he knew only one thing: he had agreed with Black Jarn that each one should return to Elney-Lovet by any route they could find, no man waiting for another. Jarn, Jarn, you are running back . . . and I need you now.

They came to Brothercrosse and stood before Beech of the Rood.

"A very useful tree," whispered Haimo between gusts of the wind. "Such a suggestive emblem on it. How came that cross there?"

Turold made no answer.

Then Haimo's men stood him against the mark of the cross on the tree and held out his arms. With mauls they hammered spikes into the shackle chains so that he stood spread-eagled to Beech of the Road.

Haimo this time had to raise his voice against the wind,

271

and it came hoarsely from his fat face. "It is going to rain, but that will cool you off. And put out that fire you set. I sent my men to the Tower to fetch that lovely maid, but she is not there. You took her from her father's men. In the morning I am sure you will feel like telling me where she is. I would like to be lord of the Tower too."

Turold laughed in his face. "You will be lord like the blacksmith in a silk apron," he said and turned his face away.

They left. Turold stood bound to the beech and looked up at the sky and thought upon his sword, with its hilt like a cross, upon which he had sworn, upon which he had prayed. It seemed that always he must lose his sword. And now his father's blade was in Haimo's girdle. I am, he thought, scarce fit to handle sword. Even Pig-Boy could do better.

The trees were swaying and groaning in the wind, the old beech shivered against his back. Now came rain and such a force of blowing as he could not have imagined. It was like some great savage animal, for it had a voice, a wild and terrible voice, a sustained screaming that tore at him as if with claws.

There had been nothing like this, he was sure, since Rollant died at Roncevalles.

> *"Tempest there was, of wind and thunder black,*
> *With rain and hail so much could not be spanned;*
> *Fell thunderbolts oft on every hand,*
> *And verily the earth quaked in answer back—*
> *Save the sky split, no light was in the land.*
> *And many said, 'We in the judgment stand.'"*

The bursting of the sheets of water through the air was like the bursting waves at sea—how the trees cracked!

Then his arms grew numb, and there was one great continuous roar that filled all his senses. He felt the old beech swaying; the great roots under his feet were moving, quivering, and they burst through the soil. The knoll where they coiled heaved up; the old tree had lost its clutch on mother earth.

As Beech of the Rood leaned and bowed, slowly, slowly going down in majestic surrender, Turold only knew that he and the tree were bound together, and must end together.

He thought . . . I am alone, alone.

But he was not alone, for someone crept to him along the wide trunk, sobbing, feeling of him, bringing him back to life and sense. He was all right; he was on top of the tree, though still shackled.

But now he knew that Pig-Boy was with him; he was not alone.

YING against Beech of the Rood, Turold saw a breaking of the day like none he had ever seen before.

Although hands and arms were swollen and numb and he knew not what the end was to be, yet when the first light fell whispering down the slope and welled about the silver boles of the beeches and the living waters of Brothercrosse, he knew peace. And far away he heard something singing.

A gentle breeze touched his cheek and stirred the yellow leaves that lay rain-beaten into the hollows between the trees and along the ruts of the Way. There was no grayness to this dawning. The wood was washed in living colors, silver, red, gold. Only some broken branches and the fallen beech showed what the night had been. He gave wordless thanks for the bowing of the tree; it had been a couch instead of a cross for him through the long dark of the night. And Pig-Boy had taken the leopard knife and dug out one of the spikes so that now he was held only by one hand, and though still shackled, could turn himself.

Pig-Boy lay close to Turold all night, when he was not digging at the spikes. When Turold asked him to leave him, to run to Elney-Lovet and get help, Pig-Boy most stubbornly refused.

Turold sighed. "Have you forgotten so soon," he

asked, "that you are now my man, not a thrall, and that of your own free will? Why do you still act the stubborn slave—instead of good vassal?"

Pig-Boy's voice quavered a little as he answered, "Yes, master, I remember! I remember. I am sworn to serve you!"

And Turold, turning his head, had seen green eyes shining in the dark by the thicket at the fordway. Perhaps it was a wolf. So he said no more to Pig-Boy about leaving him.

Aye, it was a fair morning to see when it came. And Turold still felt it to be so when Haimo and a troop of men came riding down the lane. Pig-Boy quickly laid the drawn spike in place that the Normans might not see what he had done, but when he had done that his presence of mind seemed to leave him, for he stood quivering like a bow after the arrow is sped.

The Normans rode good horses and no doubt were setting out on foray. But Haimo, it was plain, came down to Brothercrosse only to see Turold. He was resplendent in a new cap with a red feather, and the gold chain which should have kept him and all his kind out of Farthingwold was shining on his broad bosom.

As the fat man rode up, Pig-Boy stood before his master with the leopard knife in hand as if he must save him from these armed men.

Turold said to him, "Don't be a fool, Pig-Boy. Adela and Lucy—they need you. Save yourself!" And he looked up into the branches and saw that up there the sun was shining. It was worth having lived to have seen so much of beauty, to have known so much of love. And death was impossible, unreal. Hope, formless but unconquerable, filled him.

Suddenly Pig-Boy's scream rang as one of Haimo's men pricked him with a lance. As if it had been Turold who had been pricked, he sobbed, "You let him alone, let him alone!"

But Pig-Boy could not stand before them. Without warning he was jumping away from them, dodging through the ranks of horsemen, running off with arms and legs and crazy rags fluttering and flying together. Down the Way, skimming the ford, on he went toward Canterbury, shrieking, "Wait, wait!"

Almost at once his voice came back in a far thin cry, "Warn her, master, warn her! She heeds not. Master—the song of the doe!"

Haimo had heard too. His little eyes gleamed. "The sweet maid comes, I knew she must come to find you!" He set his men in ambush, some by the thicket, some by the fallen tree.

Turold could look up no longer. He turned on his side and strained to see what came along the Way beyond Brothercrosse. He sang now of hunters in ambush and of the doe who must flee away to her haven in the far glens. He sang of the stag who would die if she fell into the hands of the hunters.

And still, far in the wood Pig-Boy was wailing. Then Turold heard the thunder of horses coming at the gallop. On and on they pounded. Haimo had not hidden himself— where could such a bulk be concealed? But he sat his horse beside the fallen tree, and he watched the Way.

Now Turold could see them, two horses coming at

276

great speed. Lucy was riding the white barb, only it was white no longer but gray with mud. She rode him straight through the ford and came to a sliding halt by the fallen tree. Lucy, Lucy! And close behind came Adela, riding lightly as a boy. Foolishly, Turold wanted to shout, "Good riding, grandam!"

From the corner of his eye he watched the great man, Haimo, saw him reaching for Lucy's bridle. She turned the barb with a flick of her rein to avoid the fat hand. Instantly Haimo's men were about her and Adela, pulling them from their horses. And Haimo was whispering, "Lovely as a dream—and very rich."

Haimo was not looking down the Way and did not see the others who were coming, riding swiftly. But Turold could see them, the long unending line of knights and men, choking the road as he had seen them in Normandy on the road to the Dives.

At the head of the column, riding a huge stallion, came William. Surely Haimo must hear the thundering of their coming, the very ground shook now through all the wood. But Haimo was still looking at Lucy.

They were at the ford when Haimo turned and saw them. Then he sat very still, and his face was the color of cheese.

On came William through the ford to the fallen beech. Close to the tree he pressed his horse and halted and stared at Turold and at his shackles. The duke was pale and worn with spots like fever on his cheeks. But Turold forgot how sick the duke looked when he roared, "By the splendor of God! What is this?"

Pig-Boy was clawing at Turold in a passion of tears

277

and joy, showing William the shackles, the spike he could not get out. William roared his anger and one of Haimo's men ran and unlocked the shackles. Turold stood up, upheld by Lucy and Pig-Boy. So he stood before the duke, supported by his bride and his freeman.

"I thought I had lost you," the duke told him. "Great God! What a boon, to have you safe. I will give a jewel to that shrine back there. Doubtless it was the saint who brought you safe home. But let them take you to the brook to ease your hands in the cool water."

Then William gave commands to certain of his knights, so that afterward Turold could never remember what had happened first. Sometimes he thought it was the swift going of a troop of duke's men up the manor lane to clear out the sutler's brood. Sometimes he thought it must have been the other troop that went to the Tower to reckon with Lucy's mutinous knights. But usually it seemed to be what they did to Haimo. First they unbuckled the sword he wore. It was a heavy Saxon blade and Turold, returning from the brook, felt no shame to stretch his hand for it. He would have liked to take the gold chain, but one of William's men flicked it off with his sword point and it fell, hidden in leaves.

Then William's men slit the sutler prettily; it was hard to tell what part of him was flesh and what part clothes. Indeed, when their swords pricked his billowing girdle, they loosed a cascade of gold coins which fell, so that jests went round about his constitution. Then they took the sutler away, for Lucy was hiding her face against Turold's shoulder, and Adela was shaking her head. So Haimo was taken away, and they saw him no more.

278

About that time, as the pain from hands and arms began to ease with Lucy and Adela laving them again at the brookside, there came up from the rear a company of sappers who laid their axes to the chopping down of the ancient ambush thicket by Brothercrosse.

"The dark places must go," said William to Turold, as the minstrel came again to stand before him. "Yet I am already weary of the price I must pay for this land."

"You are like the stag of ten, my lord," answered Turold. "You go king, yet you must trample the wolf and fox and even the coney. Sometimes the hart of ten is caught and tangled to his death by that which he bears most proudly."

"The hart may pant for the water brooks," said William sorrowfully. "My soul is sick with slaughter and hatred. I do not wish to rule over a wilderness. Can they not understand that I am rightful king in Albion? That I only came to claim what is mine by the laws of Heaven and earth? The men of Canterbury . . . and others . . . they gave their submission. Yet not in love."

"It will take time."

Said William heavily, "Something great died on that hill at Senlac."

"It is done."

"It is done and cannot be changed. I must go on till this land—till your city of London especially—submits itself to me. If I live, I must do it. And I am weary! Must I go on reaping hate—and rewarding those who earn me that hate? Better to be the head of an ass than tail of a horse."

Then Adela, who was mounted again, pressed her

horse close to William. He looked at her as if he was glad to set eyes on such a woman.

"There be a remedy for all dolors but death, my lord," she told him.

"Tell me then if you know," said William, and he seemed strangely humble.

"Do not faint now! You must be strong and of great courage! Your great and stern will held you to this coming hither and to this battle. Now let it be strong to the re-making of this land. Go now to the Tower. Lucy and I will bring you healing there. But you must not fail nor falter, else the land will be in disorder, maybe for many years. All our great ones are dead. We must have your strong hand."

William's head lifted as she spoke to him. "There is healing here, that I see. I will go to the Tower and rest, to be well of the fever of body and spirit. And to learn of you how to win the love of these people. Perhaps I can get London without battering and slaughter and fire. Aye, we will camp about it. They will yield to me and I show patience."

William motioned that he wished to sit by the fallen tree. Three knights laid down a carpet and helped him from the saddle.

"Now," said William, "come here, Turold. What can I do for you? Nay . . . rather, what can you do for me? Help me to go on, come and sing your glees."

But Turold spoke boldly. "Indeed, lord, you can now do something for me, and for these people, if they be your people." For he saw that among the trees his Saxon folk were creeping up to see what would befall him now.

"Let me hold the Tower of you, for Rolph is dead, and last night I was wedded with Lucy. Let my brother hold of you our father's manor. Already I have sworn to me a number of Saxon sokemen. We will serve you, we will make the land to bloom even better than in past time. For now is broken that saying: Let us do as our fathers have done since the days of Alfred."

The duke shook his head sadly. "Did my loved minstrel die too at Senlac? Here is only a Saxon thane, careful for his people. Well . . ." he smiled, "when your own son wants to run away to be a minstrel, I hope I'm here to see it." Then with a touch of his old fire, "Splendor of God! I will live to see it!"

"My lord, what is good vassalage?" asked Turold. "Look at my men, waiting there in the trees. They serve me, and I protect them. I serve you in turn and you protect me. But you in turn—lord, to whom do you answer?"

"How plainly you put it. There are few who would dare. But your song. When the land is quiet again, you will come to court sometimes and sing for us?"

"Sing again?" Turold looked at Adela and Lucy, at his men waiting in the trees. "If you mean the old lays of glory, such I will never sing again."

"But your song of Rollant!" William seemed astonished. "The clerks at Rouen have already made a record of it—yet you will lose all the fame of it if you fail to keep before the world your making of it. Other minstrels may claim it."

"I care not. I am living a song now." He looked again at his people. "And we need good law, my lord. We need peace to grow crops and increase our flocks and raise stalwart boys and buxom lassies that this land may bloom again."

"Now you will be sorry you have set your hand to this," and William roared as if angered. "I shall make you king's officer here—and let you tend to the law." Then he bowed his head. "Now bring your men and make your devoirs to me, Turold, for I am weary."

So Turold called to them, and they came boldly to him out of the wood: Cerdic and Black Jarn, Godric of Wormhill and William the Hauker, Gerelin and Ascored and even Sbern. They all came and stood quietly behind Turold with their churls and young boys and old men.

And as Turold knelt to William, they knelt too behind him. With Cerdic and Lucy and Adela beside him, he knelt to William, laying his head on the duke's knee, giving him his hands. And the duke held the swollen hands and looked about him at the bold and bearded Saxons who were Turold's men.

So Turold swore to become William's man, to hold the lands of Rolph from him, and to give him good service. And after him Cerdic did the same in behalf of Farthingwold.

When it was done, William declared before them all that Turold should serve him as reeve of the shire, and give good law to all men. For William said he would give them law as it had been in the time of Alfred.

"And you will not oppress us with a conqueror's tax such as Dane-geld?" asked Adela.

"That I promise you," said William.

And Turold, looking about at his men, saw that they

were well content at this word. Then he held up the hilt of his sword as if it had been a cross, and kissing it, lifted his face to the sky and said, "Give me strength and wisdom for this my duty." And the others did the same and asked Heaven's blessing.

As Turold helped his lord to mount, he saw that he was indeed enfeebled in body. Taking up the reins, William leaned down. "You will come to the Tower now?"

"My lord," stammered Turold, "give me leave to look to our manor; it's sure the wind did damage there last night."

William's eyes were merry. "And leave this fair bride? Is it not unkind? Yet come to the Tower she must, for she alone knows how to order things there. I know you yield me this service for Matilda's sake."

"It is my pleasure!" He swung Lucy to the saddle of the barb, holding her close and kissing her before them all.

The duke chuckled. "I feel better already," he said.

William was still laughing as he rode off to the Tower with Lucy and Adela beside him.

Quickly the Way was cleared. The duke's knights and men, only part of the main army, had been passing along while he talked with Turold. After the last of them had passed, there was a great scurrying of Saxon folk, carrying sick ones, bringing their goods back in the soft sunshine, as they had gone down into Blean in the dark two nights before.

Turold and Pig-Boy stood in the Way to see them all safely into the manor lane. There was a glow in their faces and a spring to their steps now, and he felt the salt tears falling on his cheeks as he looked at them, saw how they stared at his hands and passed on without speaking. A young widow, near her time for childbed, walked as if in a dream. Kyndritha helped her over the rough places. She had her face to the home roof under which her child, after all, would be born. Someone was leading Ulfnoth's uncertain steps.

Last of all came men with Elfgyva in a litter. By the smile on her face Turold knew that her soul would see the seven candles they would light for her.

Then Turold and Pig-Boy were alone by Brother-crosse.

It was, Turold knew, the most fairest day he ever would see. The Way was trampled from the passing of the Normans, the wood was torn from the storm, the old beech was fallen. Yet most of the great trees held their places, and a sapling was growing near the roots of the uprooted one. Some day, maybe a hundred years hence, it would be such a tree as the mighty one had been.

Now the sun was shining through all the wood, shining like gold on the waters of Brothercrosse and on the scar of the fallen beech. Turold looked up. Aye, the sun knew nothing but its own shining. So then Turold knelt for a moment by the fallen tree, remembering many things.

As they were turning up the lane, he took Pig-Boy by the arm. The deer were coming through the forest, surging up the bank to cross the Way. The Old One, the hart of ten, suddenly bounded from among them, tossing his antlers, his dark eyes shining. He went to the fallen beech and lipped the place where Turold had lain through the night. Then the herd rushed past him, and he jumped quickly after them and up the slope.

"It takes the Old One to mind them," said Pig-Boy.

Turold laughed. "It looks that way. But did you notice that it was really an old doe—a very grandam of them all—who was really leading them? Maybe the antlers dazzle you."

Something was gleaming in the sun by the upthrust roots of Beech of the Rood. Turold went back and picked it up. It was his chain, the gold chain given him by William. He shook off the leaves, polished the leopards rampant against his cheek.

Only a moment he stood, looking at it. Then he turned and slipped it over Pig-Boy's head. It settled into place over the greasy jerkin, and Pig-Boy stood very straight.

"Now you are lord In Blean," Turold said.

Pig-Boy touched the medallion. He brushed the frowzled hair back from his eyes.

"This be a day of marvels, master," and his laugh rang out.

"Aye, a great and gladsome day!" They both laughed, then shouted, wild and free, and shouting ran up the lane.

A gentle wind stirred the forest. The Blean lay quiet with a few yellow leaves sliding down upon the carpet of a thousand Winter-Falls that had gone before.

AUTHOR'S NOTE

My deep interest in the Norman Conquest began when the librarian at Braintree, Massachusetts, handed me Freeman's *History of the Norman Conquest of England, Its Causes and Its Results,* in six volumes, volume six being the index. This was more or less a desperate measure on her part, for in trying to satisfy my hunger for source material on New England beginnings, she had run through about everything on hand.

As I plunged into these weighty volumes the great and thrilling pageant of the eleventh century unrolled before me—at times flashing like lightning over a dark landscape—at other points moving in bright sunshine. It was the discovery of a new and fascinating world —one that deserved a story.

At that time I was taking my first group of four children on Saturday expeditions (later there were two more children), and the four soon collected another four among their playmates. Sometimes I told them stories as we rested by some pond, or in bad weather on the train we took to Boston museums. At first these modest tales were based on the old happenings in New England, which swarm like ghosts around the storied places.

We had twin boys in the group, the Morcum twins, and one day they asked for a story about twins. As I looked into their eager faces, the story of Turold and Cerdic was born. It was so natural— one boy would be with King Harold, the other one with Duke William; then it could be told from both sides. And how could a Saxon lad get to the Norman court? As a minstrel.

So the story evolved, as I told it to the eight children.

That was only the top of the iceberg, and a long and happy search began for more material, more background. A move to New Haven, Connecticut, opened up the rich resources of the Yale Library, and for several years all my spare time was spent there. There was the basic source, *Roman de Rou et des duco de Normandie;* from a copy of the *Domesday Book* came place names and men's names; then I found a colorful book with pictures of the Bayeaux Tapestry—really an embroidered church piece. Then there were guidebooks, travel books, social histories, Psalters, Books of

286

Hours with their tiny sketches in the margins. I looked at hundreds of books—and used many. I discovered a translation of the "Song of Roland" that was vigorous and rhythmic, by Charles Scott Moncrieff. The greatest song of the age! Of course Turold, as the best minstrel of them all, had to be the author of that song.

I read books on hagiology, on witchcraft, on the Norse mythology, the Norse sagas, anything that could help me to understand the way the people thought, the spirit of the age—and along that avenue I discovered that vassalage was an honorable state, for when a man was a good vassal and true to his lord, he was true to himself and to God. (Turold's divided loyalty was plausible to me because of the characters of Harold and William. Rarely, if ever, has an era produced two leaders of such stature and such magnetism. Yet Turold's divided heart caused him deep inner suffering, because a true man served but one lord.)

Last of all, the United States' equivalent of five shillings sent to the British Consulate in New York brought a newly published map, "Britain in the Dark Ages." It showed the beech forest near Canterbury—which was already in the story—and called it "In Blean," as in the old records. As we don't have beech forests in America I had asked the Yale Forestry Department about it. They said that before there can be a beech forest the land must be used by man for hundreds of years—and worn out. Then the soft woods, the evergreens, would take over and hold the land for some hundreds of years. When the soil was ready, there would follow a few hundred years of hard woods. And finally—a beech forest. And the Blean was said to have been a thousand years old in 1066!

The story took shape, with tellings and readings to my children along the way—and with my interest in this period of English history ever deepening. With greater knowledge came a fuller understanding.

In England there had once been a Roman culture, but successive waves of barbarian invaders had wiped out not only the Roman civilization but a later start at a Christian culture. In the Anglo-Saxon period, the Danes raided England for centuries. Heavy taxes were the price of an uncertain peace. Before the Conquest, there was no unity in the realm; powerful lords imposed their will upon the king. The Normans had a vigor, a discipline, a genius for government that brought a needed order to the Saxons, who were individualistic to the point of lacking ability to organize effectively, even for defense. The battle of Hastings exemplified the pattern, where the ancient shield-wall, a static condition and not a force, could not in the end stand before the impact of a new, a superior way of battle.

287

Some historians claim to find no meaning in the Conquest, but to me a pattern began to take shape, not good over evil, but a victory for a better way of life, which blending with the Saxon way, brought forth a strong nation.

I would like to express my gratitude to many librarians for all the help given me and also to my editor, Esther K. Meeks, for encouragement and understanding.

M. G.
Loomis, California, March, 1968

MARGERY GREENLEAF is a native New Englander, whose ancestry dates back to the Revolution. She was born in Brookline, Massachusetts. Her husband was a civil engineer, and the family moved frequently, living in nine states and twenty-five different towns. The Greenleafs had six children.

One of their favorite recreations was traveling across the country, usually camping out. They have made back-pack trips on long trails and camped in the mountain wildernesses.

Mrs. Greenleaf has been writing almost as long as she can remember, and she has always told stories to children. *Banner Over Me* began with tales she wove for a group of children, including her own, during Saturday expeditions to parks and museums.

Research is one of her chief interests, and she has pursued it in the major libraries and archives in the United States.

Margery Greenleaf now lives in California, where she is writing a book concerning Holland's struggle for freedom in the sixteenth century.

288